HER BACKYARD

Doreen Lewis

Her Backyard

Helm Publishing

For information about this book and others:
Helm Publishing
3923 Seward Ave.
Rockford, IL 61108
815-398-4660
www.publishersdrive.com

ISBN 0-9760919-4-1

Printed in the United States of America

Dedication

This book is dedicated to hard-working women who come home from work cranky and mean, who want nothing more than to have someone who simply understands and loves them just the way they are.   I know, I know – God, I know the need.

To My Soul Mate Mark, my babies Kevin and Kelly Lewis, my mom, Adele Egbert and best friend and sister, Denise Kerbo – thanks for putting up with me all these years and loving me, despite myself.   I love you all ta pieces!   Oh, Dear Daddy – if you could only see me now, wouldn't you be proud?

Acknowledgements

No meaningful book can be written without a spark of inspiration and a whole lot of passion. So.... to all the pains in the ass bosses I've ever had that made my life miserable – THANK YOU. You made me stronger and even more contrary to fight for what I want. You know who you are!

Thank you Helm Publishing, specifically Dianne Helm, for relating to my story and taking the chance on a new writer. A hundred thousand thank you's to Paul Bagdon, a talented author, teacher and mentor who taught me more about writing and unconditional friendship than most anyone. To Denise Kerbo and Lisa Winkler, your unique personalities inspired events and characters in this story.

"The only books that influence us are those for which we are ready, and which have gone a little farther down our particular path than we have yet gone ourselves."

E.M. Forster

Chapter One

"Typical," Audrey Beane grumbled, glaring out the window. "Another New York City downpour and no umbrella," she said to the taxi driver.

He shrugged.

A mover's truck was jammed into the parking loop in front of her building. Cardboard boxes marked, *Fragile*, or, *This Side Up* littered the sidewalk. A drizzle from moments earlier had turned to a sudden hard rain. The light tan color of the boxes quickly turned a darker, wet brown.

"Ain't no room, lady. Youse gotta get out here," the scruffy driver said.

"What about pulling..."

"Maybe you din' hear me. Youse gotta get out here."

Audrey checked the meter, pawed through her purse, and found the exact change. She opened her door and tossed the money to the driver, who immediately noticed the lack of tip. She quickly slid out, slamming the door. The yellow cab peeled away, its filth and smoke behind it, along with a retaliatory wave from a puddle that splashed up just enough to get her strappy leather shoes soaked.

Ruined. No sense in running now. She refused to place her Gucci bag over her head – saving the purse instead of her hairstyle by wrapping her coat around the bag and holding it tightly to her chest.

As she walked nearly half a block toward home, her new shoes squeaked, flopped and sloshed, their leather straps wet and stretched. She noticed her breath was heavy, either from the unnatural gait, or simply from steaming anger and irritation. *Home might as well be a mile away. What a pathetic sight I am – hobbling around like this. All right, what else today? It's bad enough that the boss makes me go to lunch with that seedy auditor so we'll get a good report. Sexist pigs, both of them. Now this - the grand finale to a really bad week.*

At the building entrance with a big awning overhead, she opened the door but was blocked from entering. A tarp-covered piano was being moved out and she'd just have to wait in a tiny dry corner under the awning until it passed through. *Not! Could this burly Italian move any slower? Jesus.*

"Come on, brain boy, figure out the right angle to wheel it out – I gotta get through here. Think you can handle it?"

The mover glared at her for a long moment and looked away without responding.

"Look, Mister – I'm soaking wet, my shoes are ruined, and I'm freezing my ass off, and now you won't let me in to my own goddamn building. Move that thing!"

He looked at her, saying nothing. Shook his head.

"Do you MIND?" *What is he, retarded?*

He said something in Italian, under his breath - deadpan. Then he smiled at her, crookedly, slowly, showing off a gold tooth. His curly wet head and hairy, tattooed arms - just everything about him - gave her the willies. *Is he making some sort of a threat? Bring it on. New York cops would love this.*

"Back atcha, Guido." She would have flipped him the finger if he turned to look.

Standing on the steps. Waiting. Waiting. Her watch said seven thirty five. She let out a deep sigh, hoping the mover would hear it and catch a clue. *No hurry. La-dee-dah.* She watched. She waited.

The cell phone rang. Fumbling in her purse, she didn't get to it on time. *Too much crap – can't find anything.* She threw her bag on the stoop and dumped out her cosmetic bag, cigarette pack and checkbook to find the damn thing at the bottom. *So much for saving the bag from the rain,* she thought, as the drops blew past sideways on the steps and onto her beautiful bag. She flipped the phone open to see the caller ID. Her neighbor's home number appeared. *Jesus, why does she do this to me?*

She hit "call return" and Bella picked up.

"Well, it's about time! You didn't call me to tell me what I'm supposed to bring, Aud."

"Bella, I get busy – you just have no idea. Besides, you're not bringing anything. I told you – it's no big deal. I ordered something for delivery. Anyway, I'm right outside the building. Who's moving out? I'm blocked getting in, damn it."

"The guy from 3C, you know, the cute one except for the sleepy eye. His sister works on the same floor as Mike and she told him he got some record deal and he's moving. It didn't work out for him in Manhattan. Mike was telling me they're going this weekend to their cousin's place in Lindenhurst until..."

Ugh, that thick, annoying New York accent again. What is that? Is she chewing gum, too? She goes on and on and on. Doesn't she know I don't care? Who ARE these people she's talking about?

"Mmmm hmmm. Right. Sorry, I gotta go," Audrey interrupted. "I'm fighting this rain and can barely hear you. Let me call you later."

She scooped up her bag and all its contents and then turned her attention to the piano pushing Italian. "How much longer?"

"Whoa lady – step aside and we'll be through in no time," he said as he moved to the front of the piano to straighten it out. He put all his hugeness into it. The piano inched diagonally. The opening was a tight crack, but enough. Audrey squeezed through sideways between the door jam and the piano. She sprinted on her barefooted toes, wet shoes hanging by their straps off her index finger. Half way down the corridor she heard him call out, "Hey you! You got some hell of a nerve, Lady!"

She ignored him. *Asshole.*

Audrey turned the key in her mailbox in the lobby. *Junk. And more junk.* Disgusted, she dumped it all into the hall trashcan, and dragged herself upstairs to her apartment. Standing in the doorway, she dropped her shoes at her feet, and shuddered as she took in the sight. *How the hell will I fit a party in here? Two grand a month for a living room the size of a shoebox. And the kitchen – it's like being in a phone booth.* From the entrance to her apartment, every room was visible – the kitchen just a few steps inside, had a very small refrigerator and old gas stove in plain view. The sink was filled with dishes, as usual. Visible atop the dirty plates and glasses was a crusty pot that still had remnants of last night's macaroni and cheese dinner.

To the right of the kitchen was the living room, with its eclectic décor of traditional family antiques and treasures, elegant stained-glass lamps, and her large watercolor paintings on the walls, matted in spring colors behind glass and ornate, brass frames. A side of Audrey was art deco, so her living room also contained modern black leather sofas, and a metal entertainment center with the finest

4

stereo equipment, and a wide theater-style TV set. The windows were decorated with burgundy, bold window treatments that criss-crossed over them. Decorator vertical blinds covered in a matching floral fabric set off the curtains.

At least I try, she thought.

The apartment overlooked the gardens of the neighboring brownstones one street over. From her bedroom window, she viewed someone else's carefully pruned and blooming rosebushes, a container garden of green plants, a chaise lounge chair on the brick patio, and a birdhouse in a maple tree – collectively a pretty scene she'd painted in a watercolor picture the past summer.

Audrey was an artist. She painted as early as the days when she had a rubber-tipped baby spoon in her mouth, and a yellow stain in her diaper. Somewhere in a box, high on a dusty shelf in a dark closet, are photo albums of pictures that show a little girl with blonde curls and big blue eyes, smiling in a high chair, finger-paint all over a page. Circles of blue, red, and yellow are mixed to make brown – the same brown all over that baby's nose, cheeks and ears. There's a smile on her like a toothless Cheshire cat in a picture that tells the story of a natural-born artist.

"Artists don't get rich," her father always told her. "Use your smarts and make a lot of money." His mistake in life was not finishing college, and he didn't want Audrey to struggle as he had. Painting, for Audrey, became a hobby, not a career.

She looked across the backyard to the brownstone and its lush garden. *It's an obviously better place than where I'm living.* Her herb garden on the fire escape was pretty pathetic looking, by comparison. *Not a garden worth any amount of paint on a page – not my backyard. But that glorious garden over there, looking beyond mine, now that's something I should aspire to have.*

Shaking her head, Audrey turned and looked herself over in the full-length mirror. *Look at me! Black goop dripping down into my eyes.* She grabbed a handful of her long, blonde hair. *Sticky, smelly hairspray - a stringy, wet mess.* Her jacket was wet all the way to her blouse and to her bra. *Appalling.*

In the mirror, she saw the reflection of the back of her room – the unmade bed, four pairs of shoes – Monday through Thursday – left scattered wherever she was when she kicked them off at day's end.

It was Friday now. The place was a wreck and there was a party to prepare for less than 24 hours away. She slumped on the bed for a minute, hoping to muster some energy.

I'm not good at this. What was I thinking – a party here? She placed her hand atop her head and shut her eyes. *Gotta clean. Gotta call Bella back. No, no time. Too tired for chitchat. Sometimes, I can be a real shit to her. A real shit.* She lay there a few minutes, condemning herself for cutting short Bella's call, then decided she was hungry, tired, and needed to refuel her body to get motivated for party preps.

Somehow, the world always seemed brighter after rest, something she knew she could use right now. Audrey reflected back to her time in college over a decade ago. It used to be that her sweet love, Roger, would give her a back massage on days like these. His hands, rough from physical work, were strong and powerful against her slight build and smooth skin. She remembered those hands -- that touch. He would stroke her hair and gently kiss her neck. Sometimes he would whistle a tune quietly or hum as he touched her. *Nice, safe, sleepy and sweet.*

She closed her eyes and tried to remember what he looked like. She could see Roger in her mind's eye-- his wavy, sun-streaked, brown hair -- always a little too long in the back. She loved to run her fingers through it. The way he bounced when he walked – he'd had not a care in the world. Just thinking about him, made her want him. *God, that was forever ago.*

Twelve years ago, it was August, 1992. Roger Hollingsworth arrived on Florida College campus as a transfer student from Tallahassee. He was a senior, she - a sophomore. Audrey first noticed him behind the cafeteria, playing frisbee with Mark Anderson, a guy in her Western Heritage class. The smell of fried shrimp carried from the vent of the kitchen, and a warm sea breeze blew gently against her face. It was still summer and the new school year was filling up with new blood. Her heart felt the excitement. *Who was this Greek God? New boyfriend material?*

It might take some planning, she figured. Mark was a cut-up and a flirt; he chatted with Audrey before and after class often. He was open to anything, it seemed. She smiled, remembering how cleverly she hatched her plan to meet Roger, telling Mark he had to go to the Renaissance Fair at the end of the month. Her art was going to be on display and she wanted him to see it. Surely, he'd bring his pal along.

The night of the fair, she managed to casually bump into Mark and his new friend at the beer concession. She remembered Roger's first words to her after their introduction, "Aren't you the artist of those paintings over there?" he said, pointing to the clothesline hanging between two trees, a dozen or so paintings clipped to it. She blushed and nodded. "You're good," he told her.

It was two months until, at a Halloween party, they actually hooked up, romantically. Roger was shy; they'd only exchanged a few words between classes, but Audrey could tell he liked her by the way he leaned into her just a bit closer than casually, his voice a little softer than its normal volume, flirting so subtly. For a masculine guy, he had an asexual quality about him. *A bit rough on the outside. Inside - tender, yes, tender would be a word to describe him.* It was a contrast of the two qualities she was drawn to – in her dreams, in her thoughts.

Who knew we'd ever get together? Who knew I'd screw it up so bad? She sighed. *That was a lifetime ago. I just need to forget it all, take a bath, soak, and forget.*

She turned the faucet to its hottest setting. The tub wasn't filling up fast enough, so she jumped in anyway, just as she had done when she was a kid – feeling the stream on her feet, as hot as she could stand it.

Audrey leaned back in the steaming, perfect, strangely erotic, slightly too-hot water. The bath oil softened her in more ways than just her skin; it made her feel and smell like a more sensual woman. She felt warm inside and out – different from that thick-skinned, hard-ass New York City business manager she was by day.

Her big toe fit into the tub faucet opening perfectly and she extended her leg out straight to check for any bruises, moles or missed spots from shaving. Her leg was long and lithe and tightly muscled from her hours at the gym. *All good,* she thought, a proud smile twitching at the corners of her mouth. Unfortunately, her Florida tan was only a memory now, and the pastiness of her light Irish skin troubled her. *Brown fat is better than white fat* -- that used to be her motto in Florida, and also her excuse for needing to spend at least one day a week basking in the sun with a good book. *Not enough time for tanning these days.*

She drew in more water to rinse her hair and noticed that she was getting less limber than when she was a bit younger. As she struggled to curl her body forward to reach her head under the stream, it hurt her neck. She wondered if it was her age or just getting fat that caused her trouble maneuvering. Although she was feeling fresh, clean and anew, there was a twinge of fear within – fear about getting older and falling apart – fear of her 35th birthday arriving soon.

The big white fluffy robe she wrapped herself in was the kind seen hanging on hooks in rooms at the Ritz-Carlton. It was heavy and warm and was made of the thickest, softest cotton in the world. It came from "The Blue Victorian Inn," a bed and breakfast in Canada. She had stayed there overnight on business. She snuggled in the terrycloth, sniffing the wonderful powdery scent from the fabric softener, sorting through memories.

She was new to Manhattan in 1994. Traveling used to be exciting when she was in advertising sales. Venturing to major cities, carrying a laptop, strutting in sling-backs and short skirts through airports to meet clients – Boston, Seattle, Atlanta – it was all good. She was young; she was special and different, and the world could see it -- a woman who could talk it up like the boys, smart, but whose body was worthy of any man's consideration. But after a while, men in suits all start to look alike, and the scent of Aramis starts to stink.

Men were in their forties, some married - some not, and she, in her twenties. Maybe it was a compliment then - but they wanted her. Now, things were different. The thought of old farts after a young chick made her nauseous. *What a sad, sad cliché -- some dumb blonde gives a blowjob to get an account.* She never did it. *That shit goes on everyday. The corporate world is fucked up.*

Travel days were behind her now after being promoted to department head three months ago. The executives did promise <u>that</u> much. *Good.* Travel would lessen and the money was substantially more, but she'd be accountable now for P&L. She could do it.

*****

It was getting late. Audrey's bedroom was dark except for the computer monitor that gently lit her pathway to the mound of clothes hanging over the desk chair. On the top of the chair were her red plaid flannel shirt and gray sweat pants, which she slipped into. She put on some crocheted slipper-socks her sister hand made for her, and smiled as she did so. Her sister called them "cozies" and they surely were cozy. *Ah.*

She fixed supper in the kitchen and made her way back to her room, thinking that being single certainly had its benefits. She looked down at her dinner -- a cup of tea with lemon, sliced strawberries and a corn muffin. *No one's judging whether dinner is going to be a balanced meal, or the after-supper cigarette or two that would follow. Ah, no one home to snarl that I should quit and be thinking about my health.* The apartment was Audrey's private happy place, at least, at that moment.

Several new emails appeared in her personal email inbox. One was from Bella -- some long poem about friends in which the words were the outline of a picture of an angel. It was corny as hell, but worse was the note at the end of it to forward this email to five friends and something special would happen. *Good God – a chain email.* Audrey deleted it.

Next was a note from Avaleen, her sister in Florida. Avaleen and Audrey always corresponded or called each other by referring to the other as simply, "sister," instead of by name.

```
    Subject  -  We're  Not  Sisters  Any
More!

    Sister, we never talk any more.  I
haven't heard from you all week and I'm
dying to know if Macy's had the same
sale there as here and if you bought
yourself the thong to try it out.  Let
me know.  Oh, by the way, Mrs. Beasley
had a litter of six today.  One was
```

tri-color and the rest were sable. I
can't figure out the new digital camera
but I promise to send you some shots as
soon as Jeff figures it out for me.
The kids are ecstatic about the
puppies. Should I save one for you?
Ha. Ha.

Sister

Audrey longed to be on the farm with her sister.
Avaleen and Jeff had a big old-fashioned wood framed
house painted white with black trim. It had a porch that
wrapped around the house and there were lots of wooden
rocking chairs. The property was in Pasco County, Florida,
and surrounded by a white stockade fence. A couple of
horses decorated the back forty, and a big, old-fashioned
red barn served as a picturesque backdrop – something like
in a photo calendar or in a coffee-table, picture book. It
was a place Audrey longed to paint in watercolor.

Avaleen, a stay at home mom of two little boys
(Sammy, aged four and Josh, two), bred Welsh Corgis,
dogs whose long stout body and short legs reminded
Audrey of little pigs.

Audrey sent her email reply to Ava:

Sister:
I'll call you on Sunday and we can
talk for hours. The new cell phone
plan the company bought gives free
weekend minutes. But first, on
important matters (the thong thing),
you owe me $14.99 for a bum deal.
Yeah, I got it. It was soft and pretty
in the lingerie department. I wore it
Tuesday with my new Anne Taylor gray

pants, which lay low on the hips and tend to show panty lines. I figured this would be a good test. It looked good from what I could see in the mirror before I left for work. Then the day wore on….

Ava, I cannot believe chicks pay the price of a wad up their ass all for smooth butt lines. There's only one way I would ever continue this torture – if someone told me my ass looked fantastic that day. As you probably guessed, I got no feedback despite that I strutted around the place shakin' my boot-ay. Nobody noticed, damn it. It was nearly torture. Sheer Hell, I tell ya. Did a man invent these? I'll bet! If you wear 'em - you've got to be kidding. I'll take men's Hanes briefs any day over this shit. I'm back to my three pair for $7.99 bikinis. I'll buck the trend.

Glad to hear Mrs. Beasley survived her first delivery. I know you were afraid if she'd make it after the vet said she had hip problems. Kiss the boys for me. God I miss the family. Tell Daddy I'll call him soon. Love, Audrey

P.S. I'm having a party tomorrow night at the apartment for the team. We got the Essential Earth account! Anyway, as you might imagine, I have crap everywhere to clean up and I need to check on the menu. Gotta run!

Sister

Audrey closed her personal email account and then went to Smith Anderson's website and logged on to enter the secure site to check the office email. There was something from her boss asking for an update on the City of Glenn Park annual report project.

"Like this can't wait til Monday, Loser-man-with-no-life?" she said out loud.

She lit a cigarette. The City of Glenn Park job was a cakewalk -- fourth year in a row the team did their annual, and most everything was a template. They could drop in new photos, new charts and update the text and it would be a done deal.

"You want to play with me on the weekends, Bucko? Well, I ain't playing this time," Audrey said. She got offline. No reply.

She put Nora Jones on the Bose. It was mellow, so New York, so adult contemporary. She sang the only parts of the song she knew, "New York City, such a beautiful disease. New York City such a beautiful, such a beautiful disease." She took a drag and leaned back.

It is a disease, living here. Big job and making money – lots of it. It's addictive. Make daddy proud for what he always wanted for himself, but didn't get in his own life. I do it good!

George Beane had never had the son he always wanted. But he did have Audrey, the first born child, his strong girl who was taught to be self-sufficient. "You can't rely on men today to take care of you. You've got to have a plan. Be the best. It's a different world out there today. You've got to be strong," he'd tell her in her teen years. "Go to college, Audrey. Be smart. You're strong. You don't need anybody."

And so I learned. Daddy's got to see it happening for me and be proud. I earn in the top 6% of the United States population, she thought. She smiled. She knew her Papa was proud of her. *No place better than New York City to make it big. I'm doing it.*

Ah! That Nora Jones -- At least it wasn't that shit the kids played at the office. What do they call it, house music or techno-something? Come on, whatever happened to quality music? The bluesy sounds got her sashaying about. It inspired her to clean. Volume a bit higher -- polish, mop, wipe, rearrange.

She worked until midnight getting the apartment ready for Saturday night's party. When she was done, she stood back, hands on her hips, looking around. Her lips were tight. She bobbed her head in approval. "How feng-shui," she said, beaming. The exertion was a good workout, especially since she hadn't been to the gym in a couple of weeks.

Audrey plopped on the sofa to watch the Late Show and puffed on her last Newport Light. Her head finally let go of all the spinning thoughts that drove her crazy – the many lists of things to remember, who to call, what needed doing. It was all gone now. The workweek was wrapped up, and she was finally settling in, enjoying the whirr of the ceiling fan above, and the soft volume from the TV set. That was her last memory of Friday night.

Audrey could doze off practically standing up. It was one reason she didn't like to drive a car. Her mind would drift. She'd get into her own world, and could easily nod off. As intense as she was by day, Audrey could let it all go when sleep finally did come. So when the clock on the stereo shone 7:03 A.M. Saturday, and Audrey's eyes opened to the slit of sunshine peering through the blinds directly on her face, she wasn't completely surprised to find herself where she was, that the TV was still on from the night prior.

A siren blared outside. Sirens are certainly not uncommon in Manhattan, but Audrey personalized this one. Maybe a baby was being born. Maybe a grandma was dying. She made it a habit to offer the sign of the cross and say a quick prayer. .... *What the heck, and, Lord, if I could add one request... Help me get through tonight with grace and dignity. Amen.*

Audrey had a little crick in her neck – no pillow syndrome. *It's always something to get the day started off pissy.* Which reminded her. *Better call Bella. Make nice.*

She felt it again, the guilt, thinking Bella was a much better friend than she deserved. A petite girl and pretty, Bella was in her mid 20's with black-as-night hair flowing long down her back. She wore it most times twisted into one braid draped to the front over a shoulder. Bella was Peruvian, bi-lingual, with a thick New York accent.

In the tradition of many Peruvian women, Bella was a loyal friend and lover to her husband, always supportive, and a doting mother who never complained. Incurably optimistic, happy and good, perhaps Bella's only fault was that she was overly sensitive and easily hurt by people. Bella sometimes felt scoffed by strong, smart career women, and that's why Audrey and she had their spats. Bella was a high school dropout. They had their battles, but they truly liked each other. In most cases, Bella could rise above her feelings of inferiority, and even showed empathy for the office challenges Audrey frequently complained about.

She was Audrey's best friend. Bella had a unique way to look at what seemed like a complex work problem to Audrey, and break it down into smaller parts. Bella helped Audrey see clearly on many occasions, that Audrey had a nasty habit of personalizing minor incidents, then blowing up as an overreaction to them. *You'd think I'd learn, but I never do.*

"Hello", Bella sang when she picked up.

"It's only me."

"Oh. Hi. So. What's up?"

Audrey gave a quick run-down of her busy evening the night before, "You know, tidying up things for the party tonight followed by getting tied up online -- then it became too late to call."

It seemed to be a good enough excuse.

"I called to ask if I could borrow some of those crystal things in your china cabinet? You know, for the shindig."

Bella had many sets of beautiful glasses, dishes and tabletop décor items that were either heirlooms, or received as wedding gifts five years ago. Audrey thought it was silly - Bella registering at Saks for all that fancy stuff. What Bella and Michael really needed was furniture, electronics, or appliances. They had nothing. "What about bed sheets and towels?" she had asked when she was registering. Audrey remembered one time going over there and washing her hands in the bathroom. No towels to dry off with. When she looked into the cabinet under the sink, all she saw was a bottle of Draino and a roll of toilet paper.

Audrey thought about it, though. Perhaps Bella wasn't so stupid, after all. By now, the towels would have become ragged from years of use, and the electronics outdated. Besides, who remembers the name of the person who gave a bride a toaster? The expensive crystal in the cabinet would, more likely, serve as mementos of their wedding, with great sentimentality attached to the person who gave them. *Yeah. Yeah. Yeah.*

"Come over. Bring a box or something. Take what you like," Bella offered.

After hanging up the phone, Audrey threw on some shorts and a Florida College sweatshirt. *No need for shoes, though. The cozies are thick enough to walk the hallways.* She grabbed her Smith Anderson mug filled with tea and cream, and brought a laundry basket to collect the crystal in.

Bella answered the door in a pink running suit and her hair in her usual braid. The baby was active in her walker,

16

cooing and babbling, as she tried hard to cross the wood floor over the thick plush area rug, through the neat, organized apartment to where they were standing.

"Come in," Bella said.

"Hi, Shandra. How's my baby girl?" said Audrey in a little girl voice, kneeling to the baby's level. "She's getting big. Her hair is finally growing. I'll bet soon you can make braids."

"I can't wait til she's got enough even to put a bow in it. People still ask me if she's a boy or a girl, unless she's wearing something pink."

"Hey... I owe you an apology for being short with you yesterday," Audrey said, stepping further inside. "Boy, was I a case for the men in white coats last night," she said, taking a sip from her mug and setting down the laundry basket with the other hand.

"Naw, don't worry about it. We all have our days."

"Did I chap your ass? I gotta learn to get a grip on shit - stop overreacting to everything. I sometimes wonder if I have a real problem."

"Oh shut up," Bella laughed. "You make such a big deal about everything. You know me – I don't stay mad long. Sure, I got a bit peeved when you cut me off yesterday, but I understand. Don't you know that after all these years? C'mon."

"Yeah, I do. I just know how I come across to folks. I don't mean to. I don't mean it at all. Sometimes the brain and the mouth aren't on the same page, ya know?"

"You're a trip, girl," said Bella. "Just quit it. Now come see my beeee-u-tee-ful treasures for your table..." She led Audrey to the china cabinet.

Bella's husband, Michael, slid past the two women in his gym clothes. "Hi and Bye," he said, grabbing a duffel bag by the front door. "Morning workout. See you in an hour, Bell." He blew a kiss to the baby who was now pulling all the magazines off the coffee table.

17

"Good morning to you, too," laughed Audrey, but he was gone, the door shutting tight behind him.

They spent the next twenty minutes looking over all the crystal pieces and deciding what would go with the other pieces. They carefully wrapped the serving dishes in paper towels, placing them gently in the basket. Audrey slugged down the rest of her tea, then wrapped up the dirty mug with a paper towel and set it on top.

"Why you making this such a hoo-ha? Aren't they just your staff? Are any big wigs coming?" asked Bella.

"No big wigs." Audrey shrugged. "I dunno, I guess I feel like, I want to show them that I have a nice place, and am well-rounded with a life outside of the office. It's silly. I'm stupid. I guess I'd like them to see me a little more down-to-earth. You might not guess it, but I think I give off an air of, oh, I dunno, maybe being a tough boss lady,"

"NO! Really?" said Bella, laughing. "Not you?"

"Whaddya mean by that?"

"Oh Audrey. You're so good at playing Top Dog that it's who you are. But anyone who knows you deep down knows you're the biggest spoofer ever. Don't you think that your employees see through you?"

"I know they <u>don't</u>. Don't get me wrong, I don't want to shake up the mirage. I like the power. But, well, I guess I need to get them to warm up a bit. Be a bit friendlier. So I'm nervous about this party because I have to balance the image and let them in only a little. Not too much. Does that make sense?"

"I won't let you make an ass of yourself tonight, if that's what you're worried about," said Bella.

"Exactly. That is your assignment for tonight. Geez, I should pay you for this."

"Silly. Here, let me help you with that. It's heavy."

"I got it. Thanks again," Audrey said, holding tightly to the basket and squeezing out the door. "Bye, Shandra." She turned back to Bella, "Oh, and now don't forget, you need to be over <u>before</u> anyone else. I'm too nervous if you're not there. OK? Six-ish. That'll be enough time for you and me to do a shot of liquor to kick it off, and take the edge off my nerves. Kay?" She giggled.

"Kay. See ya. It's all gonna be fine. Don't worry so much."

Later, Audrey placed all of Bella's things on the dining room table on the red tablecloth. She kissed her fingers and spread them out – the Italian signifier of approval. She called the delicatessen on 48th Street to see if her order was ready.

"Yes Ma'am. Butch will be there with the delivery within the hour." It was to be a spectacular feast, which would start with original buffalo mozzarella, a house specialty flown in from Italy. It would be served with roasted tomatoes. The main course was also ordered from the deli, a few pounds of Scaloppine di Pollo with Marsala sauce. The deli made killer canoli, and she'd ordered two dozen of them.

Audrey started a large pot of spaghetti sauce to cook all day. She used a homemade recipe given to her by her mother many years ago. As she stirred, she drifted back to 1983 in Florida, when her mother was still alive.

A girl of only 13 then, Audrey was learning to cook. They had a small kitchen decorated in a retro 50's theme. Her mother always loved Elvis Presley. A clock hung on the kitchen wall that was Elvis playing the guitar. His metal hips swung left to right - right to left, to move the hands on the clock.

That kitchen was one of Audrey's favorite places as a child. Her mother was always in it, baking cookies or making food so sweet in its aroma, that Audrey would sit at the table, slouched on one of the metal stools with red vinyl covering with her chin in her palm, to watch her mother cook while she sang Irish love songs.

"The secret to excellent spaghetti sauce is three things," her mother once told her. "One, the ground beef goes into the pot raw and cooks into the sauce and seasonings for several hours, two, a bit of wine is added in always, and three, a tablespoon of sugar goes in, maybe two."

They would both laugh as Audrey's mother sipped wine, more than what she would add to the sauce, no matter what time of day she was cooking it – even in the morning.

Last week, Audrey saw an apron at the Crock Pot, a shop in the mall that carried unique kitchen items in it. The apron was embroidered, "I cook with wine. Sometimes I even add some to the recipe." She bought it. Her mother would have loved the humor in the saying. *Mom's been gone for over twenty years and I still pick out gifts I want to give her.* Those longings just never went away. She put the apron on and hugged herself, feeling her mother was with her, in some small way.

She had been a lady, Audrey's mom – a real feminine, polite, attractive, woman with an Irish brogue, and hypnotizing green eyes. Her name was Renny, which means grace and prosperity. A traditional Irish Catholic from Ireland, Renny was named after the patron saint of Kilkenny. She was devoutly religious, and a positive influence on both Audrey and Avaleen, who both adored her.

Men wanted Renny. It wasn't hard for Audrey to see that, when friends came calling, or even at the grocery store or beach when they were together, and men whistled. After all, Renny was kind and beautiful. *Fucking men – all of them after a piece of ass they can't have.* But Renny was loyal and committed to her marriage, even though Audrey's father had become a bit portly and balding over the years. That kind of love was rare.

While chopping onions, Audrey sniffed and wiped her eyes. She wasn't sure if the onions were causing a

20

reaction, or if she was feeling melancholy. She tried to snap out of it.

"Jesus, Audrey," she said aloud to herself. "Get a grip."

Over the years, Audrey modified her mother's spaghetti sauce recipe, once she learned how to use herbs and spices. Her herb garden on the fire escape always produced enough basil and rosemary to give her Italian dishes just the right fresh taste to make it excellent. It was cold and wet on the terrace, but she braced the weather to snip off a few sprigs and rush back to the pot on the stove.

Audrey pulled out a few more ingredients from the fridge -- some mesclun greens, goat cheese, walnuts and fresh pears. She made raspberry vinaigrette dressing, which she would drizzle over the salad mixture to make a second course for her guests this evening. The colors, the textures of the foods inspired her. She loved getting creative with fresh foods and seasonings. It made her relax.

Butch from the deli arrived. He carried the platters to the kitchen. Audrey tipped him and went back to party preps. *Music. Would the group have a clue who Elton or Bruce were?* She decided she would simply play her Italian dinner music on low volume to set the mood. Anyone who enjoyed a fine restaurant would expect to hear background music like it. She couldn't go wrong with that.

Time was getting close. She fixed her long hair in a casual up-do and used the curling iron to place wisps around her cheeks and around the nape of her neck. She put on her make-up -- a bit more than her usual look, *on account of it being a special occasion*, she thought, smiling. She slipped into a new figure-fitting, black jumpsuit made of stretch micro-fiber and cotton. Black onyx earrings that dangled – *A perfect match.* She checked herself out in the full-length mirror.

Hair, check. Turning around to view the back, *Panty lines, check. Boobs not hanging out, check. Outfit, good.*

Trendy, tight but not too, low cut but not too, soft and casual. Ballet-style, black flats gave it that look of, 'Oh this old thing? I didn't realize it made the whole outfit look complete, silly me.' The goal is always to look like you're not trying, even if you really are.

She'd pulled it off. She smiled at her reflection.

Chapter Two

Bella arrived early, alone, to help get the party started and serve the guests. Audrey giggled as she greeted her with a pre-poured shot of bourbon and another one for herself.

"I told you we've got to get this thing going," she said, opening the door wider, handing her friend the shot glass and guzzling her own down in one sip, raising the empty glass in celebration. Bella followed and drank hers, making a twisted face and crinkled nose when she swallowed. She shook her head and shivered at the taste of it.

"What? It's good!" said Audrey.

"Yeah, it's good," said Bella, looking around. "Ya look fantastic, Aud."

Audrey made a curtsy and bowed her head, teasingly.

Bella strolled into the living room. "Oh Audrey, how did you bring it all together so fast? The place looks terrific. The table setting is beautiful. Where did you get that dish with the rocks and the candles in it?"

"I made it myself," said Audrey. Another bow.

"You are so creative."

"I know."

"But you're not humble – AT ALL!"

"I know, but you love me anyway, doncha?" Audrey smiled.

Bella parked herself in the recliner and spun the chair around. "This is going to be fun. I love parties. Do you like my capris? Do they make me look skinny? You didn't even notice," she said as she extended one leg.

Audrey rolled her eyes. "Sheesh. Like you have to worry about things like that. You always look good, skinny girlfriend. Me, on the other hand, take a look-see at this!" She turned around, stuck her backside towards Bella and slapped her buttocks. "What the hell do you call this? I need lipo!"

They laughed.

"Come help me in the kitchen."

"It smells terrific," Bella said.

Together they finished getting the appetizers ready. Audrey felt warm inside, ready for the party and actually looking forward to it now. Bella gave her a sense of confidence whenever she was nearby.

Randi and Elizabeth arrived first, together – all smiles and a bottle of red wine with a bow on it.

"Hello. Hello. Hello," said Randi. "We're finally here! We took the subway and walked the rest of the way. I thought we'd be late."

Randi was the newest on the team. A young graphics artist from Queens, she came cheap because she was just starting out, but was definitely an artistic, rising star. When all the resumes for the job came to Audrey's office late spring, one of them arrived in a plastic mailbox with "Smith Anderson Marketing Department" painted on one

24

side in gold, decorative lettering. Randi's resume and a sample direct mail piece she customized for Smith-Anderson & Associates were in it. That one creative act made her application stand out among hundreds, and got her hired immediately. Randi had only been with the firm a few months, but was a fun asset to the team.

Elizabeth, a long-timer to the company, was Audrey's prodigy. She was being groomed for advancement. She would one day replace Audrey as a manager at the firm when Audrey would be made a partner. A business guru with sophistication beyond her years, Elizabeth would be great. However, Elizabeth had a reputation for being a man-eater. She was a flirt and a tease; and although this worked in her favor in securing several accounts, it might end up being the death of her career.

The final guests arrived while the others were sitting in the living room, sipping wine, and admiring some of Audrey's original paintings hanging on the walls. Raymond and Jack had met at the office that afternoon to wrap up a project; they shared a cab over. Raymond was from Negril, and handled reception and administrative duties at Smith Anderson. His Jamaican background and British accent attracted attention. It made an excellent first impression to incoming callers. He was a bit of a wild man, Audrey had been told, but he effectively played up his respectable side in the presence of the office executives.

Jack, the oldest of the support staff at 30, was suspect for being a little light in his loafers. Audrey wasn't sure if he was a true homosexual; but he was often the center of attention among both sexes. Jack had worked with Audrey for the past two years, and she'd never known him to have a girlfriend, or even a date. He was quiet in the office, and a gifted writer. He worked long hours and was a top performer.

Bill, her boss, was a no-show. He mentioned earlier in the week that he was working on negotiations for an international account - some top secret thing she'd be hearing more about from him in the coming weeks. He said he'd try to make it. *Yeah, right. Just as well. He'd probably have ruined the mood.*

With everyone present now, Audrey stood up to make a toast. "I invited you all here today to celebrate the marketing division's success at Smith Anderson and Associates. The Essential Earth account we got last week will bring an estimated 2.5 million dollars in profit to the company, as well as security of jobs for a long time to come. We couldn't have done it without all of your individual contributions and long, hard hours. This is only the beginning of our journey together on a very challenging project."

Audrey smiled, and held the smile a bit longer than she really felt it. "OK then, well... I hope you all like Italian. Let's eat, drink, and get closer to our teammates, as we'll be spending a great many hours together from here on out. To each of you and for all you do, a toast..."

Glasses clinked.

"Here. Here," Randi said.

It was going great. At one point during dinner, everyone had his or her glass raised high, were swaying back and forth to the beat of "That's Amore", singing along, or at least trying to. After the third or fourth wine bottle was opened and dinner was through, the indulgences continued. Several ashtrays were filled with butts, and everyone was feeling no pain – numb from all the wine.

"I'm calling it a night," said Bella. "Got that long elevator ride to my apartment."

"Lightweight," said Audrey, as Bella waved and walked out.

Audrey noticed things were winding down, and the group was wrapping up their conversations and discussing their transportation home.

Before anyone could motion to leave, the lights went out.

"Hold on, everyone," Audrey said.

She fumbled through the darkness, finding her way to the kitchen for a flashlight. She hit the light switch so she could see better, and sniggered when the light didn't turn on. "Aha! Here you are, you little bastard," she muttered as she felt the shape of the flashlight among the junk in the kitchen drawer. She flipped the flashlight to the on position. *Nothing.* The batteries were dead. *Rats!* Then she remembered all the candles in the cupboard and made way for them, carrying back several large ones.

"Some sort of brownout or a blackout," said Raymond. Looking out the window, he pointed through the blinds. All the streetlights were out. Residents were out of their apartments, in pajamas and robes, socializing. Strangely, the mobile phones each of the guests carried were useless, as was Audrey's landline. It looked like no one would be going home any time soon.

"Well," Audrey began as she lit the candles and placed them about the apartment. "Get comfy. It's not safe for Elizabeth and Randi to walk to the subway. Who knows if the subway isn't stopped with people stuck on it? Guys, you're also welcome to stay. We can't very well call a cab, can we?"

More drinks. More cigarettes. More talk. Everyone was sitting closely, huddled together in the small room, circling the candles on the coffee table. It reminded Audrey of good times she'd had in the past: a bonfire on the beach with old friends sharing life stories and philosophies. In her living room, she noticed how the flames from the candles cast a gentle light on everyone's face, making them all understated, as close friends, sharing innermost thoughts around a big fire.

Inhibitions seemed to be shed, and this pleased Audrey. A half a dozen empty wine bottles and empty

27

crystal glasses glimmered from the dining room where another candle reflected. Looking around at everybody, Audrey sensed that everyone seemed to feel as she did -- connected and safe -- that they could talk about almost anything, openly and freely.

Then, most unexpectedly, Elizabeth turned her face sharply to Audrey. "Audrey, how come you're such a bitch?"

"What the hell do you mean by that?"

"You know exactly what I mean. You're rude. Demanding. Completely not understanding when it comes to work and deadlines," she said.

"As I should be."

"But you're like a different person outside of that place," Elizabeth said. "I don't mean to criticize you. For God's sake, I learn so much from you and I want to be in your position one day, but you're so goddamn nasty sometimes. Take last Monday, for example..."

Elizabeth turned to the group to address them all. Audrey noticed how Liz commanded the stage on Audrey's own floor. Audrey's hands began to shake nervously. *Here comes something I don't wanna hear.*

"I was a tad bit late on Monday morning," Liz said.

Audrey raised an eyebrow.

"OK, OK, it was more than a tad bit - maybe 30 minutes late. But so? Was it really necessary to get that email fired off to ALL of us that said, basically and in no uncertain terms, something that work times needed to be kept up?"

Liz looked fearlessly into Audrey's eyes. "What made it bad," she said, "were the words in the email, that there would be zero tolerance for lateness, unless there was a snowstorm, or if someone called in advance if there were extenuating circumstances." Liz used her pointer finger and middle finger on each hand to motion quotation marks. "Zero tolerance, Audrey? Come on!"

28

Audrey bit her bottom lip to contain her upset. She paused a moment and looked at everyone in front of her, Randi sitting in a chair, the guys on the couch, all looking scared. Elizabeth, with her big head of teased, over-processed, bleached hair, tiny dancer body in some clingy knit Barnum and Bailey getup of sorts, stood there in the middle of the living room, confidently, boldly, like an actress in the middle of a dramatic scene.

Catfight? Audrey wondered.

She walked up to Liz, towering over her by several inches in height, moving closer than culturally acceptable. Looking in her eyes, Audrey said, "When you strolled in at 9:35, <u>more</u> than a half hour late, you looked like you just rolled out of bed and you had the same clothes on that you did that Friday night. What were you doing?"

Audrey turned to the group. "It didn't help that Randi also arrived late; and Raymond wasn't at the reception desk at opening time."

"Hey, wait one minute, Audrey," Raymond interrupted. "I was in at 9:00, I was in the break room heating up my bagel and getting coffee."

"9:00 start time means starting work at 9:00, Raymond, not whipping up a little banquet for yourself."

Audrey continued, "Do you know on my ride in that morning my cell phone rang. It was Bill, and he was on his way to a board meeting. He needed a figure from the marketing report and the whole side of our office building was dark and no one was there to find it for him when he got in. Fortunately, I was two seconds from the office and able to get what he needed. But Bill made a few snide remarks that our little powerful department seemed to have some issues that I needed to address. I was totally embarrassed."

"Well YOU were in the cab at 9:15, so aren't you just as guilty?" asked Randi, who retreated into her chair and cowered as quickly as she said it.

29

"Jesus Christ – what the hell is going on? You can't compare someone like me to someone in a staff position. I'm not going to sit here and defend myself. I mean – you guys practically punch a time card. I've got to light a fire under you to take on an extra overtime hour or two. But me – I'm not getting home 'til eight or nine at night. I do this shit at home on the laptop. Get a clue. I can't believe what I'm fucking hearing. Jack, are you on their side on this?"

Jack sat there poker-faced.

"Here's a real quick lesson in business and I suggest that you forgo further comment until I'm through speaking," said Audrey. "Let's just keep in mind that we've all had a bit too much to drink, we're all a little out of our comfort zones finding ourselves in a social situation, and damn it, it's a blackout and we're all stuck here together. Shut up a minute and hear me out."

The whites of 10 eyeballs shone in the candlelight against an otherwise dark room. Audrey felt the power of the silence. Raymond had his arms folded in front of his chest. Jack was leaning forward with the scared look of a scolded child. Randi and Elizabeth were standing side by side, like protectors of one another.

Audrey stiffened.

"People, I am a leader of this company. I've paid dues to arrive where I am. That includes working seventy-hour weeks, repeatedly, for many years. Unlike you, in choosing to advance my career, I lost out on a lot of personal enjoyment. I moved here from Florida, leaving my family behind. I chose this work over having a romantic relationship or a family of my own, and I traveled half the country to build profitability into Smith-Anderson. I did it better than anyone else in this firm. Don't you dare compare yourself to me."

She lit a cigarette, sipped her wine and paused.

"Audrey, wait... You're taking this..." said Randi.

"Quiet Randi, I'm not quite through yet. You all have no idea the pressure I work under working for an asshole who abuses me. There – now you know – I said it. I shelter you from my own hell and protect you when anyone criticizes the department. I take the bullets, not you. I treat you all like my children. You little, disrespectful, ignorant souls."

She shut her eyes tight. Crying. Hard. Her shoulders shook up and down. Elizabeth put her arm around her.

"Audrey...."

Everyone was silent as Audrey wept. She was able to pause with each puff of her cigarette, and everyone sat there staring at her tear-streaked face shining in the candlelight.

"You guys," Audrey said, "I'm good at what I do. I give everything to Smith Anderson. I support you and all your career aspirations. I go to bat to get funds to give you bonuses and pay raises. You don't know me well enough to judge me. I resent your comments about me being a bitch."

She continued, "Yeah, some of the men in management joked at last year's Christmas party. They said I needed a good fuck, that I had some sort of corncob up my ass, that I was uptight. Yeah, I heard it all."

The weeping became bawling.

"How would you like THAT, people? Why am I a bitch? Because I got a job to do. I can't allow myself to fall apart when the going gets tough. I gotta fight back. I gotta kick ass. Gotta win and compete like a man does. There's zero tolerance..." She made quotation marks with her hands and glared at Elizabeth. "...Or, they'll call you a wimp. Or, they'll say you failed because you're a woman. Well, no man is going to know when I have period cramps, or when I romped in the hay and strolled into work late, or if I need to leave early to find a dress for a party. I'm gonna be bad to the bone, as far as they're concerned."

31

She inhaled another long puff of her cigarette as she gathered her thoughts.

"I suggest to each of you.... Elizabeth, you especially, that you hold yourself out as you want them to think of you. If you want to be promoted or become a manager, there's a price to pay. Sometimes you gotta take the respect you get from others as your reward, and not worry if people don't like you. It's a hard one, but you learn to like it because it's all you get.

"I don't really give a rat's ass – all of you – if you like me or not. Do your job. Arrive early and leave late. Eat lunch at your desk most days, and nobody will bother you. Act like you a have a personal life, instead, and you will be nowhere, going no place, fast. Figure out the rules. Follow them. Or you'll be dead on the battlefield."

Audrey's voice was shot from too much smoking that night, and she was starting to get a headache from the wine. She simply stopped talking and sat down in a recliner. Everyone else sat silently for a long time.

"It's late. Please understand it's not easy to be a boss and also a friend. If I have to choose, as much as I love each of you, I will be your boss, not your friend. Sorry."

She stood up and grabbed a candle to light the way. "I'll get the pillows and blankets. You're welcome to stay." She brought linens to the living room, threw them in a pile, and retired to her bedroom, locking the door, finishing her cry quietly into her pillow.

It must have been about 4:30 or 5:00 in the morning when the electricity came back on. The stereo came on playing right where it left off with the Best of the Eagles. She lay there a while, trying to remember specifically what was said the night before. The bits and pieces that resonated made her cringe. She rolled over and put the pillow over her head. Her head. *Mother – it's a doozy. OW. Fucking hangover. God only knows what they're thinking out there. I want them gone. Now. I want to find a black pit to fall into and die.*

There was the sound of someone hurling, and then the toilet flushing. *Oh shit – I'm gonna be sick too.* She lay there until she heard the bathroom door open, and then ran to it so she could quickly fix her face, brush her teeth and become respectable looking. She straightened her posture, tightened her robe belt and decided she would go out there and be strong.

It was a bad scene in the living room. There was a stench of stale smoke. Bodies were strewn all over – the floor, the couch, and the chairs. She breezed past to the kitchen and started the coffee pot."

"Breakfast?" she yelled to the living room.

"Absolutely not. You've done enough. A cup of coffee and we're out of your hair," said Jack as he folded up the blankets.

Elizabeth came into the kitchen where Audrey was clearing the countertops from the food from the night before.

"Oh Audrey, I'm so sorry I upset you last night."

"Elizabeth, I probably overreacted and it's no big deal. I won't let this come between us."

"But I feel guilty."

"Don't."

"I had no idea you've done so much for Smith Anderson. I really respect you."

"Thanks. I appreciate that, Liz."

"But in a way, I want to be your friend."

"That's very sweet."

"I know you like to keep personal and work lives separate, Aud, but, you're alone. You need some friends who are like you – you know, who are professionals."

"Look, there's no hard feelings about last night. I hear what you're saying and you're right, it's good to have professional allies, colleagues, friends – whatever you want to call it. But I think you know me well enough that I try very hard to keep work and my personal life separate. That's not to say that you and I can't go to lunch now and then. It's good for the manager to spend some alone time with each teammate."

"Audrey," Elizabeth said with her lips curled down and her teeth clenched. "This is what frustrates me. I may be a subordinate today. Tomorrow I might be an equal. Why can't you break the wall down?"

"I..." Audrey replied. *Let this be over soon.* "I'm not trying to make you feel like there's a wall. Please understand..."

"Mmmm hmmm. I just... well, maybe we just need more time."

Audrey shrugged and turned to get the cups and spoons to the table.

It was the fastest coffee-drinking scene, ever. Within ten minutes, everyone was out the door.

Chapter Three

The marathon party is finally over, she thought, as she dragged herself to the bathroom to take three ibuprofens and put a few eye drops in her dried out, half-slit eyes. She tucked herself back in bed immediately, and stared out her bedroom window, thinking of nothing for a long time. Even sleep was no solace. *I will never drink again.* The phone rang several times throughout the day. She heard it, but she didn't pick up.

Rapataptap. Tap. Tap. Bang. Bang. 5:42 PM. *Who is fucking banging on the door?*

It was Bella. "I've been calling all damn day!"

Audrey said nothing, but opened the door wider to let her neighbor enter.

"What the hell happened to you? You look like crap," Bella said.

Audrey shrugged and scuffled away. Bella followed her to the kitchen. She drank down a glass of water and filled it up again for more.

"Are you sick?"

Audrey shrugged again.

"You look like you're going to cry."

Audrey's eyes welled up. "I can't do it any more. I can't be this any more. I've lost myself. I got nothing. I'm dead inside."

"What happened last night, Audrey? It was going so well when I left."

"Yeah, it was going well, wasn't it?" Audrey said, picking up a dishtowel and throwing it across the room.

"It's like I knew something was going to go wrong last night. I prayed to God for strength to not let anything go wrong. How is it, that I knew it was going to go wrong? It's like what happened was supposed to happen. I can't go back to work as if nothing happened."

"What are you talking about, Audrey?" Bella asked. "You've got to be blowing this out of proportion. I want you to tell me everything that happened from the minute I left."

"Wait. Let me get something in my stomach. I haven't eaten all day. I'm feeling dizzy and woozy, especially after that water. Why is it after a night of drinking that when you have a glass of water the next day, it reactivates the alcohol and makes you drunk again for a minute?"

"I wouldn't know about that," said Bella.

Of course you wouldn't. You're perfect. You don't do anything to excess, like me.

She put a piece of bread in the toaster.

"Want some?" Audrey asked.

"No."

As Audrey moved about the kitchen getting the butter and the cinnamon and sugar, she was sobbing.

"I just don't even remember how it started...."

"Tell me," Bella said.

"One minute we're singing *That's Amore*, the next minute there's a blackout and we get talking from the heart..." She cleared her throat and continued, "and then Elizabeth tells me I'm a bitch to work for, and no one defended me against that."

"Since when do you care if anyone says you're a bitch, Audrey?" Bella asked with a smile on her face. "You've told me more than once that you take pride in being feared and respected, and keeping your people in line."

"Bella, stop." Audrey said. "I guess I've been kidding myself. I guess I say one thing but deep down feel another way. That's why I can't do this any more. I don't even recognize who the hell I am any more. Life used to be so carefree. What happened to having time to dream? What happened to planning for a future? All I do any more is respond to what other people place before me in my life. I'm not an active participant in the direction of my own life. Smith Anderson owns me, Bella... Oh shit, I don't know what I'm even saying. I'm fucking confused. I don't want to live the life I've chosen any longer. I hate it all, and I'm beginning to dread everyone and everything in my path."

"Audrey," Bella started, "Take it easy. It's not that bad. Don't trash the things you've built in your life that make you, you – that make you successful, strong and unique. Do you know how many people would kill to have what you've worked for and earned? Do you want to throw your career away?"

"Kind of," Audrey said.

Then they both started laughing. It was a moment of only brief relief for Audrey. She put a pat of butter and sprinkled the cinnamon mixture on her toast, and started eating.

"I'm looking for divine intervention. Why doesn't God offer me assistance? Why do my prayers for peace go unanswered? Tell me! You're a holy roller. You're

Catholic just like me. Where is our God who gives us love and comfort? Why do I feel so alone? Why doesn't He direct me and help me?"

"You need to go back to church, honey," Bella said. "God is with you. He loves you. Whatever you're going through, whatever this is, Aud, He is here with you. Don't blame God because you feel confused. You need to work through this. In His time, in His way, you'll be on the path. Hard times are tests of our heart. Look deeper within. Get a grip, girlfriend. This is not God failing you. This is something else. You are in some sort of transition. You've got a lot of thinking to do and planning for your future."

"You've got it all, Bella. I'm so jealous. You have a husband and a baby, plus all this free time. I'll never get to paint or read a whole book, or drive a car down a country road, or see the beach and feel the sun on my face again, or love a man. How can I – I'm in a suit, sitting on my fat ass at a desk all day long. I've got an asshole for a boss who tells me what to do, where to go, what to say, and makes damn sure I do it his way – with a polite smile and no controversy."

Her hands waved in front of her to make her point. "I feel like somebody's robot. Nobody cares about me. Nobody cares about anybody. We are machines in the corporate world. It's cold. It's lonely, and it's not fun. Any fun you do make is against the rules. I didn't sign up for this, Bella. I – did – not - sign up for this."

Bella sat there with tears in her eyes. "Oh Audrey, what happened last night that brought you to this?"

"It's not what happened last night." She took another bite of her toast. "All last night did was confirm how people perceive me, just as I thought, and it's not who I am inside. I'm a sweet girl, a lady like my mother, who is giving and loving. But you know what, Bella?"

She was sobbing now, "You know what? Nobody has seen who I really am inside. Nobody knows me and I don't

38

even know myself because I don't get a chance be myself. I'm like an actress in a play, playing a role that isn't me. I am a fraud; and after so many years of playing the part, I've forgotten that me that I once was. That little girl, who was cute, and fun, and optimistic, and playful – where is she, Bella? What has happened to me? How do I find her again?"

Bella had tears of compassion streaming down both cheeks.

"Oh, Bella! This is why I love you so much. You may not understand the root of my pain, but you see me in pain and you have so much compassion. You never judge me, despite how fucked up I am. How can I be so smart and so stupid?"

Bella leaned over and hugged her.

"Audrey," she said softly. "Maybe you would have been happier if you were stupider, like me."

They both laughed.

"Bella, I love you. *Stupider* isn't a word – you should say, *more stupid.*"

"See." Bella laughed. "Being stupid is good. You don't know what you don't know. But this I do know, Audrey; you're a good, kind person with a lot of heart. If anyone can figure out a solution to a problem, I know it's you. You're the smartest person I've ever known."

"How can you say that?"

"Because it's true."

"Not."

"It is. Can't you take some time off? Take a breather? Go away? Paint. Visit family. You know, a sabbatical – is that what they call it?"

"Oh, right. I'll just call Bill and tell him I'm a bit tired these days and need to get away. Sure, he'll understand that when we're in the middle of a major project."

There was a long silence.

"I feel like quitting and packing up."

"So quit and move," Bella said.

Audrey nodded in quiet consideration.

"So, what are you going to do?" Bella asked.

"Nothing, I guess. Be a good soldier. Go to work tomorrow as if nothing happened. Wear a coat of armor and not show how I feel. The usual."

"That's my girl," Bella said. "Tell you what... why don't we go to shopping some evening? I'll meet you, and we can walk to the stores. Bring a change of clothes with sneakers. We'll have a light dinner at that new Bistro. I'll get Michael to stay with the baby. It'll be good for both of us."

"OK."

*****

Mondays are Mondays, Audrey thought as she walked in. *This one is no different. They were all as ripped as I was.* She checked her reflection in the glass door of her company, forced a smile, and walked inside. Everyone was at their desks on time. The usual cordial greetings were exchanged. She filled a mug with tea.

She entered her office and set up the laptop on the desk, opened the blinds to view the street below, and sat in the chair. Sipping her morning brew, Audrey checked her email, and there was a slamming note from Bill:

Subject: Glenn Park Report
See me when you get in RE: Page 27 on the attached. There are glaring errors on this report. You obviously didn't proof this. This is unacceptable and exposes Smith Anderson to a financial risk on a government project, a potentially costly mistake that we cannot absorb. I'm sure I don't need

40

to tell you the PR implications of such
a screw-up as well (Remember Charday
Cosmetics, 1998).   I should like to
know who in your department is
responsible for the mistake. Jack told
me this goes to the printers today. We
have some things to discuss before you
take any further action.
    Bill
P.S. I tried your phone this weekend,
no response.

*That sonofabitch has to bring up Charday Cosmetics
every time he wants to rub my nose in something. That was
six fucking years ago. Charday isn't even a company
anymore.*

She looked at the Glenn Park file attached to the email.
Yeah. So? She saw there was an obvious clerical error.
*Damn him. I would've found the problem with or without
him. Why does he have to constantly step on my toes,
undermine me, embarrass me, make me rant and bring
down my staff?*

Audrey grabbed her pen and pad and headed down the
hall to see him. Bill was sitting at his desk in his usual
demeanor – angry looking and serious. He was in his
typical attire – a dark coat and tie, crisp shirt, dark-rimmed
glasses, his receding hairline covered by dyed black hair,
swooped from one side over the bald spot.

"I got your email. Is now a good time?" she asked.

"Shut the door," he said. "Have a seat and tell me
why you were unavailable this weekend. I called your
mobile phone several times yesterday."

She didn't say anything, just looked at him, hoping
he'd realize himself how ridiculous he sounded.

"That's unacceptable, Audrey. In acceptance of the
offer letter of your promotion, you agreed to be available.

When I ask you a question like that, there are only three appropriate responses."

"I've worked with you long enough to know, sir," she said.

"Tell me the responses."

Fuck him. Why does he make me do this?

"They are – yes sir, no sir, no excuses, sir, and on very rare occasions, I don't understand, sir," she said flatly.

"That's right, Audrey," he said. "Why didn't you answer your phone this weekend?"

"No excuses, sir."

He smiled at her. Wickedly, he smiled.

Goddamn son of a bitch. He's probably sitting behind that desk with an erection, all full of himself about how cruel and scary he can be. What is my fucking problem? I should stand up right now. I could pound my fist on his desk. I should tell him he's an asshole, and ought to be ashamed of himself for being a bully. I should tell him how everyone kisses his ass only because they need a paycheck, and not because he earns any respect. I could take my arm and swipe it across his desk right now and shove everything on it to the floor. Then I could spit in his eye. Then what would he do? Would it shock him? Scare him? What if I just screamed? Just fucking stood up and howled, shaking my head and jumping up and down. But I won't. I won't because I'm a wimp.

"It won't happen again. Regarding Glenn Park, I saw the problem with the spreadsheet. It was a formula copied wrong. I'm proofing the document now and we'll be ready for final review at close of business. The printers can run the job tomorrow morning, and we will meet the agreed upon deadline with the city of Glenn Park. Sir."

Damn, my voice is shaking. He got to me and he knows he did. Damn it. Damn it. She dug her nails into her thigh to make it hurt, so she could get a grip on the situation and toughen up.

42

"I trust that," he said. "If it was Jack that fucked up, you need to tell him. I have no problem billing him personally against his paycheck for the cost of any mistake. Good day, Miss Beane. Please close the door on your way out." He looked at her over the top of his glasses.

Rude Bastard. Never a kind word or personal greeting. I hate him. I despise him. I hate me for being a pushover. Every fucking day is like this anymore.

She marched back to her desk with her head high and a determined pace. Her stern expression and deliberate speed would be a good cover to how she really felt, should anyone see her leaving Bill's office. Once inside, she shut the door, sat at her desk and put her head in her hands, only briefly, to allow a moment of emotion – one tear and not one more. She turned her attention to the computer to find something to look at to get her head right. She was getting good at the one-tear rule she set for herself. *One tear, then act like a leader, not a wimpy, whiny thing. OK, that's over with. Moving on....*

She buzzed the intercom for Elizabeth, Jack and Randi to come see her. Moments later, they were sitting in front of her, postures erect and at full attention.

"There's an error in the spreadsheet on the annual report. Jack, you talked about it with Bill?"

"Yes, ma'am. I.... I.... I."

"Don't worry about it, Jack. The important thing is we get this corrected by deadline. I'm going through the final calculation checks now. Randi, great work on the photo section. Elizabeth, I need you to coordinate with the printer – I want to get this over there at the latest possible time tonight to allow us to have a final read though, beforehand."

Elizabeth nodded and jotted some notes on her pad.

"Audrey?" said Jack.

"Yes."

"I saw you in Mr. Barnes office. So? How did that go?"

"Brutal." *No lyin' about it. They felt the heat.*

"Did he mention my name?" asked Jack.

"I told you not to worry, Jack. Bill's just doing his job, protecting his investors. You give me your full attention and best output today, and this little problem won't ever be mentioned again. Never happened. Should be an easy fix."

Everyone looks so serious. "Guys, c'mon. We're a team. Let's not get paranoid because Bill's boxers are in a wad today. Maybe he hasn't had enough coffee yet. Point is, we gotta knock out Glenn Park today, and then get rolling on Essential Earth. Lunch is on me tomorrow, a creative session - does that work with you guys?"

Everyone nodded.

"We'll order pizzas and soda. Well, maybe I should have a salad. I've had more than a few carbs this weekend."

Everyone grinned.

"Oh, you too? Too many carbs?" she teased. "Well, have a menu faxed over here and if you all agree, we'll get individual lunches instead of pizza. Randi, could you sign us up for the West end conference room from noon to four?"

"Happily," she said.

"Include Raymond in the lunch, but he can take his hour how he likes. Anyway, for us four, I wanna have a brainstorming session on the Essential Earth presentation. Jot this down. I'm thinking of creatives that target families. We need images, slogans, and positioning tools for the TV commercials. Think of the point of sale opportunities, and go back and look in our case history files, particularly the Beirsdale, Inc. campaign we launched in 1999. I want something like that, but better."

Audrey stood up and paced the floor behind her desk, her pencil eraser in her mouth as she took a moment to think. She then took the pencil out and waved it up and down, making her points with the wave of her pencil.

"For Essential Earth, the latest demographic study shows that married women in their twenties and early thirties are our users and target. The stats of these women who are mothers are staggering." She paused. "Be thinking in terms of reaching them in an emotional sense, through family messages. We'll start with the personal products line – the soap products, shampoos and stuff. I want to go with simplicity, almost a back-to-basics concept."

Lots of nodding. Good, they're getting this.

"Oh, it looks like sample products were delivered early this morning," said Audrey. "I saw the box by Raymond's desk, out front. Take some and try 'em out. If you have a better idea than I'm suggesting on the campaign, throw it out tomorrow, I'll always consider a new direction."

Pencil eraser back in her mouth. Then out.

"And, before I forget... This morning I will email you the research I have on Essential Earth. I put a preliminary budget together last week. Elizabeth, I'll send you that to chew on. Everyone, look over Essential Earth's website, too. As much prep as you can do before lunch tomorrow, will make our time together effective. Questions?"

"This is very exciting," said Randi.

"This is your first major company account, isn't it, Randi?" asked Audrey, smiling.

"Yes."

"This could be our biggest success ever. Really. We gotta stick together and make it work. You guys in?"

They all nodded.

"Get outta here. Get to work."

They got up to leave.

"Wait," said Audrey.

They turned, still standing. All eyes were on Audrey.

"Everyone okay from Saturday night?"

"Oh, how rude of us," said Randi. "Thank you for the lovely dinner."

"No, no. I wasn't looking for a thank you, Randi. I do appreciate it, but I want to make sure that on a personal level, well, the professional level, too -- that everyone is okay. I guess, well, I guess I was a bit over the top with the lateness thing, huh?"

"Audrey, you made the point you had to make, it was wrong for any one of us to question your authority on the job," Jack said. He turned, squinted, gave a quick look of disdain to Elizabeth, which Audrey caught out of the corner of her eye.

"Hey, I might have been a bit out of line about that," said Liz, "I don't mean to be disrespectful. Anyway, you won't have lateness issues from any of us any more."

They all shook their heads in agreement.

"Your dinner was really, really nice," said Randi. "I mean it. You were a terrific hostess."

"Thanks, guys. I guess I was a little nervous that having a few drinks together might have changed things. Glad we're all good. Let's just get this damn city job done. Then the fun starts. Are you ready?"

"Go team!" said Randi.

"Yeah, go team," said Elizabeth.

"Go team," said Jack.

"All righty, then. Get the heck outta here. Go team," said Audrey, smiling.

She took a deep breath. Somewhere deep inside her, she knew that time after time, these types of work confrontations and their ensuing emotional fixes, began to wear on her body, leaving scars and bad tastes – changing her. After the thirty-seven thousandth work issue, it becomes harder to keep a sense of calm, or humor, at that, and not be tainted the next time it happens. She wasn't sure if she, herself, was sincere, or just playing the corporate game. Truth and politics were blurred ends of the spectrum.

Despite it all, the day wrapped up nicely and the city job was off to the printers. When everyone cleared out, Audrey changed clothes in the women's room into jeans, a sweater and some running shoes. She didn't want to be late meeting up with Bella and had several blocks to walk.

Fall was becoming winter, but the maples (though few in the city) were still plenty full of leaves, still red and gold in color. The city lights were extra beautiful that night, and for some reason, Audrey was extra observant as she walked to the new Bistro. There was a smell in the air of the city – fresh pies out of the oven at the pizza place, the steaming hot dog stand on the corner. These smells were always stronger against the wind in the fall air. It made Audrey love New York and feel connected with Manhattan, like a real city girl.

By the time she got to the avenue, Audrey was already five minutes late. She could see the Bistro's neon sign in the near distance, *Les Mis* glowing in green lights. When she opened the heavy wood door to the restaurant, there she was -- sitting next to the hostess stand, in a Yankees jacket, sporting the unmistakable braid, her face in a paperback.

"How the heck can you see the pages in this dim light?" Audrey asked.

"Jesus, you scared me. I'm just passing time waiting," Bella said, putting the book back in her bag. She looked nervous.

"Why didn't you go to the bar? Let's grab a stool until they call us," she said, and then told the hostess, "How long is the wait?"

"About twenty minutes."

"OK. Bella, did you already put our name in?"

"No, sorry."

"Beane, party of two, please. A booth."

"Got it."

"Let's get a drink," Audrey said, turning to Bella.

Bella followed her to the bar.

"Why you acting like you've never been out before?" asked Audrey.

"I dunno. It's just, well, I would never go sit at a bar alone to wait for you. Would you?"

"I guess I never thought about it."

"This is the city, Audrey. You better watch yourself. Jesus, I mean, Mike would..."

"Oh what, he'd have a fit if you were at a bar – alone?"

"Uh... YEAH! Girlfriend, you need to find someone to watch over you. Sometimes I think you've been single so long, you don't have any instinctive fears. That worries me."

They took the two stools at the end of the bar. The bartender was a young guy with long hair tied into a ponytail and wore two gold hoop earrings, one in each ear.

"What's your poison, ladies? It's happy hour. Two for ones on house wines and drafts. Call brands regular price."

"Glass of Burgundy or whatever your house wine is – red and dry," said Audrey.

"Me too," said Bella.

"You wanna split the two for one or get two each?" the bartender asked, taking down glasses from the rack overhead.

"Two each," said Bella. She turned and smiled at Audrey. "What the heck, how often do we go out?"

"Fine. So anyway.... back to this girl in a bar alone thing you were talking about....I'm amazed," said Audrey.

"What of?"

"You are one hundred percent right, girlfriend. I should take better care of myself. I suppose if I got here early and you weren't here, I would have gone to the bar alone and ordered a glass of wine." Audrey turned around full circle in her chair to check out everyone in the restaurant.

"See that guy over there in the booth, sitting alone?" said Audrey.

A man with red hair and a beard, slouched at a booth, was sipping a draft beer, and cracking open peanuts with one hand.

"Yeah, I see him," said Bella crouching in closer.

Audrey whispered, "That's the *Le Mis Bistro* Mad Man, incognito. He waits for his prey to enter, finds a seat alone, then, when she turns her back...."

Bella started giggling. "So who's the guy that just came out of the men's room and sat down next to him, then?"

A blonde man about twenty slid into the booth across from the bearded man.

"His accomplice, of course," said Audrey, now sitting up straight, her eyes wide and her mouth open, as if she were in fear.

"Oh Audrey, you're always playing," Bella said.

"Beane, party of two," sounded across the room.

"I'd say that was hardly twenty minutes," said Bella, carrying two wine glasses. Audrey followed.

Audrey got up close to Bella's ear so the hostess couldn't hear. "They always do that. Those hostesses only make seven bucks an hour. They make up the answers to the questions about how long. It's always twenty minutes, whether it's five or thirty minutes. It's a safe number."

They sat down, giggling.

"Let's split a big ass appetizer and just drink so we can quick go shopping," suggested Bella.

"Great idea."

They ate a plateful of chicken fingers and cheese sticks and drank, planned their course for the night, and hit the streets within an hour.

"I've got a whim for a new pair of shoes," said Audrey as they entered Saks.

"Mind if I start early Christmas shopping?"

"Fine," Audrey said.

They spent some time in the baby clothes section, and Audrey watched as her friend matched up tiny tops with little skirts and tights for her baby. *I want a baby to buy clothes for.* The thought was more of a flash – a quick image in her mind – but it startled her with its intensity. *Where did that come from?* She let the thought breeze by, headed to the shoe department and ended up with a pair of new Mootsy-Tootsy pumps for herself. *Something new always makes me happy.*

Chapter Four

Weeks passed. Audrey returned to workaholism. Bill was leaving her alone, *probably picking on some other poor soul in another department.* Surprisingly, the Glen Park project ended up being the best work for the year. Smith Anderson was recognized for it at the City's Annual Party. Audrey attended alone, and received a plaque on behalf of the company. *How goddamn ironic,* she kept thinking. She wanted to put her mouth to the microphone at the podium and tell everyone the real story.

It was two weeks before Thanksgiving. Bella invited Audrey to spend the holiday at Bella's mother's house in Long Island with them. Bella's family was quite large, but there was always room for one more at the dinner table.

"I'll go only if I get to bring the wine and make my special vegetable casserole," Audrey said.

"Sounds like a plan."

Things started slowing down at the office and requests for vacation for holiday time came across Audrey's desk.

And what about me? Audrey thought, as she approved her staff days off. The five of them were all pretty tired from the major account they were on. It got her thinking. *Maybe a few leisurely days at home, painting on canvas?* It had been so long she worked at her craft.

It was a cool November weekend and Audrey was working on a Smith Anderson report in her bedroom, listening to the television set in the living room. "Jets versus Bucs - no greater sporting event than a New York team against Florida," her father used to say. She closed her eyes and remembered. Her heart felt like there was a hole in it. She put her hand on her chest and laid her head down. *Missing somebody like that is a physical pain.* She lit a cigarette. *It's official. I'm calling daddy tonight to talk about the game.*

Later that day, Ava called.

"That's so weird, I was just thinking about calling home tonight, I mean I was just sitting here thinking about daddy..."

Avaleen interrupted and there was a strange tone to her voice, unfamiliar to Audrey. "Come home."

"What? What's wrong?"

"It's daddy."

There was a long pause.

"What do you mean?"

"Trouble. They checked him into the city hospital. Tests. They don't know."

"Ava, tell me what happened," she said.

"I went over to his house this morning. We picked up some things at the grocery for him. He said he wasn't feeling well. I invited him to watch the Bucs game with us and stay the night at the house. He agreed.

"We packed up his things and I drove him over. He said he was having a migraine. He got tunnel vision before we got home. He was sweating profusely. Then everything was blurry. He started slurring his words. We

52

didn't even get to the house. I drove him immediately to the Emergency Room," she said.

"Where are you now?" Audrey asked.

"I'm in the waiting room at the hospital. They're checking him in. I thought he was having a stroke or something."

"Did he take his blood pressure medicine? Maybe that's all it is, his blood levels are out of whack." Audrey said.

"No, I already thought of that. He took them. Audrey, I'm fucking scared. He's all we've got. Get on a plane. I need you. Jeff is keeping the kids calm, but I need to scream. I need you. Daddy will be asking for you."

"I'm coming," Audrey told her. "I'll call you with the flight number. Should I rent a car or will you pick me up?"

"I'll pick you up."

"I'm coming tonight," Audrey said before hanging up.

He's going to be all right. I just need to keep the faith. Dear God, please let this be okay.

Audrey was unusually calm in emergencies. She was a melodramatic freak in other situations, but in cases of emergency, her head was always clear. She knew how to take control and get done whatever needed doing.

She fired off an email to Bill, copied her staff and blind-copied Bella.

```
Subject:  Scheduling This Week
All,
     I have a family emergency in Florida
and  am  taking  the  next  flight  out.
Elizabeth   will   have   to   lead   the
campaign  presentation  on  Wednesday  -  2
PM  at  their  office,  7th  floor  on  5th
Avenue.   Please  send  my  regrets  to
Nancy  and  Don.   I  will  follow  up  with
them  on  my  return.   I  expect  to  be  only
```

a few days. I will call you, Bill, as soon as I can tomorrow.

Liz, the files are on my desk in the right hand basket. I am attaching the budget that I completed today. Jack, make sure Elizabeth proofs the storyboard for the commercial before Randi does the graphics. Randi, I can view a .pdf on my laptop, which I'll take with me. I'd like to see the print ads before they are presented.

Wish me luck, my father is in the hospital and I don't have too many details yet.

Regards,
Audrey

Audrey checked flights to Tampa and the rates online. The last flight would be leaving La Guardia in a couple of hours. It didn't give her much time. She booked the flight, charged her Visa account, and scrambled to pack a suitcase. She did a final check of the electrical appliances in the house, grabbed her laptop computer, suitcase, handbag, keys, and then called for a cab. She chain-smoked while waiting, until the yellow car pulled up. "La Guardia," she said.

It was an hour before boarding. *A book. That'll help.* She walked into the newsstand and scanned the titles of the bestsellers rack. *Same shitty authors, same shitty stories. Ya got your romantic, cookie cutter stories, girl in Manhattan travels to foreign country, meets Fabio-type, has passionate sex, they break-up, boo hoo, then he rescues her from her foreign conspiracy and takes care of her. Geez. Look at the cover. It says it all.*

Oh here's a winner, another bad ass detective finds a dead body in a ditch and it's a cousin of some ambassador and the world is going to come to halt if he doesn't bring the secret he found to light. Puhleez. Who reads this shit?

She settled on a light, chick lit book about three girls who reunite at a twenty-year reunion.

In all her rushing around, the importance of the events had not yet sunk in. She was running on pure adrenaline. She grabbed a seat at the gate and dug in her purse for the cell phone. *Of course, not in the right pocket.* Digging, digging. *Fuck.* She brought out her sunglasses, keys, cosmetics bag, calendar, calculator, and spread them out on the empty chair next to her. *There you are.* She phoned Ava's cell phone while she put everything back in her big bag.

"Hey, it's me. I'm boarding Jet Blue Flight 143 to Tampa, arriving 10:12. Ya got that?"

"Got it, 10:12," Ava said.

"What's happening now, Ava?"

"He's checked into a semi-private room. Thankfully, there's no one in the other bed so it's just us. I'm here with him now. Want to say hi to daddy?"

"Hello," said her father.

Audrey held back the tears. "Oh, daddy!"

"Now Audrey, don't worry. I can't see right now but they think it's temporary. There might be some pressure around my brain. They gave me something and it doesn't hurt any more. I'm just really tired from the drugs."

"Daddy, I thought of you today before Ava called, I wanted to watch the Bucs with you! Now I'll be there soon and I can't wait." That was all she could think of to say.

"Fly safe, Aud," Ava said. "I'll pick you up, curbside."

"I'll say a prayer." Audrey said. "We're boarding now."

The flight felt like a year. She had forgotten about the novel in her bag, which might have distracted her. Instead, she looked out the plane window and stared out to the blackness of the night, feeling blind, just like daddy. She imagined his fear and pain. *My poor, poor daddy.* She put her hand over her mouth and took a breath.

The flight attendant asked if she was okay or wanted anything.

"Vodka?" Audrey asked.

"Sure." she said. "Tomato or Orange juice?"

"Tomato," Audrey said, handing over a ten spot. "Keep the change."

She opened the mini bottle of vodka and poured half into the iced cup with some of the tomato juice. She felt the burn of the alcohol as it reached the back of her throat. But it was good. It calmed her. She sipped it until it was gone and then requested another, and then another. It probably was enough to get drunk off of, but the effect was merely a sense of numbing. *I can do this.*

The plane made a smooth landing and the cabin lights came on. Sleepy passengers took their bags from overhead and Audrey began losing patience with the pace. *Move your fat asses, you losers with nothing but vacations on your mind.* She wanted to strangle every last one of them. *You're all just extras in the movie of my life. Drop dead, for all I care. Get me off the damn plane and to the hospital.*

When she was curbside, her sister was waiting for her with the car running. They exchanged a sideways hug as Audrey climbed in, throwing her bags in the back seat.

"Are you okay? I can't believe this," said Audrey. "Anything else going on since you left daddy? How is he? Tell me."

"Ooooooh. It's bad. He ain't right. He ain't right."

"Ain't right? Ain't right what? How?"

"I don't know how to describe it. They don't know until they run tests. A stroke? I don't know. We'll get the medical scoop tomorrow. For now, all I can tell you is that the headaches and passing out are major. He can't even put

56

words together one minute. The next minute, he's pretty lucid. He was resting good when I left the hospital. The nurse wasn't too bad, so I didn't feel too bad leaving him."

Audrey looked out the window at the familiar long highway. "I've been away too long. I feel disconnected. I can't wait to see him. I'm so glad you called me today."

"I'm glad you came so fast, I know how busy you are," Ava said. "How was the flight?"

"All those fucking tourists wearing Mickey Mouse ears, all bright and cheery like life was just a breezy boat ride on *It's a Small World*," she complained.

"You crack me up!" Avaleen laughed. "I think *It's a Small World* finally closed down."

"Let me bitch without correcting me, will ya? You get my point. Sister, why is it when something is happening bad in your life that everyone around you seems to be happy and stupid, and you want to kill them?"

"I know exactly what you mean," she said.

During the drive, the conversation covered much ground from what was new with the kids, Audrey's disgust with her job, to Ava's concern about dad's health and still not knowing what was wrong.

"I thought we were going right to the hospital. What are we doing at your house?" Audrey asked, as they pulled up the driveway.

"They said we couldn't go back. It's too late. They said after 10:00 it wouldn't be a good idea to see daddy. He needs to sleep, and the tests would start at 6:00 A.M. tomorrow. If we went there, they'd refuse to let us go up and see him."

"Well, why the hell didn't you tell me that at the airport, Ava? I thought we were going to the hospital, damn it."

"Jesus, Audrey. Don't start snapping at me. Just come in the house and we'll talk some. It's late and we'll go over as soon it's light out. For the love of God, you sure haven't changed with your impatience," she said.

"Fine. I need a cigarette before we go in. Will you sit on the porch with me?" Audrey asked, remembering that Ava wouldn't have anyone smoking inside.

"Sure."

It was a beautiful Florida November night. Warm. The sky was filled with stars. Out here, there are no streetlights. A dark sky in the country is truly black. An owl, somewhere in the distance, hooted. It felt like home. Audrey was calmed as she inhaled deeply, taking in the fresh warm air.

"Oh Sister," she said, lighting her cigarette.

"You don't have to say it," Ava replied. "It feels good to have you here."

"Exactly," Audrey said. "Do you think Jeff is awake?"

"Nope. He went to bed before I left."

"Are you sleepy?" Audrey asked.

"Completely not. I'm wired."

"Me too."

"Does this remind you of when mommy was in the hospital?" asked Audrey.

"Mmmm hmmm. I feel nine years old again, Sister. Scared."

Winter 1981. Renny Beane was 34 years old in 1981 when she died, the same age as Audrey now. It came so unexpectedly. Everything was storybook perfect in the Beane family before the pneumonia took her life.

They were a happy family living in a large southern-style farmhouse in New Port Richey on five acres. The house was a large old, two-story traditional architecture – wood frame, stone fireplace that went up two floors, oak hardwood floors, with the 1950's retro kitchen. The house on Oak Drive was decorated modestly with many garage-sale trinkets. The trinkets were Renny's treasures. She could take anything old and rusty and make it an artful décor item in the house. An aluminum watering can became a vase for dried flowers. The can had painted on it, "The Beanes – Established 1969", as one example of her many projects.

There were many homemade pretty things in the house. Renny was a seamstress, and made all the curtains and window treatments in the house. Lace was everywhere, from the white tablecloths on the formal Queen-Anne style dining table, to the sheers behind the formal, gold brocade drapes in the formal living room. The old couches that were worn from years of children's spilt milk, pet hairs, and sticky fingers had been cleaned, and recovered with new tapestry custom-fit fabric, hand sewn. The floral print was like something seen in a homes and garden magazine. Renny had a knack for taking anything in any state of disrepair, and making it beautiful again. She crocheted afghans by the dozens – anytime she was sitting, she was making something. She could crochet in the dark, watching a game with George, or pretending to be involved with a show the kids were raving about.

The formal living room toward the front of the house had a wrought-iron gate at its entrance. Renny kept it clean in case guests came for a social call. The rest of the house could be a disaster with the children's toys, Renny's latest sewing projects, or a mound of clothing awaiting ironing, but not that front room. Guests always commented how she was such a terrific homemaker. But all they had to do is step a few feet further to the other rooms to find out the truth of the matter.

The holidays at the Beane house were especially lovely. They couldn't afford the latest in yard decorations or lighting. Renny was artistic, George was handy, and between the two of them, they could come up with decorations better than most any store sold – for cheap, too. One year, they carved out of wood, eight life-size reindeer, a sleigh and a life-size Santa Claus carrying bags of presents. George was an incredible carpenter and he had only the best in electric tools. His handiwork was amazing -- he completed the outline of the wood figures that would stick in the ground and hold lights to shine on them.

Renny took George's creation to the next level. Using acrylic paints in vibrant colors, she made the reindeer come to life. It took the two of them months to get it done. To this day, that reindeer set is still used in the Beane family. Ava kept them in perfect condition in her garage at her farm.

"Remember Christmases on Oak Street?" Audrey asked Ava.

She nodded.

"Inside that house, Christmas screamed throughout. Do you remember even the bathrooms were decorated? We had hand towels with embroidered pictures of snowy scenes. Candles were everywhere. Can't you just smell the balsam or cinnamon that filtered through the hallways? Mommy always had potpourri or cinnamon-scented pinecones in a basket on the fireplace hearth. She loved Christmas."

Avaleen said, "It sounds sappy, but mom inspired me to want to keep a nice home. It's so silly, Jeff really doesn't care, but I want a place that looks nice, and smells nice. It makes me feel like a good woman to keep a clean house."

"Must be nice. My hamper is empty, but that's because the dirty clothes didn't even make it that far. They're on the floor. When I have no more underwear, I either do a load, or simply buy another pack of underwear."

Avaleen laughed, "You're not like mom was."

"Yes I am. Well, I think I could be."

"No, you're not. You're more like Dad. And after mommy died, you were even more like him in how you dealt with it all. Strong – like a man. I wish I could be like that."

Jesus, is that what she thinks? She doesn't know me, either.

When mom died in 1981, George was 37 years old. He worked for the telephone company his whole life. He wore a uniform -- a golf-style shirt with 'General Telephone' embroidered on one side along with his name.

"Did you know I thought that because daddy's work shirt was blue, that's why they called him a blue-collar worker?"

They laughed.

"I remember 1981 like it was yesterday," said Audrey.

"It's foggy for me. Tell me more."

"New Port Richey was still a best-kept secret. Not like it is today. Most snowbirds hadn't heard about the place. The tourists on this coast went to St. Petersburg and the Clearwater beaches when they came. They didn't realize how beautiful it was right here. The beauty of the countryside was different than those overpopulated cities, with all their concrete and shopping malls. The private beaches along the coast were hidden. You do remember the picnics at Green Key Beach, don't you? It was great! White sandy areas for spreading out a blanket to relax on, or cooking on the city grills. They had a great swing set. Remember?"

"Of course I remember. I haven't been back there in eons. I should take the kids. It was our favorite spot, Audrey, remember? It had nothing to do with the family spending quality time together, blah, blah, blah, as mom and dad probably thought. Hell, they could've just dropped us off alone for all I cared. The water at the beach there broke on the shore with such force. It was scary-fun. Know what I mean, Audrey? There was one point of the beach that had big rocks and the waves would blow over us and we'd fall down laughing. Why did mom and dad let us go over there? There were signs around that it was a no swimming area. Somehow we always got away with it, sneaking over by those rocks. We'd laugh until it hurt as the waves hurled water over our heads and make them lose our balance standing in the soft sand."

"Those were good times," said Audrey. "I'm so glad we got the boat the summer before mommy passed away. It was great memories."

"I remember that part very clearly," said Ava.

They exchanged more stories.

"Ya know," said Ava. "I have trouble remembering parts of mom's sickness."

"Let's not remember that part, then, okay? How about only the good parts," said Audrey.

They went inside and sat at the kitchen table. Ava broke out the photo album and they chatted about old times for a while, and looked at the latest snapshots of Ava's kids.

"Time sure marches on."

"It does," said Ava.

Audrey yawned. "Exhausted," she said.

"Well, you can have the guest room."

"I'll see you in the morning."

A few minutes later Audrey was in the guest bathroom where she could privately cry in the shower and not be heard. *It's okay, sometimes you have to release the tension to keep going.*

The roosters out back awoke her with their early morning cock-a-doodle-doos. And she felt sick -- literally sick. Her head was pounding and her muscles ached like she had the flu. She thought she might have a fever. She – who never gets sick – was sick! *Good Lord, not now.* Her throat was dry and one side of it in pain. *It must be those fucking Mickey Mouse tourists on the plane ride, spewing germs. No wonder it caught up with me -- rundown from being upset, overwork, and lack of sleep -- all factors.* She rolled over and groaned. *God forbid anything should ever be easy.*

The smell of bacon lifted in the air to reach Audrey's room and nose. She heard the sounds of little children playing and the tiny cries of puppies. Despite feeling lousy, she was excited to see her nephews. She quickly got dressed and threw on a face of minimal make-up, enough to pass her sister's inspection for not being a total slob. When she walked to the center of the living room, Sammy saw her first.

"Aunt Audrey!" He ran over to her and jumped in her arms. Josh was too young to remember who she was, but being two, he was quite curious to walk over and check her out. Puppies were everywhere, sniffing and jumping and circling.

"My goodness! This is a crazy house," she said, teasingly.

"Hello Audrey," said Jeff from the kitchen. Audrey picked up Josh and ran over to Jeff to give him a hug and a kiss on the cheek.

"Good to see you, Audrey," he said. "Don't look so sad. We'll deal with your father's situation as best as we all can. I'm taking the kids over to my mom's today. You and Ava can spend time alone with your father, for as long as you like," he said.

"Thank you."

Ava must have been showering and getting ready, while Jeff whipped up a big country breakfast. He was like that – a happy guy who was helpful around the house. He was able to make a good living selling farm equipment, so that Ava could stay home, comfortably financially, with the kids.

"The farm is prettier than I remembered it," Audrey commented. "I want to paint it."

"So paint it, Audrey. It's not the heat of summer, you can set up your old easel on the back porch. Don't you still have your brushes and pallets and stuff in dad's garage?"

"I think everything is still over there. Do you think I'll have time?" Audrey asked.

"How long is your visit?" he asked.

"A few days," she replied.

He turned from the stove to look her in the eye. "A few days?" he asked, as if that weren't long enough. "Audrey. Can I be real with you?"

"Be real," she replied.

"I think what's wrong with your father is serious," he said.

"Why?" she asked.

"Did Ava tell you he's lost weight?"

"Yes, but he was overweight."

"Audrey, he's lost like forty pounds. And he wasn't trying."

"You don't think...the big C?"

"Yes, I do think..." he replied.

"No," she said, not wanting to believe him.

"I'm just saying Audrey, this isn't a stroke, like Ava thinks. This is chronic. Something is advancing in him. The blood tests he had at his regular check-up were fine. It's something in his brain, I'm thinking."

"Maybe we shouldn't speculate," Audrey said. "Jeff, let's not invite trouble."

"I just want you and Ava to be prepared and open-minded in case it isn't good news," he said.

"How do you ever prepare for anything like that? You don't. And you know what else? When you do lose someone, you're never, ever, ever, ever the same again. I'm sure you've seen that with Ava. It's been twenty years since mom died. We're not over that yet. I don't think Ava and me will ever get over it. So in essence, Jeff, you can't ever prepare. It sucks every time. I hope to God you're wrong about daddy."

"Let's just keep this conversation between us, Audrey," Jeff said. "Ava gets easily upset about dad. He's getting older and needs to be looked after now. Ava has been very involved with him every couple of days. Did you know he hasn't driven in about a month? He blacked out pulling into the gas station in October. Sat in his car for about an hour until he could see again. That was that. Ava started driving him places the last four weeks."

"Why didn't she tell me?"

"From what she tells me, you've been a bit aloof. I know she said you were working on a major project and couldn't get distracted. Some two million dollar profit deal or something, that's what she said. She thought dad would just get better and why worry you during this busy time for you."

"Because I'm family, that's why! Family first, Jeff! If she ever pulls that shit again you tell her to lay all the cards on the table. And to think I took for granted that everything was just hunky-dory here – now I'm pissed. Not so much at Ava, but myself, for giving the impression I'm too important to deal with real problems in the family. Well, I'm here now, aren't I?"

She stopped talking. Ava walked into the kitchen, dressed for the day. She took a piece of bacon right from the frying pan and ate it.

"Audrey, you look like shit," she said, chomping on the bacon strip.

"Well, thank you, Miss Shiny Happy People Pants," Audrey said.

"Knock it off. I don't mean you look ugly, for crying out loud. You're sick, aren't you?" Ava asked.

"How can you tell?"

"I can tell just by looking at you." Ava placed her hand on Audrey's forehead. "You have a fever," she said. "You're burning up. Well, you can't give that to daddy. You're not going to the hospital this morning."

"I'm fucking going," Audrey said.

Ava put her finger over her puckered mouth and then sharply pointed at the virgin ears of her babies. "Watch the language, sister."

"They didn't hear me."

"Well, watch it. That's all I'm saying."

"Sorry."

"Alright then. No ifs, ands or buts, stay back this morning. Get your shit together, Audrey. I'm ready to leave in five minutes. You look like you need a few hours in bed."

"I'm just a little whipped from the flight and lack of sleep. I'll be fine."

"You have a fever."

"I'll be fine."

"It's not you I'm worried about. Daddy can't afford to catch a bug."

"Fine. I admit it. I'm sick. So, what are you saying, I came to Florida to be sick at your house? I need to see daddy."

"Audrey, I'm just saying, stay back, rest, and shake off the fever for a few hours. I'll go check on him this morning. We'll go back again to visit around dinnertime. Hopefully you'll be feeling better by then."

"Fine. You win."

Jeff and the kids kept their Sunday plan to see Jeff's mother. When everyone left, Audrey fixed a cup of tea, had a morning smoke, and collapsed back into the bed.

It must have been well after noon when Audrey awakened. The sleep had done her good. *It's just a little cold*, she told herself, and she would be fine. She got herself dressed and ready for the day. She unpacked and hung up her clothes in the closet. Grabbing her pack of cigarettes and cell phone, she headed out to the back porch to a rocking chair to call Ava.

She started dialing, but hung up. Her attention was drawn to the view before her. *Awesome.* The sights and sounds of her sister's farm were beautiful. The sun was hot, like a summer day, and she leaned back to feel the therapy of the sun's warm rays on her face. A gray mare was standing regally with its mane impeccably groomed to one side. There was a black horse behind the barn, hardly visible. She might not have noticed him had he not neighed. Audrey could only make out the shape of its backside as the head was partially hidden by some trees and azalea bushes.

"You can set up your old easel on the back porch." Audrey remembered Jeff's words. Her heart beat fast just at the prospect of it.

The sound of her sister's car pulling up interrupted the daydream. Audrey went inside to greet Ava, who by this time was barreling her way in the side door with an armful of bags. There was a juggling of some groceries and Audrey assisted in the delivery of them to the kitchen. There was a worried look on Ava's face when she said, "Hi."

"Hi." Audrey replied.

"The tests were taken this morning. I was there when the doctor interpreted them. There is a mass on daddy's brain. It's quite large. He needs surgery," she said.

Audrey sat down at the kitchen table, placing her head in her hands. "OK," she said. "What else?"

"Isn't that enough?" her sister snapped.

"Well there's one question I'm thinking is a pretty big one, Ava... DUH!"

"Oh. Sorry. I guess I'm not thinking straight. The good news is that they said the mass is benign."

"How big is it?" Audrey asked.

"Big," Ava said.

"Stop with the half-assed answers. Quantify."

"I don't know, Audrey – they said in centimeters, I didn't know if that was circumference, diameter, or what. I don't get all the medical mumbo-jumbo," she said.

"What now?" Audrey asked.

"I really don't know. Why don't you give them a call because I don't understand this. They say he needs surgery immediately, or, he could consider a program to shrink it with chemo and radiation. There's risks with each of the choices."

"What risks?" Audrey asked.

"I would say there's a risk associated with brain surgery, Audrey. I think you know the side effects from chemotherapy or radiation. Or shall I educate you on that?" she said.

"What's with the attitude? Sit down. Let me make you a cup of tea."

"It's hot out, sister. I'm sweating. I don't want hot tea, for crying out loud. Why is it you always think sitting down, having tea and a cigarette solves things?"

"Uh. You don't have to get snippy, Sis," Audrey said, her face becoming red and hot.

Here we are, just the two of us, facing a family crisis. Behaving badly. It's just like when we were kids – the way we snap at each other. Audrey felt 12 again and wanted to pounce on her sister, knock her down to the floor and hold her shoulders to the ground, until Ava screamed for mercy. She took a moment to indulge in a fantasy of beating the crap out of her sister. *She could be such a bitch!*

"I'll be on the back porch when you want to talk some more," said Audrey.

She slipped out the sliding glass door from the kitchen and found a rocking chair with the same pretty view of the farm. She sat and stared, unblinking. *So I wonder what we'll all be doing three months from now?* Her heart was beating fast, and there was a lump in her throat.

Her thoughts drifted. Ungodly as those thoughts were, she fantasized about daddy dying. Then she could come to Florida and sell his house and have enough money to allow her to not work so hard. Then she would have an excuse to

68

have a sabbatical. She'd be so filled with grief, everyone at the office would feel so sorry for her. They would all be nice to her, for once. They would soothe her and tell her it was going to be okay. Her boss would insist she take a few months off. She'd spend that time in Florida. She'd paint pictures that expressed her pain. She'd get much sun and rest. She'd make a vegetable garden.

What the hell am I thinking? She shook her head to get such an evil thought out of her mind.

Just then, she felt something cold on her neck and stood up and looked behind her. It was Ava behind her, teasing her by placing a cold glass of iced tea to her skin.

"Rude!" Audrey snapped.

"Not rude – funny!" replied Ava, giggling.

Audrey threw her head back laughing. It was their own way of making up from spats – teasing one another. It worked every time.

"Let's hang out here a while," suggested Avaleen. "Later, I was thinking we could swing by daddy's house. He asked me to bring him a couple of personal items. Maybe we could sneak a slushie in his room for him for a treat. He can't wait to see you. Fever gone, I hope?"

"I'm good. Fine. Do you think we could take a quick look in daddy's garage for my easel and paints?" Audrey asked.

"You're going to paint?"

"The backyard here. It's beautiful."

"Great. But I want to keep the finished product, frame it and hang it on the wall."

Chapter Five

Later that afternoon they drove up to their father's house. It had been years since she had been to his home, a small place he downsized to shortly after Audrey and Avaleen went off to college. The house needed a paint job. The canvas awnings were in need of cleaning. It looked like nobody had edged the walkway to the front door for quite some time. Audrey hoped that the inside would give her a better feeling.

The inside of the house looked the same as it ever did, but now it seemed like just a house. *Where is the love?* "Ava, it's dead inside here. I can't remember ever being here without that blasted TV being on some news program at an ungodly volume."

Audrey moved through the house to the back door. She could see from the small window that the garden wasn't the way she remembered it. She opened the back door to the screen room to view the yard.

The garden was overgrown. There used to be landscaping in the back that looked like it came out of a home & garden magazine. She reached down to where the garden used to be. *Why? Why?* Now, there were weeds, brown patches, and where there was once a pond filled with Japanese gold fish, was now a piling of mulch-covered dirt, where it looked like some sort of plant was trying to grow, but failing, miserably. The concrete benches were green with fungus and the pathways that Audrey had helped her father carve in the yard blended with the rest of the grounds. It was shockingly different than Audrey remembered.

Ava must have noticed Audrey's reaction. "Daddy's been too sick to take care of it, Audrey."

"It's alright," Audrey said, pretending it wasn't a big deal to her.

They loaded up the trunk with Audrey's art supplies, and Ava filled a tote bag with some of dad's things, his mail, and a book he was reading. They stopped at the convenience store to pick up a slushie for their father.

"I'll just run in," said Audrey, "keep the car running."

Audrey made her way to the slushie machine and filled her cup, when she noticed an old familiar face getting a six-pack of coke out of the nearby cooler. *Could it be him?* Tall, dark, thin, blue eyes, muscle shirt and board shorts. *It had to be him.* She walked by to glance sideways without him seeing her.

"No way!" she said loudly.

He turned to look.

"Audrey Beane?"

"Roger Hollingsworth?"

They embraced. It was only a moment, but long enough for Audrey to swoon in his muscular, tanned arms. It was his familiar cologne fragrance that brought her back in time to her college days with him. He still wore a gold ball earring in his left ear, just as he had a decade, or more, before. *He is cute, cute, cute.* He'd lost some of his boyish look and was a real man now, as evidenced by some facial and chest hair. He wouldn't have needed to say anything, just a tug and she would have gone arm and arm, any where with him in that very moment.

"Audrey, I thought you moved to New York?"

"I did. I'm just here visiting. I'm staying at Ava's place for a few days," she said. "What are you up to?"

"Got a bungalow downtown in the old section by the River," he said. "Started my own brokerage. Got married last year," he said.

"Married? Anyone I know?" asked Audrey.

"Nobody you know, Audrey."

That was all he said about her – this woman he called his wife. *Oh please tell me more*, but they were standing in the Quick Mart, and it was becoming weird.

"Congratulations. You look well," she said.

"You look wonderful, and it's good to see you," he said.

There was a pause. Their eyes met momentarily and each looked away, almost as if they were guilty of something.

"I gotta go," she said, holding up the slushie. "Kinda melting."

He smiled. His dimples were revealed.

She felt goose bumps all over. Her heart ached for him.

She paid for the slushie and wanted to look back at Roger to see if he was watching her, but she was afraid he might see her looking back, and think she was looking at him. So she didn't. She hustled to Ava's car and got in.

"What the hell took so long?" Ava asked.

"Un-fucking-believable," reported Audrey. "Look. Look. Look who's coming out of the store in the red shirt. Do you see him?" she asked.

"Is that Roger?" Ava asked, looking over the top of her sunglasses.

"Yes! I just saw him. Oh Ava, isn't he beautiful?" Audrey asked. "Oh Avaleen, I fucked up my life big time. Look at him! I want him."

Ava shook her head and turned up the radio. *How Do You Talk to An Angel* was on. Audrey closed her eyes and pretended that Roger was singing to her. They didn't talk about it any more in the car. They just listened to tunes and drove with the windows down, relaxing.

They drove through town and it wasn't long until they were back to the open country road. Ava picked up speed. The sunroof on the Toyota was open as far as it could be. Tunes blared. Audrey reclined the seat to better feel the warm, setting sun on her face. Its heat contrasted against the cool, intermittent November breeze, intensified by the car's speed. The sky was an azure color that turned radiant shades of pink and orange around the perfectly round, yellow sun. The fresh air had an aromatic hint of freshly mowed grass. There was no traffic, no sounds of old car mufflers or mac trucks, just the perfectly balanced bass and treble of an old favorite song. She shut her eyes and made a memory of this feeling.

Ava slowed. The car meandered down an S-curved road to the hospital entrance. When it stopped, Audrey was conflicted about getting out -- about being there at all. It had been so long since she'd seen her father. It would be a happy reunion, yes, but the circumstances of this meeting, however, were surreal. She wondered what Ava was thinking. They had spent the past twenty minutes in the car without sharing a word. She was probably as far away from reality as Audrey had been, immersed in the ride and the music. Who wouldn't be trying to forget, if only for a moment? Darkness surrounded both their worlds now.

Before going into the patient room, Audrey asked the front desk if they could provide her a surgical mask so she could cover her mouth, so as not to give her father her cold. They obliged.

When the two sisters walked in, their father was laying flat on his back, hands on his stomach, one on top of the other, and the covers were perfectly tucked around him and under his hands. Audrey hated herself for her morbid thoughts, but he did look completely, peacefully dead -- just lying there. Just seeing his fingers resting there with his class ring on his right hand that he was always so proud of, it made her sad. His hands she knew so well.

Ava and Audrey stood at the door silently for a long time, without saying anything. Afraid to wake him, or afraid he was dead, they just looked at him. His hair was thin and a colorless white, gray. He had many more age spots on his cheeks since Audrey had seen him last. His lips were parched. He looked so small on the big hospital bed. An IV was in one arm. It looked like the life had been sucked out of him.

It was an off-white, barren, sterile room that smelled of bleach and medicine. The window overlooked the parking lot and trash dumpsters. Next to the bed was a tray with a water pitcher and cup of water with a bendy straw. *How sad that hospitals use bendy straws because patients obviously have trouble managing a cup. Depressing*, she thought.

No flowers in the room? Suddenly Audrey wanted to kick herself for not picking up some, or at least a balloon to brighten up the place. She looked down at the blue slushie melting in the plastic cup and thought how distasteful it was that this was her offering of love to her one and only father. *All the way from the Big Apple on a jet plane to come here with – with – with – this.* She immediately had the urge to hop on the elevator to the first floor and buy something respectable at the gift shop. She would have done it too, except the dead man on the cot opened one eye

74

and looked right at her, one eyebrow higher than the other. It was apparent his vision had returned.

"Why are you hiding behind a mask? You can't catch what I have, daughter of mine," he smiled.

She ran to him and touched his forehead and kissed him through the mask.

"You're ice cold, pop!" she said.

"It's like a refrigerator in here," he said.

"I'll get some blankets," said Avaleen, and she left to find a nurse.

"I guess this was a dumb idea, daddy," Audrey said, holding up the stupid blue slushie that was now a disastrous cup of melted, over sweetened, dye-colored water. The plastic cup was sweating and dripping moisture down her arm.

He smiled sweetly at her. It made her feel better, and confirmed to her that he knew she had remembered he loved blue ice. *It's the thought that counts. That's all that ever matters anyway, really, ever.*

Audrey set the cup at the little sink near the bathroom and pulled up the chair as close as she could get to him. But it felt weird to be in his presence. Everything seemed formal and tense. This wasn't their normal greeting. Dad was always center stage with some sort of funny and animated story to tell. He was so subdued now.

"I'm glad you're here, Audrey," he said, gently closing his eyes.

Her eyes welled with tears. It just didn't seem like him. *Where was his character and spirit? He was acting like he was on his last leg. Was he?*

"I love you," she said, sobbing.

"I love you," he said.

The formal exchange of words is way too real. In the past, sure – we had exchanged "I love yous," but those times were in a silly way – like when you say goodnight and I love you, it's kind of silly. Not real. Not like you're telling someone I really, really love you and you must know this before you die, kind of a thing. When his eyes opened, she could see his soul. Maybe she was imagining it, but he was different now. Very different.

Ava returned with the blankets and parked herself right on the edge of the bed near her father. Avaleen's face was contorted. She, too, must have been sensing that things were different. She just sat there, staring – first at Dad, then at Audrey, and again. Daddy's eyes blinked, and each blink was deliberate and hard.

"Can you see okay?" Audrey asked.

"I can see," he said. "There's clouds around lights, though."

"What did the doctor tell you?" Avaleen asked.

"He was in here again after you left, Ava. Can't remember what he told me. There was a nurse with him. Something about wanting to see you when you got here."

"The nurses didn't say anything to me when I asked them for blankets. Who was she, Daddy? What did she look like?" Ava asked.

"Don't remember. Dr. Martin...making rounds after dinner...said he would stop by..... in case you're here."

"Good," Audrey said. "Want anything?"

"No. I'm so tired," he said.

"Rest. We'll just sit here with you," Audrey said.

He shut his eyes and quietly repeated, "Thank you so much for coming here."

"Oh, Daddy! I know if the tables were turned you'd come to see me on the first flight out," Audrey said.

He smiled, saying nothing. His breathing got very regular. He was quickly asleep, deep enough that Audrey and Ava could talk in normal volume without waking him.

"I should bring my laptop here when we come tomorrow," said Audrey. "I could set it up right over there." She pointed to a chair by the window and an A/C floor unit coming out of the wall that would have enough

76

width to hold the computer upright. "I could at least review the presentation for the Essential Earth account if I download it tonight, and still be here if daddy wanted to talk..."

Ava looked at her, cocking her head. "You really are a piece of work, Aud. I mean really."

"What do you mean?"

"I could shoot you," said Ava. "I could just sit here and shoot you."

Audrey's brow furrowed. "Why?"

"Because," said Ava.

"I don't understand what you mean."

"Could you forget about the damn job for one fricken day?" she said.

"Don't start with me," said Audrey.

"I mean, a time like this..." Ava's voice trailed off and she shook her head.

"What does it matter if I'm sitting here reading a book or if it's a file on a computer screen?"

"You just don't get it, Audrey. You really don't. You are so caught up in yourself. It's all about you, isn't it?"

"Why is it, Ava, that you think you can just say anything you want to, never thinking you're going to insult someone?"

"Hullo Kettle – you're black," said Ava.

"You're so fucking funny."

The sisters dropped it. They sat there silently watching their father breathe. His chest rose and fell with every breath. Audrey found herself breathing along with the same rhythm, getting sleepy. The mask on her face was like breathing into a paper bag – her own exhaled carbon dioxide. Sleepy. Dozing off...

Suddenly...."Good evening."

Audrey sat up, alarmed. Standing at the door was a stout, short man, with pink cheeks and big blue eyes -- stethoscope around his neck, white lab coat, and a dangling badge from his collar that said, "Dr. Richard Martin." He smiled, approached, and without a word, checked the chart at the end of the bed and took his patient's pulse.

"You must be Mr. Beane's daughters," he said.

"Yes," they both said.

"I discussed your father's condition with him earlier today and explained that he will have a long treatment – the course of many months. The tumor on his brain is quite large." He held out both hands in an open prayer position to make an oval shape much larger than the size of an egg to indicate the size. "Your father has elected to try chemotherapy and radiation and forgo surgery. A social worker will be scheduled to meet with you to assess your family's need for his care. There are community services that will help you – such as for a hospital bed for home, bars for the bathroom, diapers, if necessary." He noted the pulse rate on the chart on his clipboard.

The sisters sat there silently – Ava was on the other side of her father across from Dr. Martin, rubbing her father's frail arm, caressing his hair. He was still asleep, heavily sedated.

"The dosages of the treatment will be as high as he can tolerate. We want to be swift and aggressive and shrink the tumor quickly. His condition may worsen simply because the prescribed dosages are toxic to good cells as well as bad cells. The nurse can provide you some booklets about side effects of chemo and radiation, so you will know what to expect."

"When will he go home?" asked Avaleen.

"Tomorrow, maybe by the end of the week, as long as there's no seizure. There's not much we can do in a hospital for him other than stabilize him. He'll need someone to be there for him at home. You might consider a visiting nurse."

A million questions later, Dr. Martin said he had to go. He left a telephone number for them to call at 8:00 in the morning to coordinate a meeting with the social worker.

The ride home was desperately silent. A cold front had blown through and the heat from their breath fogged up the inside car windows. Ava struggled with the vents and defroster settings, dramatically sliding the buttons left to right, from heat to cold settings to clear the windshield. Nothing was working so she took her hand and wiped a big circle in the window, clearing some of the condensation. Her jerky movements expressed her frustration. She started crying – a child's type of crying - snorting and shaking, hyperventilating, saying nothing, just boo-hooing and not holding the tears back any longer.

"It's going to be all right, sister," Audrey said.

Ava shook her head. "No, it's not all right."

*****

The next day, they arrived at the hospital to meet with the social worker. With all the back and forth traveling, sobbing, bouts of silence or spats between Audrey and Avaleen, one day was running into the next and a sense of time was lost. It all ran together. They took a seat outside the social worker's office in a waiting area that was otherwise empty.

"What day is this?" asked Audrey.

"Tuesday, I think."

"Did I brush my teeth today?" asked Audrey. She put her tongue across the front of her teeth to see if they felt gritty. "Ava, I'm losing it. I can't remember if I brushed my fucking teeth!"

Ava put her nose in a fashion magazine and was hardly paying attention. "Mmmm hmm. You probably did. Who cares? Check out this outfit Britney is wearing."

She held up a magazine photo of the star who appeared half-naked with a pink fuzzy jacket over her shoulders.

"Ew."

"Ew."

They both started giggling.

The door opened. Audrey and Ava straightened up. A short, redhead with half-glasses across her long, long nose and an attached chain extending from the glass frames to around her neck, peeked out, "If you are George Beane's daughters, please do come in." She had an English accent and enunciated every syllable. "I am Saundra Pruitt, and I need to assess your home situation before your father can be released."

Released? She makes it sound like he is incarcerated..

Pointy, persnickety Mrs. Pruitt uncapped her ballpoint pen and began writing on a form. Her tiny, white, left hand with trimmed nails, wrote in perfect penmanship. "Number One, will George Beane be going to one of your homes?"

"Mine," said Ava.

"But I'll help all I can," said Audrey. *Could I sound any more insecure? Geez! But I will help all I can Miss Social Worker, cuz I'm a good daughter, too. Oh, puhleez!*

An hour later, they were out of there. They left Mrs. Pruitt's office with a long list of names and addresses, and places to go to pick up this and that, that daddy would need for his return home. His prescriptions would be extensive as well, and these needed to be ordered. Jeff had called Ava's cell phone on their way out. He needed to get to an appointment, and she'd better get home to take the kids off his hands – right away.

There was so much to do! They had to split up tasks and decided to meet back at the house in the evening.

"You take the car and pick up the medical supplies. I'll go home to the kids and make a couple of phone calls to coordinate visiting nurses. We'll meet back for dinner," said Ava.

Audrey agreed and she took the car from her sister after dropping her off at home.

*****

When Audrey got back several hours later, it was still early, but autumn turns dark early. She unloaded an armful of bags from the car, leaving several behind in the back seat.

The kids were asleep and the puppies were huddled together with Mrs. Beasley, in the utility room, nursing. The light was on from the master bedroom and Audrey could see that Jeff was reading in bed. It was a chilly night – good for turning in early.

Ava came out of the bathroom and met up with Audrey in the kitchen. "Hey," she said.

"Hey."

"I'm exhausted," Ava said.

"Lord, me too, what a day. The car and trunk are loaded. I got a lot. We should wait til the morning to unload. I'm too tired, and it's too dark and cold now."

Ava nodded. "I went on the Internet and printed out information about brain tumors." She slapped down a large stack of papers on the counter. She had tears in her eyes. "All I can do is cry."

"Me too."

"What if...?" asked Ava.

"No, don't."

"I can't help but want to be prepared," said Ava.

"You'll never be," said Audrey. "Try to balance it all and not worry. Really – try to find some peace. We need to conserve energy and not get worn down and sick. There's a road ahead."

"Look, I really appreciate you having me here and it's a hard time for us, but I don't want to infringe on your marriage. Go talk to Jeff before he goes to bed. Let's call

81

it a night. I want to sort through my head and figure things out. I'd like to take a shower and read. I'll be up early. We'll figure it out in the morning and it won't seem so bleak after we let this all sink in."

Audrey glanced at her sister. *So pretty, but sad.* She'd aged – practically since the day before. Her face looked beat -- make-up was streaked down her cheeks. Her eyes were puffy. Her neck had red blotches, just like when she was a child and would get herself in a tizzy about something.

Ava nodded and gave a tap on Audrey's back before she locked up the front door and went to the bedroom.

Audrey took the bags with her to her room. She quickly showered and got changed. She decided to clean up a bit, especially if dad would be coming home this week, maybe even tomorrow. She removed all her cosmetics and hair care products from the dresser top and put them back into her suitcase, then back into a closet in the adjoining bathroom where the stuff would be out of sight and out of the way. Replacing her perfume bottle, moisturizing lotion and lipsticks on the dresser, she emptied the shopping bags she had brought in: bottles of pills, liquids and potions of all sorts, cups with bendy straws, a tube of Ben-Gay, a kidney-shaped plastic pan, a thermometer, and other assorted home medical devices and remedies. She sat on the edge of the bed, cupped her head in her hands, and looked around the room, shaking her head in disbelief things ended up this way.

She'd call it an early night, too. The bed was large with lots of pillows. She arranged them against the headboard so she could sit up and unwind a bit.

Unwind, my ass, she thought. She wasn't quite sure what to do with herself. *OK, I'm not going to borrow trouble until we talk to the social worker in the morning. I'll just do a little bit of work and then go to sleep. Just a little work....* she told herself. She had been thinking about

82

work all day and hurried in from the medical supplies shopping to finally get on email.

Yet, the guilt was enormous. *Just how enormous? Apparently not enough*, she thought, as she quietly plugged in her laptop and placed it on top of the bed.   Ava and everyone were asleep, to her knowledge, and no one would suspect she was still awake in her room. *It's ridiculous that I'm hiding working. I'm no criminal for being dedicated.* On the other hand, the words her sister told her earlier that day were repeated in Audrey's mind – over and over. 'You're a real piece of work. Can't you stop working for one fricken day?' "Is it true?" she asked herself. *Am I workaholic? Am I screwed up? Am I so obsessed with myself and work that I don't fit in with the mainstream of society any more?*

Just like smoking, she thought. *The times I've thought about quitting, I pondered it all over a lit cigarette. The irony of it all! Sitting here. Beating myself up over the fact I'm not one hundred percent giving my thoughts to my father. Is this a sin? Oh God, am I bad?*

A wireless card in the computer allowed her an internet connection from any location. *I'll only be fifteen minutes,* she promised herself. *I'll just go in and out of the email, send an authorization of approval or changes to Randi's draft on the Essential Earth account. Surely, all would be going smoothly. Then I can think through the Dad Situation.*

The first Smith Anderson email she saw made her sit up straight. It was marked "urgent" from Randi.

```
Subject:  READ AND DELETE
    Audrey, Hope you're ok and your dad
is, too.
    I thought you would want to know
what's going on here. Elizabeth brought
in someone today – a cousin of hers who
```

is an intern from the Academy of
Graphics Arts. "Just to get us through
this project," she told me. They
wanted something different, so I'm just
retouching photos and doing limited
creative work. I've been helping Jack
on proofing his write-up for the
Wednesday presentation, which has
changed significantly, literally
overnight.

We don't have anything to show you –
Elizabeth seems to be keeping controls
on everything, and she asked us not to
email you directly. She and Bill were
behind closed doors yesterday for a
couple of hours. They had a two-hour
lunch today with some guy in a suit
that Bill picked up from the airport.
He's about your age, and from England.
When I asked Elizabeth what was up, she
said she could not tell me until it was
time, but it has to do with a new
account. All she said was Guy (yes,
that's his name) would be in for a
week.

I don't know if she has corresponded
with you, Audrey, but I wanted to give
you a heads up. Call me if you like.

I hate dumping this on you knowing
your dad is in the hospital, but I
thought you should know. You didn't
hear this from me – I ask that you read
this and permanently delete it from the
company's server.

Wishing you well!
Randi

Hmmmm, thought Audrey. *Very suspicious.* She looked through her inbox for further clues about what was going on. There was an email from Elizabeth with tonight's date on it, 7:04 P.M. "The party girl is working late," Audrey said as she sneered.

```
Subject:  Marketing Update
Audrey,
Hope all is ok.  Do not worry about
the Essential Earth presentation.  Bill
and I had a pow-wow today.  We're going
in with a little more splash.  Not to
worry - we're handling all the details.
You just take care of you and your dad.
     I    pulled    Jack    from    the
scriptwriting, and Randi from graphics
just  for  the  moment  -  we  needed
something splashier.  They will work on
technical  clean-ups  with  a  new  TV
concept that I am spearheading, working
with Bill and a temp from the Academy
we got for the next month.  The theme
will be edgy.  We are changing from the
family focus theme you pitched to MTV,
Hip   Hop   to   target   a   younger
demographic.    It's   going   to   be
fantastic  -  increased  late  night  TV
spots and radio, less print and point-
of-sale.
     Now don't get into a tailspin about
this.  You always said to me that,
sometimes,  new  ideas  are  hard  to
swallow, but we are certain that the
client  will  be  impressed  with  this
improvement.  We will be in the office
late all this week - Feel free to call.
```

The meeting has been changed to Friday, and a dinner afterwards. Not sure what your travel plans are, Audrey, but Bill said with this last minute change and all that is involved, that I should lead this one, just til you get your personal situation under control.

We'll talk more soon. There is an opportunity in London for a new large account. We need to pitch ideas on that within the month. Hopefully you and I can meet on this when you return.

Don't worry about a thing. Take care.

Liz

Don't worry, my ass. Sounds like Elizabeth cozied right up to the boss and totally made a mess of things. MTV Hip Hop? Now what?

Keeping to her self-imposed rule for only fifteen minutes of working tonight, Audrey sent a short note to all marketing staff that was only a few sentences long.

Subject: Update

I am entrenched in family details with father's brain tumor. Will call tomorrow. Continue keeping me apprised of all matters via email. Hope to be back within the week.

Audrey

She clenched her teeth as she watched the computer power down, the familiar Microsoft tune playing as the screen returned to a solid bright blue sheen before turning off. Her hands were in fists, and tightly placed under her seat so she was physically restrained from powering up again. She had kept her promise not to work long. She wouldn't fire off words she'd regret saying later.

There was a whoosh of blood running through her – adrenaline. Her heart started pumping fast. Audrey recognized it as a panic attack – like she used to have as a child. *Oh no. Please. No. I thought I outgrew this.* Small, shallow breaths followed. She brought her knees up a bit from their Indian-style position, wrapped her arms around her legs, hugging them, and swayed gently front and back. She shut her eyes and told herself to relax. *Shhh. It'll pass soon.*

The experience was almost always the same, from the first time, through the years of panic attacks. That adrenaline feeling. She could actually hear it in her head. She could feel the blood through her veins, wondering if there would be an explosion inside of her.

She reached to wipe beads of sweat from around her hairline. Her face was wet, yet at the same time, clammy and cold. She could feel the beat of her heart in the back of her neck as the pounding slowed, until she couldn't detect the beat any longer. Her face was getting circulation back. Her hands, which were cramped and stiff, were now relaxing -- going limp. She dropped her head back on the pillow in defeat. As quick as the attack came on, it was gone. She lay there, quietly. Lights out.

At night the eerie darkness and the silence always made her problems seem larger, and life scary. On this night, she felt like a tiny boat with a hole in its hull, slowly filling with water. There's safety ahead – land, a dock – so close yet so far, but the boat is being carried the wrong way in a raging sea during a tropical storm. The tiny boat is sinking – drowning - not going to make it.

She adjusted her head on the pillow and closed her eyes tightly. Her held-back tears filled her nasal passages. She wished for her father's presence next to her to comfort her, just like he used to do when she was a little girl. Many times he'd come into her room to check on her before turning in to bed himself. He'd see her eyes wide open, shining in the glow of her Mother Mary nightlight. She remembered how she would be staring blindly into nothingness; or, she'd be crying softly to herself, and he'd hear her sniffles. Either way, he would come in, lay next to her, caress her long, blonde hair, or rub her back. Sometimes he'd ask what was wrong, other times, he'd say nothing. Sometimes Audrey couldn't tell him what was the matter, sometimes she, herself, didn't know. She was a worrywart as a child and at night, little things became big things and overwhelmed her. It's how she felt right now, like then, only this time there were no little things – only big things to worry about.

"Daddy, daddy, my poor, poor daddy," she sobbed softly. "Who comforts <u>YOU</u>?" She imagined him alone in his hospital room, cold, unable to sleep. Was he suffering? Was he scared? Her heart felt physical pain, breaking into little bits. She wanted him to be there on this bed, her strong daddy to comfort her. Yet he, himself, needed someone strong there for him. *Sadly, so sadly, I don't know how to reach out and give you comfort, daddy. I am so weak.*

"I was just like you as a child," he'd say to make her little girl head feel better. "You wear your heart on your sleeve." She was too young to understand what that meant. She knew now it was paradoxical that not too many people knew her – not enough to describe her <u>that</u> way. Her dad knew her though. He knew her, like he knew his own soft heart.

"Once upon a time, long, long ago," he'd start saying quietly, as she would lie - perfectly still - looking up at ceiling, imagining pictures in her mind as he described things. "There was a big, ferocious lion in the forest." He would tell the story of the lion and the mouse and how a tiny mouse convinces a lion to spare him his life by promising to return the favor one day, which he does, when the lion steps on a thorn and the mouse pulls it out. It was this part of the story that Audrey loved. Her father's big hand would lift in the air -- his fingers spread widely open, firmly. He would take his other hand and pretend to be the mouse struggling to pull the thorn out of his palm, the lion's paw. *Those hands – those big, safe, wonderful, daddy hands.*

Thinking back to decades ago, she enjoyed the story because it was her father's voice and animation, not that she knew what the story meant. Yet, every story has its moral, and now she knew why the story of the Lion and the Mouse encouraged her.

She suddenly had a strong desire to call Bella. She needed to hear her voice. Her phone was in reach on the bedside table. She picked it up and dialed the number she knew by heart, as she lay in the bed, still in the darkness.

"Hello?"

"It's only me," said Audrey.

"Oh my Gawd, how are you? I'm worried sick here."

"Oh Bella,"

"Honey, you okay?"

A long pause, then, "No."

"How's your dad?"

Another long pause and Audrey swallowed and collected herself. She gave Bella the *Reader's Digest* version of the week, her hand shaking as she held the phone, her body curling up in the bed into a fetal position in the dark, as she described how thin and weak her father looked in the hospital bed.

"Did I call you too late, Bell? I didn't wake the baby, did I?"

"Aud, you're good. It's fine. Just let it out."

"I haven't....I haven't.... Bella, this is the first time I've just opened up and let the tears flow. Sorry to unload.

I've been – I've been trying to be cool about it all. It, it, it hurts too much to even go there."

"It's alright, Hon," Bella said. "I'm praying for you right now, Sweetie. I know you've got a lot going on, just let me know what I need to do to help. Are you staying there a while? Should I send down some clothes? You want me to forward the mail? Pay any bills? What can I do? I'm all yours."

"Let me figure things out. Can I call you tomorrow? I might need to ask for your help. I don't know. I can't think right now. I just wanted to – to hear your voice. To know I've got a friend out there. I'm so out of touch with my world, my work. I'm a zombie."

"Audrey, get some rest. Tomorrow will be better. Rest. Sleep. Call me any time. I mean it, night or day. I love you."

"Thank you."

"Anytime. You hear me? Anytime, no matter what or how late. Anything you need."

"Thank you. Bye, Bella."

"Good night, Audrey."

She wept, and then settled her shaken body. She rested, but her mind was still racing.

If I fall asleep right now, I'll get eight hours of shut-eye, which I need to shake this head cold. Eight hours until morning. Dad comes home. He'll need to have his bed moved in here. How to arrange the furniture to get the bed to fit? Bed against the window? I'll take out the end tables. Move all personal items to bathroom. Personal items, do I have any cigarettes left? Have I smoked at all today? I need one. Maybe it's not too late to make tea. I could bundle up and smoke on the back porch.

Where is that packet of papers Ava printed about brain tumors? No, that will depress me. Or do laundry? Might wake Sammy and Josh. Clothes. Clothes. I need some.

There's one clean outfit left in the suitcase. How far is the mall? Can I squeeze in an hour at the mall tomorrow?

Lights on. Sitting up straight now. Eyes as big as pancakes. *Fuck. Fuck. Fuck. I can't fucking sleep.* She found a pack of cigarettes – an emergency pack in the side pocket of the suitcase, placed there for moments like these, when she got caught up in life, forgetting to replenish her stock. She looked at the pack and reconsidered.

Lights out again. Try harder to sleep. She lay back down and got under the covers. She tossed and turned until sleep finally came.

Chapter Six

The phone rang as loud as a freight train, interrupting her sleep. She trembled. Her eyes opened wide, darting to the clock on the dresser. 3:00 exactly – *a bewitching hour.* Again, another ring. She listened – then there was nothing. She sat up and pushed her bangs out of her face. She waited in the silence. *The deafening silence. Dear Heavenly Father, please let it be a wrong number. Please let it be a crank caller. Watch over daddy.* She clasped her sweaty hands together tightly. *Our Father, who Art in Heaven, hallowed be thy...*

The bedroom door flew open and a hand flipped the light switch on the wall. Audrey squinted at the brightness. A mass of green and blue flannel dove onto her bed, and she realized it was Ava. She landed parallel and put her face deep into the pillow, screaming into it, crying hysterically.

"Oh, no. Oh, no. What? What? Tell me. What? Is it bad? Ava, Ava. Talk to me," Audrey screamed.

"Daddy!" she said. "Hospital called. Pressure. Something called herniation, or something. Critical. Massive something. Emergency. Imminent."

Audrey wailed. "Daddy, daddy, daddy, please, no," she cried. She got on the floor on her knees, her head at Ava's head, stroking it. "What? What's imminent?"

"Not expected. Not.... expected to..." Ava's words were garbled. She began to hyperventilate.

"Help, Help, Jeff!" Audrey yelled across the house.

"Ava, sit up, breathe, relax," said Audrey.

Jeff bounded into the room. He, too, was crying.

"Ava's not breathing right," Audrey said. "I don't know what to do."

Jeff quickly located a paper bag on the dresser and dumped out the prescription bottles in it. He crumpled the top part of the bag to make a mouthpiece. "Avaleen, put the bag over your mouth and nose, and breathe into it. Hold it tightly over your nose and mouth. There. There. Not so fast. Slow. Relax. Normal breathing."

She was trying. Her legs were stiffening. Audrey rubbed her back. She looked at her sister's body shaking all over. The fingers of her left hand looked like sticks – unnaturally tight. Her lips looked blue.

"She's not calming down," Audrey said.

"I'm taking her to the hospital," Jeff said, lifting Ava, and cradling her body, as she gasped.

"But the hospital is twenty minutes away," Audrey said.

"There's a 24 hour clinic two minutes from here. Call them and let them know we're on our way," Jeff said. He carried Ava through the living room, picked up keys on the counter, and Audrey ran behind them to get the front door open.

"What about 911? Ambulance?"

"I'm faster. Call them. Say we're coming," he yelled back.

"What's the name of it?"

They were out the driveway now, and it was cold and windy. Audrey noticed that Jeff was wearing a white undershirt and red sweatpants. He had no shoes, only white socks. Ava was in winter flannel pajamas, no socks, and no shoes.

"Medical First, or something, on 54th Avenue." He got Ava on the passenger side, and ran to the front of the car. "Go, Audrey. Now!"

She ran back to the house, crying hysterically, trying to keep it low in volume. The boys would be still asleep. She ran to the kitchen phone and called information for the number. Then she called the medical center to provide Ava's name, address and an explanation of the situation so they could expect their arrival. Before hanging up, she asked if they had the phone number for Community Hospital, where her father was. They did.

Her hands were shaking when she dialed Community.

"Community Hospital, how may I direct your call?" a husky voice asked.

"Nurse's station for George Beane in Room 410B, please."

"One moment, I'll transfer."

Three rings. *Fuck it. Answer the fucking phone.* Four rings. Five. Six. She stamped her foot on the floor. "Answer!"

"Fourth Floor, Patient Information" a young woman said.

"George Beane in 410B, someone just called here, I'm his daughter. What is the information?"

"Name?"

"Audrey Beane. Please, hurry." She was shaking.

The sound of pages turning on the other end. "Um,"

"Yes? What?"

"Um, I need to get my supervisor, please hold."

This doesn't sound good.

94

Audrey walked with the cordless phone back to her room. She reached to the pack of cigarettes and lighter on the nightstand. She lit up and went to the bathroom so she could use the sink as an ashtray. She sat on top of the bathroom counter, smoking. Waiting. Still nothing. It had been at least five minutes.

"Damn."

She went back into the bedroom and located her cell phone and picked it up, cradling the cordless phone in one ear. She went back to the kitchen to find the number to Community Hospital. She put the cigarette out in the sink, and then dialed her cell phone. It rang. She had the both phones to her ears.

The husky voice again. "Community Hospital, how may I direct your call?"

"Fourth Floor nurse's station."

"One moment."

It rang. Two rings. Three. Four. Five times. Still ringing.

Then on the kitchen phone, "Ms. Beane?"

"Yes, yes."

Then the cell phone answered, "Fourth Floor, Patient Information" a young woman said. Audrey hung up on her and returned to the kitchen phone.

"Yes, this is Audrey Beane. Are you the supervisor?"

"I'm the head nurse. Yes, I have your father's file here. There've been some changes in his condition."

"What, specifically?"

"He's been transported to surgery. I have no details about his current condition, but there was an emergency about fifty minutes ago."

"What?" Audrey started biting her thumbnail.

"I spoke with... um... Mrs. Avaleen..."

"Yes, my sister."

"Yes."

"I didn't get all the info from her. She started hyperventilating," Audrey said.

"Oh, dear."

"Hurry. Please tell me the situation!"

"He's in critical condition. I'd recommend that you, or a member of your family, come to the hospital. We have someone who can provide you details on the patient. I just don't think it is appropriate to... well, go over this on the phone."

"I... I..."

"Ms. Beane, please stop at the lobby and ask the volunteer to direct you. I see in the file, we're looking for a copy of any living will. Do you have that?"

A pause.

"Miss Beane? Are you there?"

Silence.

"I.. I... I'm Here. Did you say... a living will?"

"I'm afraid so. You'll need to come to the hospital with it, or sign as representative. Please drive safely, but don't delay."

"I...I. OK."

She hung up the phone. She opened the laundry room where all the puppies were sleeping, to get through to the garage. Mrs. Beasley growled, and the puppies squirmed a bit.

She turned on the garage light and saw Jeff's truck parked. She peered in the truck window. "Aaaargh. A fucking stick shift," she said to herself, which she didn't know how to drive, even if she did have the keys.

She went back into the house and tried to think of someone to call to come watch the kids, so that she could get to the hospital. Ava lived far away from where their childhood house was and people she knew. Audrey had been gone for so long, she had no contacts in Florida. She didn't even know the names of Ava's friends or neighbors to hunt someone down.

Ava or Jeff's cell phone! Aha! She picked up her cell phone and speed dialed Ava's number. The phone started ringing, coming from Ava's purse on the kitchen counter. "Damn it." She tried Jeff's phone. It went right to voice mail, obviously turned off, not with him. She then called the Medical Center where Ava was, to get an update on her sister's condition.

"The patient is in with the doctor right now," said the voice on the line.

"Is she okay?"

"Yes, she's going to be fine."

"May I please speak with her husband?"

"He's with her. I'm sorry, this is not appropriate and I cannot release patient information. I will tell them to call you when they are through with the doctor. I don't think it will be too much longer, if that helps," she said.

"Please, it's an emergency."

"I will relay the message."

Audrey hung up. She made use of the time putting on some clothes to go to the hospital in. She plotted her plans. *If Jeff doesn't call here in ten more minutes, I am going to call a cab and wake up the boys*, she decided. *Tough choices, it could traumatize Sammy and Josh to be stripped from bed with their aunt, and get hauled off to the hospital. But daddy's life depends on it.*

She sat on the couch in the living room looking out the window to the street. Waiting for Ava. Waiting for an eternity. It was torture.

The phone rang. Audrey picked up on the first ring.

"Ava? Jeff?"

"Ma'am. This is Community Hospital calling. I'd like to speak with Mrs. Avaleen Gooding, or, uh, an Audrey Beane concerning George Beane."

Chapter 7

On November 17th, at 5:13 A.M., Audrey's world stood still. That was when she learned her father was gone forever. She never even got to say goodbye. Somewhere between that awful night and now, four days later, they didn't speak of the death -- not Jeff or Ava, the boys – no one.

Audrey wondered how all of them had gotten to Monday morning in one piece. An unusual strength seemed to overtake them. *Or, maybe we're all cried out.*

"It's here," said Jeff, calling to everyone from the living room. He peered through the front window, holding the curtain open, so he could see the limo pulling up. Audrey noticed the morning sun was struggling to shine, mostly hidden behind a few large, puffy clouds. She turned her attention to the hall mirror, and adjusted her new black hat and buttoned her suit jacket in front of it. She grabbed her bag and headed outside to the car.

Numb. That's how she would describe herself. She had taken a Valium, which had been prescribed for Ava the night she hyperventilated. Audrey climbed in the back of the limo to the rear-facing seat, then sat with her arms crossed, curled up in the corner, staring out the back window.

The kids bounced into their seats, their excitement about a stretch limo quite visible – ear to ear smiles and squeals of delight. *Babes – too young to understand today's significance.* It annoyed her.

"Please quit playing with the controllers," Audrey said to the boys, not looking at them. They were adjusting all the car's interior lights. "This isn't playtime," she said, snapping her fingers to get their attention. Sammy gave her a strange look. He wasn't accustomed to his aunt correcting him.

Finally, after Ava and Jeff locked up the house, they got in the car. The limo pulled away. Audrey looked across to her sister, who was facing her. *I wonder if I look as doped up as she does?* Ava's eyes were glazed over. Audrey noticed her sister's character lines, the way her mouth lines extended downward to a frown. She knew she had similar features and aging marks. She and Ava very much looked like sisters. She could see the pain on Ava's face, and it was like looking into a mirror, with her own reflection staring back at her.

Jeff was doing the worst of everyone. His eyes were red. He hadn't stopped shaking his head in disbelief and moping around for the past four days. *Shoulda taken a Valium. Just get through it,* Audrey thought as she looked at him, next to Ava. He was looking like a lost puppy, *sad and pathetic.*

Nobody spoke during the drive. Instead there was an exchange of fake smiles between the adults and the children, who were now quietly thumb-wrestling. They hadn't expected a large showing at the services; there wasn't family living in the area, and George had lost touch with many of his old pals over the years. Only a few neighbors were expected to attend, a few of Ava and Jeff's closest friends, and anyone else who might have seen the obituary in the paper the day before.

There was a small funeral home co-located at the cemetery, so the funeral and graveside services would take place in one swoop, quickly, which would not be soon enough for Audrey. They pulled up to an old, white wooden building. It looked like a restored 1920's house or an old church. There was an open, manicured hill behind it. Down below the hill, Audrey saw a line of tombstones, each with a small bouquet of yellow carnations, or so it looked from the distance, sticking in the ground. *Daddy is going into the ground,* she thought in complete disbelief. *Gone.*

There were large floral sprays and small vases of mixed flowers everywhere in the chapel. *I never knew flowers could stink so badly. Carnations mixed with roses, mixed with everything else. It hurts my nose. I can't stand it. I could get sick right now.* Her hand grabbed the back of a wooden chair lined up in the back row. She was dizzy, sweating. *Oh no.* Her heart -- beating faster. A little gasp. She grabbed the next chair to guide her along to the corner of the room. Adrenaline pumping. *OK. Ok. Go with it. Breathing returning. Nobody saw. Whew. It passed.*

She pulled her skirt down a bit and straightened her jacket. She corrected her posture. Stood a minute. Gathered up some courage. She walked up to the casket and knelt before her father. His hands were holding rosary beads, placed gently between his forefinger and thumbs. *His hands. Those hands.* She turned. She looked at his tie.

Daddy, I can't look. I'm looking at your tie, not your face, no, not even your hands. I know you understand. I can't see you dead. I don't want that image imbedded in my brain. She stayed kneeling, not because she was praying, not because she needed the time there to say goodbye, but because she wanted to give the appearance to the people in the room that she was paying her dutiful respects.

Have I been here long enough? Can I get up now? Can I go sit down and put my head in my hands? OK. Just another 30 seconds. Waiting. Now. Now I can go. I'm good. She made the sign of the cross and turned away. *No tears. No tears,* she kept thinking.

The front row was reserved for the immediate family. She took her place next to Ava. Jeff had Josh on his lap and his arm around Sammy on the other side. People kept coming and touching Audrey's hand and giving a nod and a kiss. She knew some of the faces... *But damn it if I can remember their names.*

Father Murphy officiated and read a few biblical passages. He had a heavy Irish brogue.

What's he saying? What the...? Too much to handle. Just tune it out. Almost over.

The process of drifting away from what the priest was saying reminded Audrey of mass every Sunday when she was a child. It was always too long. She didn't get anything out of it. She didn't relate to the priests. Most of the Fathers were elderly, monotoned, self-important, and more focused on formal prayer recitations than trying to speak the language of the congregation. To cope, Audrey spent virtually every mass daydreaming. This funeral, like a mass, was no different.

Well of course it's different. Daddy's gone. She realized, however, that what hadn't changed much since childhood was <u>how</u> she coped. She was good at daydreaming – all the while giving off the image of being attentive.

She started looking at the stained glass window and imagined making one from scratch, like assembling a jigsaw puzzle. Tiny colored glass pieces would be matched up to make a picture, then glued together. It was the same daydream she'd had when she was six or seven years old. *Maybe I'll try a smaller stained glass project as a little hobby. How many times have I thought that in my life and still haven't tried it?*

Audrey looked over at Ava, who seemed to have a staunchness about her – posture erect, tight lips, staring straight forward, holding Jeff's hand tightly for strength. *Something about conservative clothing, pantyhose and pumps does that to a person.*

"Ladies and Gentlemen," said a tall man in a black suit standing at the back of the room, "the funeral service will take place in fifteen minutes directly behind us. There is a walkway from the exit doors and our staff will guide you." Everybody crowded out the one door as if they couldn't wait to get to the fresh air, away from the noxious flower fumes. *Or maybe it's just me*, thought Audrey.

Graveside, everyone who attended was given a yellow rose to place atop George's casket, while at the same time, they said their own personal goodbyes to him. Each person stopped by Audrey and Ava, and offered a hug, kiss or an extended hand, even those who had already greeted them inside.

As they turned to leave, the sun peeked out between the clouds, touching Audrey's face like gentle, warm fingertips, noticeable against the cool day. The sun had found its way through the big clouds. *As if daddy was saying goodbye, and be well.* The sun was now hot on her face. She believed in signs, and that loved ones spirits stay around to help those left behind through the grieving.

Audrey was the last to get back into the limo and while she waited for Ava to scoot in to make room, she glanced down the winding road of the cemetery. A red sports car was parked about 500 feet away from the limo. Its driver, wearing a black sports coat, was standing next to the door. It was not anyone Audrey could remember seeing graveside. She squinted to see better, and tried to identify the strange man standing there looking over at George's gravesite.

The limo drove off. As it passed by the sports car, Audrey looked out to the man next to the red car. His face came into focus. It was Roger Hollingsworth -- the man in the black coat. *My old, dear love*, she thought, a tear forming in the corner of one eye. She put her hand to her chest as she felt herself getting choked up, touched that he had come to pay respects to her deceased father.

Roger's visit puzzled her, yet at the same time, intrigued her. Nobody had bothered to call Roger to tell him about George's death. He must have heard the news elsewhere, or had seen the obituary. *Why didn't he come speak to us? Very strange.*

Audrey didn't mention the Roger sighting to Ava, who seemed to be in her own world at the moment. *She'd probably accuse me of making this event "all about me" anyway, and this is no time for a spat.* Jeff had his arm around Ava, and her head was resting on his chest, her manicured hand under her cheek, protecting his suit from her make-up. Ava's eyes were half-shut, as were Jeff's, and the smooth motion of the limo added a hypnotic purring sound that left everyone sleepy and quiet the entire drive back home.

*****

"They say the best thing to do when you're dealing with grief is stay busy with your normal routine," Audrey told Ava at the kitchen table the next morning, trying to be upbeat. "Could you pass the sugar?" she asked. Ava handed her the container of Equal and nodded, as she stared into her coffee cup.

"I know," Ava said. "It'll be easier for you than me because you'll travel far away from here and be, well, you know, removed from it."

"You do know I've got to get back to New York."

Ava nodded. "We have some things to wrap up with the estate, you realize."

"I can come back."

"When?"

"I could maybe come for a weekend. I could easily come a couple of weekends – just commute back & forth. That new airline has pretty cheap rates and if you do a Saturday night stay, the prices are even better," said Audrey, sipping her tea. "But, I gotta get back to Smith Anderson. I'm thinking things really got messed up on my big account."

"It's the holidays. It won't be easy getting weekend flights."

"It'll all work it out. Relax. I'm checking the flights this morning and seeing if I can get back within the next day or two."

"Really? So soon?"

"Do you realize how long I've been here already? I thought I was going to be a couple days, maybe. It's been weeks now. I'm out of clothes, I have bills to pay."

"Kay, then," Ava said with a pout. She got up from the table and put her cup in the sink. Jeff walked in at that moment.

"Audrey has to leave," Ava said to him.

"What about Thanksgiving?" They all sat at the table and discussed it. There would be no Thanksgiving this year. *At all. Whatsoever.* It was Audrey's idea, and Avaleen was quick to agree. The last thing either of them wanted to do was celebrate anything, or cook, or eat. "The boys would be just as happy with mac and cheese," Ava had said. Jeff was fine to go along with that, too.

"I need to go back home," Audrey told them.

"Thanksgiving or not."

They understood.   So it was all settled, *Fuck Thanksgiving.*

"What about painting the backyard? You said you wanted to," Ava asked. Jeff grabbed his coffee, kissed Ava and waved and blew the boys a kiss on his way out, not interrupting them.

"I don't know. It's a mood thing. I paint when I feel creative and relaxed."   Audrey looked out the kitchen window. "The skies are such a pretty, deep blue color in the winter time. Everything green is turning brown, though. I suppose I could visualize it and enhance the real thing to make it greener. I'm going to try to fit in some time to paint – today? Tomorrow, maybe. But if not, you don't mind storing the easel, maybe I'll start it the weekend I come back."

"Mmmm hmmm," Ava said, her back still towards Audrey.

"Don't be mad at me," said Audrey.

"I'm not," said Ava, but it was so obvious she was.

"Can I take you and the boys shopping and lunch at the mall today? Last chance for us to do something together. They've been through a lot these past days. Let me buy them something they want. It will be so fun for me to watch them pick something out at the toy store. We can have lunch at that place the kids like – where they crawl through tube mazes and costumed characters walk around with balloons, what do they call that?"

"Oh, not Chuck's Pizza Place, Aud. It's so loud there and the bigger kids always push Sammy and Josh around. It smells like a locker room with all those shoes off those nasty kid feet. Disgusting."

"What the hell do I know? I'm no mom. I was just trying to think of a place we could let the kids run free and we can watch them and sit back."

"McDonalds by the mall is fine. They have a playground."

"If you like."

Ava went to the boys' room. They were getting a bit rowdy and noisy. Ava started to threaten them, "Aunt Audrey wanted to take you boys to the toy store today, but the way you're behaving..." The kids stood at attention before their mother, both with their lips tight, silent.

Audrey smiled. She scooped up one of the puppies that was sniffing around her legs under the table. She took him to her bedroom, shut the door, and placed him on the bed with her. She brought him in close to her chest. Just to hold something warm up close to her like that – a life – a puppy – a baby – a gentle squeeze. *Everybody needs hugs. God, do I need hugs.* She teared up. *No hugs for me. No hugs I can really call my own.*

She lay on her back with the dog on her belly. He settled in, sleepily. So did Audrey.

As she drifted, the boys opened the door and jumped on the bed. "We're ready," said Sammy. Josh said nothing, but was all smiles in a long-sleeved Hockey shirt and his hair parted on the side, wetted down with some gel. *Absolutely adorable!*

"You boys are the cutest things I've ever seen, even cuter than this puppy," she laughed. "Are you ready to go to the toy store?"

Their heads moved up and down quickly.

"Then let Aunt Audrey get dressed and we can go. I need privacy."

She was amazed they knew what that meant. They both left the room and shut the door behind them.

It's a good hair day. Audrey remembered how rare days with low humidity were in Florida. Her hair needed no special handling. It was clean, straight and shiny. She brushed it and noticed how long it was getting. She hadn't thought much about what style to be aiming for lately.

106

She put on her jeans and a pink cashmere sweater. She accessorized the look with large, silver earrings. She spent extra time on her make-up this morning. *I need all the help I can get*, she thought as she noticed her eyes looked tired and her skin a colorless, gray, depressing shade. Finally, she put on her last pair of socks from the suitcase, making a mental note to buy more today, and threw on some walking shoes.

Ava drove Audrey and the boys to the toy store, just as planned. The mall was crowded. The parking lot was filled to capacity. Inside, Christmas shoppers were poking around the stores in search of bargains, and it still wasn't even Thanksgiving. *Pathetic souls desperately looking for a cheap price.* The mall was decorated with lights, and large, plastic, glittery candy canes were hanging from the ceiling. The sounds of school children singing carols at the center of the mall chimed through the corridors. Josh and Sammy were squealing and excited just to be there.

Audrey was distant. She wanted to be a cool aunt to Sammy and Josh so that they would remember her that way, but mustering up a smile took energy she couldn't find anywhere within her. *My toes. My feet.* She didn't want to complain about it either, because Ava was grieving and surly, tired and cranky, too. *But....*

I brought all the wrong shoes on this trip. It's torture. Torture -- Traipsing the mall in these expensive walking shoes. There needs to be criteria for labeling shoes, WALKING shoes -- Like a test by real women. To hell with restraining myself from complaining, she thought.

"Ava, damn it. Have you tried this brand of walking shoe?" She stopped short -- right there in the middle of the shopping mall, in front of Penneys. An elderly couple who'd been walking behind Audrey unclasped their hands and passed her on either side to avoid bumping into her. Audrey kicked off one of the shoes to show her sister the brand name inside. Ava bent down to read the label, going along with Audrey's drama. The boys peered into her shoes too, not sure what they would find there.

"Oh, yeah, I heard of those. I never got 'em, though. Aren't they expensive, like $100 a pair?"

"Yeah, that's right."

"Why? What's wrong? Are they hurting?"

"Hell yeah, they're hurting," Audrey said, pointing to the insole of each foot. "Like walking with a tight rubber band around my feet and toes."

"So, return them."

"Can you do that? I mean I'm wearing them."

"I would try."

"I don't have the receipt or the box any more."

"You know, you could learn a lot from me, sister. You'd do a hell of a lot better if you got over the name brand obsession," she said. "Look," she pointed across the middle of the mall. "Let's go over there."

"Payless? You're joking."

"I'm serious," she said, grabbing Audrey by the arm, with the boys following close behind. "Git joself some real comfy shoes, and put those bad boys away," she teased. "If they don't take 'em back, sell 'em on Ebay. That's what I'd do."

"Ebay? That auction website?"

"You're so out of it. Yes, Ebay. You can sell anything and make money and ship the crap to the buyer. I do it all the time. I bought a lot of our horse supplies on Ebay. Good stuff. Like new. You'd be amazed. I'll show you how to do it. It's great for selling stuff, and not having to mess with a wasted weekend having a garage sale, not that you could do a garage sale in Manhattan. I think I made, like, ten grand last year selling shit. I'm talking -- shit."

"Shut up! You did not." Audrey pushed on her sister's shoulder in a teasing way.

"It's true."

"Show me. I've got purses that cost me hundreds and I

hate 'em now. They're just sitting in my closet. You're saying, I could make money on them?"

"Ebay. I'm telling you. It's the only way."

"Cool."

They walked together into the store. A checkout girl no more than sixteen nodded as they walked by. Ava ignored her and kept talking.

"Josh's old baby clothes -- some of them were brand names. I had, like, two or three moms fighting for the lot of it, in the last seconds of the auction. I sold one box of his clothes for $200."

"Sign me up," said Audrey, as she followed Ava through Payless, checking out the racks of sales, grabbing a pair, trying them on, then putting them back.

"What? Are you going to try on every pair in the store?" Ava laughed.

"Yep."

After twenty minutes, they left the store, and Audrey was smiling and wearing new sneakers. She had a shopping bag in each hand. One bag contained three new pairs of shoes, and the second bag held a pair of boots, plus her old shoes in one of the new shoeboxes. *All this and in twenty minutes flat.*

"I'm shocked and amazed," Audrey said.

"I told you. Stick with me, you'll be just fine."

"I miss you. I miss things like this. Little things," Audrey said.

Hmmm. Little things. Little things - to make a mood good or bad. As they strolled to the other end of the mall, Audrey remembered the title of a book she had read once, a few years back. Something about not sweating the small stuff, and, it's all small stuff. She shook her head, disagreeing with the premise. *Everyone always says to just let shit roll off your back. Not me. I'm a digger for the meaning beneath everything. Why does small stuff break me? Why does something so tiny that's good, change crankiness to happiness? The small stuff is symptomatic of big stuff,* she decided. *We should pay attention.... Small stuff is really big stuff expressed in small ways - over and over again. Maybe that's why I'm so.. so...*

"Hello. Earth to Audrey. Did you hear me? Did you want to get the toys now? We're here."

They had walked right to the toy store and Audrey was oblivious.

"Oh, oh, sorry, I was just thinking. Yeah. Sure. Toys. Whatever."

"You were a million miles away. What's on your mind?"

"Nothin'. Well...the shoes, I guess. And making money in other ways. The simplicity of living, and how it could be. And, being happy or cranky with little things. I fixed my shoe problem and now I'm happy, whereas twenty minutes ago, my day was ruined."

"Mmm. Hmm," Ava smiled. "Doesn't it feel goo-oo-ood to find a deal? Isn't it great when you find something right?"

"Yeah. I mean.... It's so different in Manhattan. I spend so much money for everything."

"You can afford it," said Ava.

Audrey shrugged.

They were in the toy store now, and Ava let the boys run wild, alone. Audrey and Ava walked a hundred feet behind them, chatting.

"You should be happy you can make choices what to do with money."

"I actually wonder what it would be like living a little simpler. Money's good, but earning it is a bunch of shit. Bella knows. Bella, my neighbor. She knows me pretty deep."

"The job too intense?"

"Not the work, in and of itself," Audrey said. "The politics."

110

"Isn't this what you always wanted?"

Audrey shrugged. "What is it about America that you decide what you're going to be when you're twenty years old, and then you're stuck being that for the rest of your damn life?"

"America didn't say that. Nobody did. You're limiting yourself if you think that," Ava said.

"Whether America said it or not, it's prevalent thinking. If I decided today I wanted to be an artist, it might be too late, who'd take me seriously?"

"That's ridiculous. Of course you could change careers. People do it every day."

"I would have to start all over and give up the big salary," said Audrey.

"And so? That old saying about the cream always rises to the top -- you'd have to give yourself some time to get established in that new direction, and then you'd make it - eventually."

"Who can afford to make a life change like that?"

Ava touched Audrey's arm. "You might think I'm nuts saying this, but once we get daddy's estate settled, you might be able to afford new choices, Aud."

Audrey's mood turned sour. Her lips tightened. "I...I... I can't believe for the past hour I forgot that he's gone. Ooooh." She dropped one of the shopping bags and put her hand over her mouth and started a quiet sob.

"Shhh. It'll be weird like this for a while, I guess," said Ava. "It's okay to digress from the mourning time. We've got to clear our heads," Ava said. "That's why we're out today shopping, being together. If daddy is looking down, he'd be pleased -- seeing us together like this -- like old times."

The boys were now reaching for figurine robots and a collection of weapons.

"Would you like to get these?" Audrey asked. She turned towards Ava. "You're not one of those moms who

111

refuses her kids certain toys that the right-wingers say instill aggression?" she asked.

"Oh, we're right-wingers, but only an inch or two from center," teased Ava. "I think it's good for kids to have an outlet and exposure to most things, and it's the parents' duty to provide guidelines."

"You're a good mom, sis," said Audrey. "I wonder if I'd be good."

"I can't see you as a mother. No offense."

"That was a stinky thing to say."

Ava shrugged.

"C'mon," Audrey said to the boys, abruptly, and grabbed the boxes of toys from Sammy's arm. "Do you want one of these toys too?" she asked Josh.

"Yes, he wants the green one," said Sammy, running back to the shelf to pull it off. Josh didn't know the difference between the robots, or if it was a ball or stuffed animal, and Audrey knew it.

"I was the older sister once," she said. She looked at Sammy, then Ava. "I know what you're doing, Sammy," she said, winking.

"Oh, just get it," said Ava. "Josh doesn't know one toy from the other. He's still at the age he likes to play with the box the toy came in. It's all the same to him."

Audrey slid her credit card out of her wallet to pay and looked down at the boys. "Hungry?"

They both nodded excitedly.

When they got to McDonald's the boys hardly touched their Happy Meals and were much more interested in the tubes and slides to play on in the playground. It was a nice day, so Ava and Audrey finished their salads outside to watch Sammy and Josh chase each other through the maze of colorful, plastic, jungle gym equipment.

"There's something I wanted to tell you," said Audrey as she sipped her drink.

Ava looked intrigued. She cocked her head and leaned

in closer.

"Um. At the cemetary.... Did you notice a red sports car parked across the street from the old house, building, whatever it was, funeral parlour?"

"No. What car?"

"There was a convertible there, and a man standing next to it."

"Did he come to the services?"

"No, that's what was so curious," Audrey said. "He just stood there, watching all of us. But he was dressed in a suit, like he was going to come. I keep looking to see who it was because he looked young, well, relatively -- like us."

"Now I'm really curious. So?"

Audrey smiled. She took a bite of her salad and wiped her mouth with a napkin. She paused for a prolonged period. *For effect, actually, and it seemed to be working.*

"He was delightfully handsome," she said, putting her right hand to her heart and patting her hand on it.

Ava crinkled her forehead and pursed her lips. "Hmmm, I don't know anyone like that."

"R.H." said Audrey.

"R.....H....." repeated Ava, slowly. She paused, thinking. "Roger? YOUR Roger? You're kidding?"

Audrey nodded. "Can you believe it?"

"I can't believe it. Why didn't he say anything?"

"I was going to ask you that," said Audrey, putting her plastic fork into the salad container, shutting it and tossing it into the garbage can a few feet away. "I thought we could analyze the situation together, and come up with the reasoning."

"That - is - really, really weird," said Ava.

"I'll say."

"Well, he was close to daddy when you dated. Didn't he help make the garden out back of daddy's house?"

"He did. They loved to watch sports together, too. Daddy really loved him, like his own son, I even think."

"Why do you think he didn't come up to the casket and pay respects?" asked Ava.

Audrey shrugged. "What's even weirder is that he came alone. Where was his wife?" Audrey's eyes opened wide as she looked at Ava, inquisitively, searching for some sort of explanation.

"Well, that's an easy one, sister. How could he bring his wife to a funeral of a man who was the father of a woman he once loved?"

"Loved? Do you think he really loved me?" asked Audrey, desperate for validation.

"Oh Jesus, Audrey. Is your ego so shallow you need to hear the answer to that?"

"I guess so."

"Of course he loved you. And didn't he tell you that a lot?"

"Mmmm. Hmmm."

"If I recall, YOU broke HIS heart. He wanted you to stay in Florida and marry him."

Audrey turned her head away from Ava. She pretended to be watching the boys on the jungle gym.

"Audrey? Are you listening?"

"Yeah," she said, still not looking at Ava.

"You're not over him! Are you? You still have a thing for him! I can see it."

Audrey kept her face blank, watching the boys. *Focus.*

"Audrey, look at me."

There was a pause, then finally, Audrey turned.

"You just broke your cover, girl. I see the writing."

Audrey shrugged. "It doesn't matter, does it? He's married."

"If he's married and so damn happy as shit, why did he put on a suit and drive to the cemetary?"

"Because he remembered a man who was like a father to him," said Audrey.

"Oh, that is such bullshit. I don't believe it," said Ava.

114

She tried to throw her salad container into the trashcan, but missed it. She got up to pick it up and put it in. "I think we should look up this wife person - you know, drive by her work, check her out. See what she looks like."

"Ava, you have gone mad. I'm thirty-four years old, not sixteen. We grown-ups don't do that shit any more."

"Oh, puhleez. The day you're too old for a good investigation is the day you're dead. Where's your sense of adventure?"

"I'm neither a stalker, nor desperate for a man. There are plenty of men for me in Manhattan. Plenty, I tell ya."

"Name one."

"Um..."

"I'm waiting..." said Ava.

"Fuck you. There was this guy, John, who worked for the company on the sixth floor where I work. We went to a cocktail party together. I met him on the elevator and we flirted every day for a week or two. He asked me out. We had fun. He's an attorney. He came into my apartment that night for a night cap and we continued our date... very intimately, if you must know....." she trailed off.

"When was this?" Ava asked.

"Hmmmm....Last June," said Audrey.

"We're like five months out from then," Ava said. "Who ya seen lately? So what happened to...this guy, John, whom you never previously mentioned?"

Audrey was silent.

"Well?"

"Um, he never called again. I don't see him on the elevator either. Maybe he transferred."

"Ah hah. So, why did you even mention him in this conversation?"

"I'm just saying... I get around plenty enough," she said. "Enough for me, at least. Geez, I'm no whore, you know. But I have no trouble getting dates."

Ava turned her head and under her breath, softly said,

"Doesn't sound like it to me..." and she rolled her eyes, which Audrey quickly noticed.

"I heard you."

Ava shrugged. "I'm just sayin'....."

Audrey opened up her bag, pulled out her lighter and lit a cigarette.

"When are you going to quit smoking?" asked Ava.

"Fuck you. I'm totally imperfect. I don't get laid, and I smoke cigarettes. So sue me."

"Sensitive, aren't we?"

Audrey didn't reply. She took another deep puff on the cigarette and extinguished it in the tin ashtray on the concrete table. "Let's just go, now. I gotta go online and check flights back home."

"Fine, then."

"Fine," said Audrey.

They didn't speak to one another during the ride back home.

Chapter Eight

These prices are outrageous. Audrey checked all the airline websites and the discount travel sites. Rates were triple the normal charge because of the holiday week and almost all the coach fares were sold out. She took what she could get, which meant flying first class - *probably the cost of actually buying a small plane* - and it was a day later than she actually wanted to leave. She grabbed a pen and wrote down the flight information on the back of a receipt and put it under a magnet on the refrigerator door for Ava.

She made a few calls to the office, but had trouble reaching anyone. She left a few voice mails to let everyone know she'd be back in the office on Monday, and that she would be available to work remotely over the weekend, if anyone "wanted to or cared to give her the details and an update on the Essential Earth account," which was exactly how she asked the question, filled with attitude. *Cripes,* she thought. *Everyone is so elusive. What the hell is up with Essential Earth?* Even Randi hadn't given her the skinny on things lately. But then Audrey remembered, the staff was taking time off this week for the holiday. She didn't want to call her boss on his private cell number. Talking to him always made her nervous. She much preferred voice mails or emails, so she left him a brief message, too.

Audrey took her calendar out of her purse. The five by seven inch black book was scuffed and filled with loose inserts, receipts, and business cards -- all held closed by a rubber band wrapped around it. She opened it and turned to the month of November, scanning each day. All the meetings and luncheons she'd had scheduled for the month were missed and had expired. The month of December was practically clear because she hadn't been around the office to fill it up with new appointments. She had no clue when the office holiday parties were scheduled. *I might as well be on Mars.* She closed the black book and put the rubber band back around it, and stuffed it back in her bag.

The sun was beaming through the bedroom window and she glanced out and noticed that her old wooden easel was resting against the porch post. There was a tin can that held an assortment of paintbrushes. All she needed was some canvas and new paints. *The backyard beckons.* The corners of her mouth twitched until she smiled. She ran into the kitchen, calling, "Ava... Ava... where are you?" Whatever Audrey had been ticked at Ava about earlier was now lost in the excitement of the imminent art project.

Ava came out of the boys' room with her index finger over her lips. "Shhh. Damn Audrey, I just got Josh settled for a nap."

"Can I borrow the car to get canvas and paints?" she asked. "I'll fill 'er up with gas for you, and pick up anything you need for dinner. Or, hell, let me pick up Chinese for everyone. I want to paint. I could do a small painting -- today, even. And if I have to, I could finish it up tomorrow. She pointed to the flight information under a

118

magnet on the refrigerator. "The best I could do, but it buys me some time to paint the backyard."

Ava handed her the keys. "We like shrimp fried rice and make sure you get the boneless spareribs, not the ones with the bone in it. Oh, yeah, egg drop soup and ask for an extra bag of the crunchy noodles - they always forget. Get lots. Jeff can eat a pint or more of the soup by himself."

Audrey grabbed her bag, and headed toward the door.

"Oh, wait, Aud.." Ava called.

Audrey looked back.

"Would you mind if I called a realtor to schedule for us to meet at daddy's house before you leave for New York? I need your help on getting a price if we want to sell it, and I'd like to do that while you're still in town."

Audrey shrugged. They hadn't really talked at all about what to do with the old place. "Whatever. I'll be back in a couple of hours. See ya."

Driving the car alone, with the sunroof open and windows down, is bliss. Utterly divine. Audrey loved maneuvering through the country roads in Pasco. This was quite a contrast to how she got around the city streets of Manhattan, and she had enough cab fare receipts to prove it. *The way those freaks drive in New York -- too scary for me.* Here, things were paced far slower.

To think in a couple of hours I'll be at the back porch painting Ava's backyard. She was completely removed from reality - the sad reason she was in Florida. Instead, she was completely alive, and somehow very spiritually connected with George Beane, who might be looking down at her and understanding this moment of joy and her excitement for art.

Something, maybe-- just maybe he underestimated in the physical world. Maybe now he knows the depth of my love for painting, that I'm more than just a successful businesswoman.

In the distance, Audrey noticed the beautiful palm trees

119

in the highway divider. Along the right side of the road were huge old oak trees, showcasing gentle golden autumn leaves, shaking and falling off their branches by the dozens as the wind blew. As Audrey observed her surroundings on each side of the car, she noted the beauty of these parts in Florida. It was far enough north that some of nature had a feel of a more northern state -- North Carolina, with hills and pines and oaks with all their ruggedness. Yet, there was still plenty of signs of Florida's typical southern horticulture - the palms, the citrus trees, and the aroma of the beach reaching her nose, even though it was still three miles to the shore. This time alone on a long drive was treasured. And needed. *I can't wait to paint.*

Later, when she pulled into Ava's driveway, it really should have been two trips from the car to the house, with the number of bags to bring in. *Gotta paint. That's all that matters. Now.* She loaded up the bags of Chinese food on one arm and her purse and paint supplies on the other arm, one bag held in her teeth. She barreled her way through the door, dumping everything on the kitchen counter. "Dinner!" she yelled, and everyone tromped into the kitchen.

"Enjoy...See ya. Save me an egg roll. Gotta paint." She quickly walked through the house to the back porch.

Finally. Finally. Alone and painting. She placed her hands outward in front of her, making them into the shape of a picture frame, then panned the landscape until she composed the right view. The afternoon sun, what was left of it, lit the barn, making the metal roof different hues of silver, red, and blue. The chicken coop, although far from the barn, would be moved in the painting to appear as if it were closer to the barn.

Audrey was lost in the next couple of hours, stopping only for one cigarette and a glass of iced tea. It was dark when she finally came back inside. All she could think of was a hot bath and reading her book in bed. *The perfect*

120

end to a nearly perfect day.

*****

When she awoke the next morning, she noticed her head was completely free of that nasty wet head cold that had hung on for weeks. *Something about being out in fresh air all day lends itself to a night of hard sleep.* For the first time in a very long time, Audrey had slept the night through, well beyond dawn, and more than ten hours total - she counted.

She adjusted her oversized tee shirt, which had twisted itself around her during sleep, and unraveled herself. She got on her knees to look over the headboard and windowsill, out to the back porch. *There she is! My painting. Lovely. Just a few additions and it'll be done.*

She jumped off the bed like a child excited for a day on summer vacation, and she reached for a large bag on the chair. Out of it she pulled a big wooden frame she had picked up at the supplies store. She ran her fingers over the smooth edges. *Oooh! Perfect! My present to Ava and Jeff, with my love.* She smiled. She kissed the frame.

Again, she looked at the painting out her bedroom window. She looked into the picture, placing herself within it in her imagination, a girl, a much younger, sweeter girl, carrying a pail to the horse's trough to bring some feed or drink. And she wondered, *What if? What could have been, had I stayed in Florida? I could've been her. A sweeter life, perhaps.* She could see herself stepping into that life and making it real. A part of her wanted a more serene existence. She had lost track of time in this fantasy.

The clock said 10:38 A.M. and it was quiet around the house. "Where the hell is everyone?" Audrey asked out loud. She quickly washed her face, brushed her teeth and threw on a pair of jeans and a freshly laundered, long sleeved, black tee. She twisted her hair into a flip and put

121

on her cozies. She headed to the kitchen to hunt for some tea, or coffee, or anything with caffeine. *Late start this morning, better kick it up to full speed.*

Nobody seemed to be in the house. No puppies were running around. She looked in the garage, and Jeff's truck was gone. Just a few tools hanging on hooks, organized. *Probably in alphabetical order, knowing Jeff.* She went back in the house and looked out the front window. Ava's car was still parked out front. "Anyone home?" she yelled. No answer. She came back to the kitchen and started the teapot. There was a handwritten note on the counter:

```
Sister - Took pups to vet for shots.
Jeff's working in Tampa all day. Took
me & boys to his mom's for the day. Be
back at 6. Realtor at daddy's house -
2:00, please meet him. Sorry can't
come. Call on the cell if you need
anything. Love, Sister
```

Audrey called Ava, "Hello?"

"Where you at?"

"We just left the vets'. We're in the car to Jeff's parents'."

"How come you didn't tell me what's up?"

"I fuh-got. You got my note, right? It's not a big deal, is it?"

"Yeah. That's fine."

"OK then, you'll drive over to daddy's?"

"Yeah."

"Great. See ya tonight, Aud."

"See ya. Bye."

Audrey hung up the phone and looked out on the porch where her paints were. *Still time to finish up around here...* She quickly made a cup of tea and brought it with her to the back. *Yards with gray horses and pallets of paints, a big cup of tea and fresh air to breathe. Brown paper packages tied up with string. These are a few of my favorite things....* She laughed at her attempt to reword the lyrics to a classic old song.

The sky was filled with fluffy clouds, the kind Audrey as a child would pretend she could see animals and people in. Her eyes darted to her cloudless painting. *It isn't right yet.* She mixed white paint to add clouds to the picture - final touches. She stepped back, looked at it from a new view, and nodded. *Almost done.* She needed one last thing. That girl -- that younger version of herself -- holding the pail in the picture.

Her hand trembled as she dipped the paintbrush into the water, then the colors, and dabbed off the excess. She bit her bottom lip as she painted her own being into the scene, slowly, carefully. Her hair was longer, blonder, and she was a bit thinner. She painted her ideal self. It made her want to work on getting that look for herself back, for real. The warm sun danced on her hands as she moved them to paint more life into the picture, fixing here and there, getting it just so. She stepped back again and looked. *Done. Officially.*

"OK, now what?" she asked herself, then decided to get ready, then drive over to her father's house early to look around, then meet the realtor there. She did a quick clean up of her supplies on the porch, came inside, made the bed, and then to the bathroom vanity mirror. She applied a fresh face of make-up and some lipstick and a dash of perfume. Nothing too glamorous. In Manhattan, she was much more fussy about how she looked, but here in Florida, she felt more in touch with the earth, and natural. She remembered she had new boots from Payless and quickly searched the bags in her room to find them and put them on.

On her way out the door, she caught a glimpse of herself in the hallway mirror. It might have been the new boots, the way her eye make-up set off her well-rested look, no bags, no sags. She hadn't looked so rosy and fresh for months. *Indeed, I'm a natural girl.* She smiled.

Her mood turned melancholy as she drove up to dad's house. She wept as she turned the key in the door. It was so empty, despite all the furniture. She sat in his old recliner and listened to the sound of the silence. She remembered happier times.

The spring of her college junior year, Audrey returned here from the Florida College campus to spend the Easter holiday at home with Ava and her father. It was the first time Audrey brought a boy home to meet the family, and she had indicated on the phone, "to please be extra nice because I really, really like this one." Being Catholic and all, it was certainly an issue whether Audrey should broach the question of their sharing her old room together since they'd be there a week, or if another arrangement should be made. She had hoped the old pullout couch wouldn't be the solution.

"Oh, Audrey," George laughed, when she had called him from the dorm the night before her visit to inquire. "Now, if your mother were here, it certainly would have been a different story, but, my dear, precious princess, I'm not judging you. If you're comfortable having your friend in your room, I'm comfortable."

"Thanks, daddy. It was on my mind and I didn't want to presume anything. It's not like we're... we're going to, you know, well, do anything..." she trailed off.

He chuckled. "You don't have to even say it. I know. The walls are paper-thin. Don't embarrass your poor, old, broken-down daddy."

"Thank you. Thanks much for understanding. You're really going to like Roger," she remembered saying.

"You're welcome, honey. Of course I'll like him. I love you, so what you like, I like."

Audrey remembered when they arrived at the little house on Pineapple Avenue, they were greeted by George, and Ava and Jeff, who was Ava's fiancé by then, and everyone embraced, as if they were all family who had waited many years for this moment of reunion. *That's how life should be - all the time. Home - Home Sweet Home. Everything it represents. The American Dream.*

Audrey reclined further in the chair and lit a cigarette, looking around the room at the family photos on the end tables, remembering happier times. She closed her eyes. *If I could turn back time*, she thought. *Oh, the things I'd have appreciated more - things that are gone now. And the years that followed, the things I'd do differently, the things I'd say, the kindnesses I'd show.* She swallowed hard, thinking of what she had made of herself, and being not too proud of it - despite the financial success. How she really was most days in Manhattan -- nasty, cranky, witchy. *A real piece of work, just like they all say. And it's true, I did think I was hot shit for being a piece of work -- that, at least I stand for things, have opinions, not like those wishy-washy go-along-with-phonies.*

It started to rain, softly, gently. *Just a little sun shower, so common here.* The weather was turning colder and there was a little draft in the house. Audrey watched the drizzle out the window and thought about how the angels in heaven were mourning this loss of George Beane, how this house once so filled with life was empty now, and would never be the same again.

She went into the kitchen and saw dirty dishes in the sink, where dad had left them the last day he was there, a large stein that dad drank coffee out of. It had written on it, "World's Greatest Dad." She washed all the dishes by hand and put them on the sink to dry, wiping her tears with the dishtowel.

She went through each room, turning on the lights and opening up closed doors to bring life back in. There was a memory for every corner of every room. *It's sooo hard.* When she entered her old bedroom, there was a photo of

Roger and her, arm and arm, a picture taken after they had completed digging and setting the Japanese pond in dad's backyard. In the snapshot, they were filthy, sweaty, but most of all, happy. And the picture told the story of two kids - mad for each other. She picked up the photo in the dusty old leather frame and ran her fingers gently over it. She blew the dust off of it. She put it near the door on the floor so that she would remember to bring it back to the living room and stuff it in her purse to bring home. One day, she'd paint daddy's beautiful backyard the way she remembered it.

The big mahogany desk in her room had lots of little drawers. She pulled the top one open. It was filled with treasures and trinkets from decades ago. She took the drawer completely out of its holder and placed it atop of the bed and lay next to it. She took the first pieces of paper off the top of the pile, and unfolded the pages to see what was written on them.

The first piece of paper had on it:

```
Audrey - Roger called for the 5th
time.  Please call him back, Damn it.
Ava
```

She smiled. She turned the paper over, no date or year on it.

There was a card in a blue envelope, marked "Audrey" in flowery writing. She opened it. The front of the card was a photograph of a beach scene, and footsteps in the sand along the shore. In it, was a poem called, "Footsteps, by An Unknown Author", in which the poem described there being only one set of footsteps during the darkest hours of one's life. The last line read, "You were not alone. For when you saw only one set of footsteps, it was then that I carried you, my friend.".... as if the poem were authored by Jesus. It was signed, "Mom" and the note read,

```
Our Dear Daughter, Audrey,
     On    this,    your    auspicious
thirteenth   birthday,   our   beautiful
precious daughter, we wish for you many
good things, but most of all, we wish
you peace and joy of living all your
life.  Pursue all your dreams.  You
have so many gifts lovely daughter, you
are  blessed.   And  we  are  blessed  to
call you our own, our sweet Audrey, our
first born, our love.
     We love you always,
     Mommy and Daddy
```

She wept again. *Mommy and daddy are together now.* And it made her want to have her own daughter or son, to love as much as she was loved by her parents. She imagined that as she looked out the window. The rain picked up a little, and tapped against the glass.

Her confidence, her strength of character, all her goodness, no matter how deep she had to search to find it, came about because she was loved. Audrey knew it. *What's wrong in the world is the unhappiness from feeling unloved. You cannot love a child enough.* And knowing, that inside she was still a child, as everybody is, *all this world needs is to feel loved.*

Audrey sat on her old bed and wondered for a long time, how she could make things better. She wanted to return to her younger, more graceful days, where she had received life's little gifts so frequently when she was a child, a teenager, a young adult -- things that helped her to build her confidences to become anything she chose. It was all too deep. Her head was spinning. Yet, she felt she was on to something meaningful. Some new desire to make a life that gave back. *Corny as hell*, she thought, but *Fuck'em all in Manhattan. There's great stuff in simplicity. It's definitely underrated.*

Next in the batch of papers from the drawer was a yellow Kodak pack that had a dozen or so photos in it. She took them out. They were pictures of Roger and her at Disney World. He was standing on one side of Tweedle Dee, a dressed up character, and Audrey on the other side, with Tweedle Dee's hand on Audrey's ass (which couldn't be seen in the picture, but Audrey knew, and at the time she was horrified that the character was making a play for her).

Audrey Beane then - sweet and shocked. If it were Audrey Beane today who had Tweedle Fuckin' Dee's hand on my ass, I would've filed a lawsuit against Michael Eisner, Disney's CEO, and let the whole Tomorrowland hear about it, or whatever land I was in when the picture was taken. Today, a million years later, she just had to laugh it off. She put the picture aside on the bed to show it to Ava later.

Somehow, this trip down Memory Lane at Pineapple Avenue is enlightening. Audrey took a minute to light a cigarette and look in her father's wine cellar. *Well, what he called a wine cellar.* In reality, it was a little cabinet that had a few bottles of wine, mostly given to him as gifts. She found a bottle of Woodbridge Merlot, her favorite, at least for an every day type wine. She opened it up. *I'll just pour me a bigass glass. Perfect with my smoke.*

She plopped herself into the overstuffed sofa and threw one leg over the armrest, the way she used to when she lived there. She inhaled a puff from the cigarette. She looked around the place and wondered if it would be hard to let it go. *Just sell it, that's the practical thing. How much could this place bring?* She wondered. *A hundred grand? Maybe we should keep it. I could live here.*

She took inventory of the home and how she'd do it up. *First, the wood floors would need to be refinished. The walls? Taupe? Red and green accents? She could see herself fitting in here. Maybe....*

The doorbell rang. She jolted, practically spilling her glass of wine. *Is it 2:00? Already?* She set her glass down on the coffee table and ran to the door to greet the realtor.

Chapter Nine

The most handsome man in the world stood before her, wavy blondish-brown hair, a long-sleeved, button-up tan shirt with a real estate company logo on it, black pants and black shoes. His eyes were sparkling -- blue, and he had a tanned face with dimples on his cheeks. He was carrying a legal-sized folder at his left side. A tiny, flip-style cell phone was hooked onto his belt loop. He gave her a polite and formal nod when she opened the door.

A powerful flush of heat waved over her and she felt her face turn red. She didn't expect to see him, of all people. Her jaw was frozen and she couldn't find a syllable to utter. She stood before him, staring. *Staring like an idiot.... Say something, stupid.*

"Um... Ava didn't tell me you'd be... um... Jesus, I'm just so surprised to... to... uh... can I please buy a vowel?"

He laughed. He reached his hand to her. "Audrey, my Audrey."

She put her hand out to his casually, as if to shake

hands. His was calloused on his palm, but had soft skin on the outside of it. *Big. Strong. But this isn't a handshake. Awkward.* He held her hand lightly, holding it longer than a typical business shake. Unexpectedly, he turned her hand and lifted it slowly to his mouth, gently kissing it. She took a deep breath. He held her hand to his mouth for several seconds. *Getting nervous.* When he released her hand, she was relieved a bit and put it in her pocket.

"Roger!"

"Hi."

"Ava didn't tell me it'd be you. I should've figured. You did tell me you had your own brokerage firm. I don't know why I didn't think of you, myself."

"Avaleen called me yesterday and all I had available was today. She said she'd find a way to make it work, even if only one of you could make the appointment. I'm kinda glad it's you, old friend, it's been a long time."

She nodded.

"Well..." he said.

"Well," she said.

"Um... are you going to invite me in?"

Stupid, staring idiot. "Uh.. of course, lost my head there. Step inside."

He looked a bit nervous, too. His eyes were big and he was standing there a moment, his feet together, his body swaying back and forth. Then, shyly, he took a step in. He looked up at the ceiling and then at the floor, and then into the living room from the hallway. "It's not too much different than I remembered."

He looked into her eyes, her eyes that only he of anyone else on the planet, could see deeply into her soul. Or, so it felt. *God, can he read my mind? Is my chest visibly vibrating as my heart pounds?* The intensity of the emotion was almost embarrassing, and she was struggling with all her might to conceal how very un-cool she was feeling inside.

His stare into her eyes was riveting, burning a hole through her. He looked so sad, so sweet, yet intense. She, like he had over her, had insight into his heart, and she thought she knew what he might be thinking.

"What is it, Roger?"

"I...I...I thought about this moment and how uncomfortable it might be, but that is only one one-hundredth of how really uncomfortable this is. It's hard. It's hard to see you after all this time." He took her hand again and brought it up to his face and placed it on his cheek. Again, he looked down at her, deep into her eyes. "I am so sorry about your daddy, Aud. I.." His eyes were watery. No tears, but she could tell what he was feeling.

He was still holding her hand to his cheek, his soft, tanned, clean-shaven cheek. She brought her other hand over her mouth and started crying. He reached for her to put his arm around her. "Shhh. Shhhh."

"Oh, Roger!"

"Shhhhh. Quiet. I'm so sorry. So sorry. I know. I know."

He smelled of a familiar Calvin Klein cologne. She couldn't remember the name of it. Her face was nuzzled into his neck and shoulder. The way he held her close, his strong arms, his tight hold, she couldn't decipher if her legs were turning to jelly because of the emotion and sadness she shared with him about the loss of her father, or if she was so shaken to be in the arms of the only man she ever loved. *Which was more earth shattering?* She didn't know. She did not know.

He pushed her back gently so that there was about a foot between them. He kept looking at her, her face, her body. She was beginning to feel a bit uncomfortable. After all, he was here for business reasons, he was married, he was holding her out before him, and seemed to be adoring her. And she -- adoring him, as well.

"Um, well, I guess I should get down to business," he

132

said. He took a pen out of his pocket and jotted a few things. He stepped inside a little closer and peered into the living room. "Can I measure this room?"

"Sure." She stood back and watched.

I'm going to kill Ava. This was a set up.

She stood back while Roger measured. *Well, this is awkward as shit.* She needed something to do with her hands. *I look like a dope, just standing here. We're not saying anything! Not anything! We just had this incredible greeting, and I cried on him, and now we're not saying a thing!* She went for her glass of wine.

"Um, I know you're working, but if this your last appointment, maybe you'd like a glass of wine with me?"

He smiled.

"Is that a yes?"

"That would be super."

"Super?"

"Super."

She giggled. "I haven't heard that word since I last saw you."

"Oh, I guess I'm stuck in the 90's, or is that from the 80's?"

"Possibly the 70's, old guy."

"Hey, now, if I'm remembering correctly, another couple of weeks and a certain someone hits her mid-30's, right?"

"You remember when my birthday is?"

"Audrey? My God, of course."

She handed him the glass. "It's really good to see you, Rog."

He smiled. "Hey, how's that garden we made out back? Still there? Got any Koi left?"

Audrey shook her head. "Sadly, daddy was too sick to keep it up."

"Aw, that's a cryin' shame," he said. "I know that would have been a deal-sealer for the house sale. It was spectacular, like...like... Sunken Gardens. Hey, remember that place?"

Audrey laughed. "Yeah, I think we misbehaved there, but they sure did have some beautiful gardens."

"We misbehaved everywhere we went. Oh, shit. Look at me. Audrey, I don't mean to keep you, you want a comparative market analysis done. This isn't a social call. I've got a folder here with some numbers in it and it has your name on it. Shall we take a look, or finish up going through the rooms?"

"Rog..."

He looked at her. "Yeah?"

"Um... nothing."

"No. What?"

"Just... nothing."

He laughed. "What?"

"This may be out of line, but it'd be great to hang out a little while, I mean. I know you're married and stuff, but, man -- we go way back. Old friends, ya know? Ya know, Roger? What? You look sad? I'm sorry, I didn't mean to..."

"No... No.. Not you. Um, yes, I'm married. But let's just say... um... not for much longer."

"What?" Her eyes lit up. She cleared her throat and toned it down a bit to cover her reaction.

"Here." She reached over and grabbed the bottle of wine to pour more.

"Do you think this is the time and place?" he asked. "Maybe I should call you, you know, schedule time and take you to a restaurant or something, I mean, I'm here to give you real estate information for you and your sister. It's business."

"Don't be ridiculous," she said, filling up her own glass with the last bit of the wine. "Besides, I'm going back to New York. This is pretty much my last night here."

He jotted a few notes, nodding. He looked up and

gave her a plastic smile. The mood seemed to change. "Well, then, it was good to see you today, if only briefly."

Is he sad I'm going back to New York? Does he want to spend time with me?

She gazed at him. Part of her wanted him to read her innermost thoughts without her having to find words that were so hard to find. She wanted him to know, just by knowing, what she couldn't say... *I've missed you. I've wanted you. I've needed you. For so long...* But she would never, never, ever articulate those words that she knew to be the only truth.

There were so many uncomfortable pauses as they walked through the rooms. *Here's a guy I've bared my soul to, with whom I've been intimate for a significant number of years, whom I've loved and (maybe?) still do. And we can't talk? This sucks.*

"Mind if I smoke?" she asked.

"Still smoking?"

"Oh shit, not you too - another ex-smoker?"

"No, I'm just a sneak-smoker. May I?" He put his two fingers out to receive one from her pack. She handed him a cigarette and the lighter.

She grabbed an ashtray off the buffet table and they headed to her old bedroom.

He threw the folder on the dressing table and sighed. "Wow."

"Blast from the past, huh?" she said as they both looked around the room.

"It's like back a dozen years ago," he said.

The room was a little musty and dusty, but Audrey pulled open the curtains to let the daylight in. It was still raining softly, but the sun was shining at the same time. She took a puff and extinguished her cigarette.

"What's all this?" He pointed at the desk drawer and messy papers strewn all over the bed.

Suddenly she was embarrassed. "Uh... I was going

through things, cleaning up. I found a lot of memories in the desk."

"Hmmm... any pictures of me?"

"Actually..."

She sat on the bed and pulled out the yellow envelope of the Disney pictures. "Maybe you'll remember these." She handed him the photos and he put out the cigarette to free his hands to look over the pictures.

"Come sit," she said and patted the bed. "There's some more in here I hadn't even gotten to." She handed him another envelope with photos in it that she, herself, hadn't looked at yet.

He walked over, sat next to her.

"Closer?" she asked, so she could see the next batch of pictures with him.

He squinted, looking in her eyes, then at the photos. *Maybe he thinks I'm leading him on? Am I?* She saw the squint and realized it herself. *Jesus, Audrey, don't get too comfortable. You've got a lifetime of space between you. Assume nothing*, she told herself.

He looked at one of the pictures and kept it hidden from Audrey. He started laughing and lay on the bed, rolling over, holding his stomach.

"Oh c'mon. What? What's so funny?" she said.

He reached toward her to hand the picture to her, then teasingly swiped it back close to him quickly so she couldn't see.

"Gimme that, what's that a picture of? Let me see." She reached over to him, but he put the photo in the other hand and then in his shirt pocket.

"It's a funny picture of you," he laughed, holding his hand over his pocket.

She jumped on the bed and tackled him, the way she used to. He was flat on his back and she was sitting on his stomach. She took both knees and pinned his elbows down at each side. He wriggled. He surely had strength enough that he could have turned over and thrown her off of him, but he let her win.

She grabbed the photo out of his pocket and looked at it. They both sat up. It took a minute to remember that weekend spent with him that was captured in the picture. She rode a horse at the Sunshine Stables in Clearwater. The horse's head had turned away from the camera, and when the picture was snapped, the image came out that the horse's head couldn't be seen. It looked like Audrey was riding a headless horse.

She studied the picture, turning a bit serious. "Oh, Roger! Remember that day? I was so afraid of that horse. How did I ever get him to stand still for you to take that picture?"

He put his arm around her and pulled her in closer to him on the bed. "I haven't been horseback riding ever since that day."

"Me neither," she said. "I'll probably never go again."

She turned her face to him and they were as close as they could be without kissing. She could feel his breath on her. They were both a bit out of breath from the wrestling, *or am I breathless because I am sitting here next to this beautiful man?*

He reached his hand out and ran his fingers around the outline of the side of her face. He didn't say anything. She didn't say anything. His face turned to a serious look -- no smile, big sad eyes, some wrinkles around his eyes that were new to her. *Very sexy.* She stayed still, engrossed in the moment, hoping it would never end.

Yet, it was all she could stand. She looked down, away. *How could something so good, hurt so bad?* He kept caressing her, her face, her hair, her neck, and the outline of her lips. She sighed deeply.

His gentle fingers that caressed her became his whole opened hand, massaging her arm, her back, her hips and then her thighs on the outside of her jeans. They both lay back on the bed, their feet still touching the floor – not completely on the bed, not completely off either. He kissed her tenderly, and they lay in an embrace for only a few moments. In those brief moments, she decided she would let whatever was going to happen, simply happen. He could have her. Married or not, his touch was so powerful over her, it wouldn't matter.

Her whole body shook as he gently lifted her shirt to rub her belly and waist, and over the top of her bra. As she lay there, loving every second of his sweet touches, she turned toward him and placed her hand on his cheek, and looked sadly into his eyes. And at that moment, when their eyes connected, she was overcome with guilt for leaving him so long ago, and she felt a strong desire to reconnect with him, both physically and soulfully.

"Audrey, you're even more beautiful than..."

"You are. I've almost forgotten."

She couldn't take it any longer. She kissed his neck. At first, just her lips, then her tongue. Gently -- his neck first, moving to his ear.

He reached around. His forefinger and thumb lifted her chin to his face. He tilted his head, closed his eyes, and gave her an open-mouthed kiss. And it was long, and sensual and passionate. And she embraced it. And she tingled in places she had long forgotten could tingle.

She remained attuned to the surroundings....the rain pattering on the window, that it was getting colder, and she felt that this would be a lasting memory in her lifetime. They lay in each other's warm caress for hours. Still fully clothed, just kissing, touching, holding.

"Roger," she muttered.

"Audrey," he whispered.

"Oh Roger, let's stay here forever."

"OK."

"It's been so long," she said, "so very, very long."

"Audrey," he interrupted. "I want you so badly. I

138

want you more than any man ever could want a woman."

"...and I, you," she replied, hopeful.

"...but... this isn't right," he said. "Um..."

"Um, what?" she asked.

"Nothing."

"Nothing?"

"I dunno. Um...I'm getting a divorce, but I'm not divorced yet."

She sat up and looked at him.

"I don't understand your loyalty, then."

"Shit, it ain't that..." He got up and walked out of the bedroom to the living room.

Audrey jumped off the bed and followed him to where he was standing – at the sliding glass door. He was looking into the backyard.

Is he upset?

"I don't get it," she said, standing behind him. "What's wrong? What just happened in my room?"

"It's got nothing to do with the marriage bullshit. Um...just nothing."

"Roger, can you talk about it? Can you tell me who she is, what happened?"

"It's a long, sad tale."

"It's just a long, sad, rainy day. Unless you have something better to do, I'm here." He said nothing, so she asked, "Want some more wine?"

"OK"

Audrey opened another bottle of wine and changed the subject for a minute. He took a chair at the dining table.

"So, tell me," she said. "How much will the house sell for?"

"You won't believe it," he yelled from the other room.

"Really? What does that mean?"

"Things really went up in this town. Hugely. The market is booming, especially in Pasco, since the addition of the new parkway. People can now live here and commute easily to Tampa for the professional jobs. I can't think of a better place for a real estate broker to be. Business is good, Aud. Sales are great. It's a good living and I never aspired to as much as I've been blessed with."

"Really? That good? You always were such a simple person, I don't mean that as some sort of a crack, but making lots of money wasn't ever where your head was at."

"I think whatever you pursue with a passion, even if it isn't traditionally a money-maker, that you'll do well."

She washed her hands in the sink and wiped them dry on the dishtowel. "That's a profound statement, Rog. In fact, it's sort of parallel to some thinking and soul-searching I've been doing lately."

"What's up with that?" he asked.

"Oh, I wouldn't want to bore you. Besides, you still haven't told me the numbers for daddy's house."

"Could you grab my folder from your room? I left it on the dresser. I'll go over it with you."

She brought the folder to the dining room table, where they both sat, drinking wine and having cigarettes.

"Here," he said, his pen pointing to recent sales in the neighborhood. A list of twelve addresses showed homes selling from $167,500 to $179,900.

"Holy shit," said Audrey.

"Holy shit is right," said Roger. "This area is averaging 10-12% value increases every single year. It shows here that your father paid off his mortgage several years ago. The home is free and clear. I have no doubt we can sell it quickly for a very good sum. They say Christmas time is a down time for real estate, but you'd be surprised. I've done awfully well historically this time of year, especially in January."

"I have a lot of packing up and sorting to do of all this personal stuff," Audrey said, looking around.

"If you're going back to New York and your sister is

too busy with her children, I could recommend a company that handles estate sales. There are quite a few antiques in here that would bring in some dollars and it might be worthwhile to have a third party handle it for you."

Audrey started crying and went to the kitchen.

Roger was right behind her. "I'm sorry, did I say something?"

"No, it's not you. You're very sweet. I...I... I dunno, it's hard to part with sentimentality. Much of this is my family's history. She pointed at the antique buffet. "That was my father's mother's mother's furniture. We saved it from the junkyard, and daddy and I stripped the old finish off of it, sanded it down, and by hand refinished it to its glory days. Look at it. Just look at it."

"It's a beautiful piece."

There was a pause. Then Roger suggested putting the important pieces into storage. "You could ship to New York what you wanted to keep. Maybe Avaleen could store some of it for you."

She wiped her nose and nodded. "I guess I just need to put more thought into this."

"I understand," he said. "I deal a lot with people who need to sell a house that they weren't expecting to have to sell. There are a lot of personal items to consider. It's pretty much an issue for most people, especially for folks who lost a loved one. It's hard to let go of stuff."

"Roger?"

"Yes?"

"Why don't we do this, can I just take the property comparables to go over the numbers with Ava and Jeff? I'll take inventory of all the furnishings and personal effects. It's something I guess we have to do, not you. Then we can let you know when we want to list."

"If that's the case, Audrey, let me review with you the commission structure and how it works," he said.

"I don't care about that, Roger," she said. "I trust you

completely, and I would never entrust my father's home more comfortably to anyone else."

"Well, thank you very much. That is truly a compliment."

She put more wine in his glass, and then hers.

"What are you trying to do, get me wasted?" he asked.

"Seduce you," she said, teasingly, but regretted saying that after she did. *A bit aggressive there, Aud. Not pretty.*

He laughed.

"Come here," he said, patting his lap. *He's sitting on a hard-backed, wooden dining room chair. Where the hell am I supposed to plant my fat ass?*

"I don't want to break the chair."

"Fine then," he said. "No seduction."

She walked over and sat on his lap. "Well if you put it that way..."

He took her in his arms. He touched her chin to turn her face to his and he kissed her, long, softly, and with his tongue. It didn't take her long to respond - tingling again in all places, and she felt him hard against her leg.

"Oh, Oh, I can't believe you're doing this to me," she said.

"Me doing this to you? You're doing this to me!" He looked in her eyes, sadly. "I don't mean to... I can't help myself."

"You're torturing me.." she said.

"You mean you want to...like we used to."

"Oh God, more than anything."

He held her tightly. "Me, too. You'll never know how much."

He looked at his watch.

"What, is it late? Do you have to go home? Is she waiting for you?" Audrey asked.

He laughed. "SHE...is gone. SHE left ME. I got no place to be. My secretary locks up the office at 4:30. I was just wondering...." He leaned to look out the window. "Is

142

it still raining?"

She looked. "No, but it's cold. What did you have in mind?"

"Well, if it were nice, I would've offered to take you for a ride out on the river on my new boat."

"Oh, I would definitely have enjoyed that! But it's awfully cold out there."

"Yeah. It is."

"Um... Do you have plans this evening?" he asked.

"I don't."

"Can I buy you dinner? We could go to Hooters, on the water. Have brewskies, wings, a grouper sandwich."

"Oh, that sounds terrif," she said.

"I should call Ava and let her know."

"OK," he said. "Now if you don't mind, I need to use the facilities."

She stepped out the sliding door to the backyard. It smelled like wet grass and a fireplace some place blowing burning wood. Her hands shook, she was a little buzzed from all the wine, and very excited as she dialed Ava's phone.

"Audrey," she answered.

"How'd you know?"

"Duh, caller ID." Ava said.

"Oh. Where are you?"

"At Jeff's mom's place, in the jacuzzi with a glass of wine."

"I should have figured. You bitch! You sneaky, rotten bitch. You set me up."

Ava laughed. "Well, what happened?"

"He's still here. I only got a minute."

"So... tell me everything."

"Are you interested in daddy's house price, or, or..."

"Well, I guess I'm more interested in the OR, part. Wait. Wait. I need more wine."

There was the sound of some splashing as Ava poured

herself some more wine.

"So.... it's after four now, what the hell went on for the past two hours?"

"Well, we went through all the rooms - you know, taking measurements for the sale. And, well, we got to my old room..."

"Yeah...so...what happened? Did you or didn't you?"

"Did I or didn't I what?"

"Do it, damn it."

"What the hell do you think I am?"

"Oh please. It's a fair question."

"Well, we made out a little."

Ava started laughing. "You sound so seventh grade."

"It's probably been that long."

Audrey told her sister what really happened – nothing much. She didn't feel like embellishing what wasn't true.

Ava yawned loudly.

"You're such a bitch. I suppose we could have. I didn't push. Anyway, he tells me he can't do it."

"Can't do it? Is there a problem?"

"Not that way. He can't do it cuz he's still married. It's something like that. It sucked because by this time, I'm hot and wet and..."

"Ew."

"Ew what?"

"TMI."

"What the hell is TMI?"

"Too Much Information."

"Oh, sorry, but you get the point. Anyway, I'm just calling to tell you I'm going to Hooters with Roger."

"Oh, you mean Hookers?"

"Hookers? No, I said Hooters."

"Well I call it Hookers," said Ava, "Why would you want to go there? The waitresses wear short-shorts and tight tee shirts. Hooters means boobs."

"Oh, please."

"Well... I got nuthin' else. What are you wearing, anyways?"

"Why?"

"I hope you wore something cute to see him in."

It hadn't occurred to Audrey what she was wearing, or if she even looked halfway cute. She looked down at herself, to see what she had on. "Oh shit, I haven't really taken inventory. Maybe if you told me to cutify myself, I might've. Um... I'm wearing my long-sleeved black tee..."

"That's good. Black hides all sins. Go on."

"...and my jeans - the low riders. The ones I wore the other day."

"Do you have your black belt on?"

"Yes."

"Good. Those make you look skinny. What else? What shoes?"

"You're making me feel really insecure. The black boots from Payless."

"Oh, that's very good. Very good. Jewelry?"

Audrey put her hand up to ears and neck. "I forgot a necklace, damn it. I got big, silver hoop earrings on."

"Not to worry, that's all good. You don't need a necklace. Are you wearing a thong?"

"Didn't we already have the thong conversation in an email? I hate those damn things."

"Hmmm... This could be a serious error. What underwear do you have on?"

"Never mind."

"Just don't get naked with him tonight, do you hear me? I'm serious. You need a lesson in proper undergarment dressing first. Anyway, you go to that Hookers place now."

"It's Hooters!"

"I know, I know, I'm just making a point."

"I hate you, Ava."

"I love you, too, sister."

145

After the call, she needed to get her purse and get to the bathroom to check her make-up. *How careless of me. I'm ten years older than he last saw me and I haven't even fixed my fricken face.*

She went back in to the house.

"A year later..." he teased.

"Sorry. We had a few details to talk about. Sister stuff."

He walked up to her and hugged her. "I'm looking forward to dinner."

"Me too," she said.

He kissed her.

"Rog, I need to use the little girl's room, there's some wine left, would you refresh our glasses?"

"Sure," he said.

She grabbed her bag and went into the hall bathroom.

Horror of horrors! Look at me. She dumped out her bag into the sink to find her Clinique ultra-hide, super double cover, fixer-upper concealer, and some blush. She spent an inordinate amount of time totally redoing her face. *It needs it.* And she cursed her sister in her mind for making her feel so ugly. In her bag, she found she had a bottle of Yves Saint Laurent's Paris (her favorite scent), and she sprayed some on her neck, between her breasts, and on her wrists. She stepped back, adjusted her hair to the front, and was satisfied.

She stuffed all the cosmetics back to her bag and shouted, "I'm ready," on her way out.

Roger was sitting in the living room. "Why don't we finish up this wine and get going? Maybe they'll be a pretty sunset when we get there."

"Great," she said, sitting next to him.

He grabbed her hand and clasped it. "It's so good to see you. I've missed you. I thought I'd never see you again."

"Me too," she said.

146

They sipped on their wine, and looked at each other and smiled.

"It really is great to see you," she said. "You've hardly changed a bit. Any signs of age you do show make you better looking. I'm serious, Roger, you're one good-looking man." She looked down, embarrassed for her open appraisal of him. She hated about herself how easily she revealed herself.

"Well, I don't see any flies on you," he said.

"That's sweet."

"That's me," he said.

"To old friends?" she said, lifting her glass.

"To old lovers!" he said, clinking.

"Um... speaking of which..." she said.

"Y-e-e-s-s."

"What the hell are we doing here? I mean, together, like this? Is this as weird for you as it is for me?"

"We have no idea what we're doing." He held back laughter. "We really have no idea."

"This reminds me of that time we got stoned on campus."

"Oh, God, here we go... I know this story," he said, throwing his head back.

"No, I'm serious. I think that joint was laced with something."

"It wasn't laced with anything, Audrey. You just never smoked before, and you have the wrong personality to smoke marijuana. People who already think too much are not good pot candidates. We talked about that."

"Well, I remember how it felt, I was all paranoid and stuff. I was saying things before I thought through the idea. That's how I feel right now. Did you put something in my drink?"

"Oh God. Audrey, you're a trip just being you. A glass of wine gets you wound up. No, there's nothing. You're just naturally weird."

147

"Well, I don't understand why being with you makes me feel woozy."

"Woozy? And you made fun of me for using the word super? What does woozy mean?"

"You know... dizzy," She swayed back and forth, "off kilter, unsteady. Is it not a word?"

"I don't think it's a word, but you would know better, you were the Scrabble Champion of 1992."

"Oooh, I think there's a scrabble game here somewhere."

"I'm not playing with you ever again. Remember the last time?"

"Oh. Oh, yeah. The fight."

"Uh huh. We promised we would never, ever play again unless we had a Scrabble dictionary and an egg timer and set the rules up front."

"Oh, that's right."

"When's the last time you played Scrabble?" he asked.

"In 1992."

"Me too."

They laughed.

"Are you hungry yet?" he asked.

"Why, did you want to go?"

"Um... This wine is kicking in pretty good, and I'm afraid what I might do to you if we stay here much longer."

"Oh, why do you tease me? I could always open another bottle and see what you do after some more."

"Now you're testing me. You're the tease."

She drank the last sip of her wine and set the glass on the table.

"Nope, I respect that you've got some secret reasons for celibacy right now. Let's go to Hooters." She got up and grabbed her bag.

"Want me to drive?" he asked.

"I do. You're ok to drive?"

"Yes, I'm ok."

148

The little red sports car pulled away from George Beane's house, on its way to the restaurant on the river.

Chapter Ten

"Whaddya think?" he asked.

"About what?"

"About anything at all."

"Don't know."

"Me neither."

They were standing on the dock at Hooter's, each holding a beer, and waiting to be called for an inside table. It was cold. She didn't have a jacket, and neither did he. She huddled in close. He put an arm around her shoulders.

"Sunsets in Manhattan - it ain't a happening thing. Just take a look at that," she said, waving her arm over the horizon.

"I never tire of them. Does it make you sorry you left Florida?"

"It really does."

He pulled her in closer. "Shit. It's really, really cold."

"Wanna wait inside?" she asked.

"Then I won't get to hold you close like this."

"Alright then."

They had avoided the important questions and answers all day. How long can we flirt like this? She didn't want to jinx it. The attention felt good. She would follow Roger's lead, wherever it would take them. *Let fate take this*, she thought. *Something I've never allowed.*

The orange circle over the river slowly sunk, until it was half a circle, and then only a tiny crescent shape, and then it was gone. "Another day," she said.

"Not just any day. A very special day," he said.

"Because you got a new listing?" she asked.

"Oh, you are so funny. No."

"Then why?"

"You're going to make me say it, aren't you? You're a sucker for romance, aren't you?"

"Is this a romance, Roger?" She looked into his eyes. It was a serious question.

"You tell me."

"Um.... I think you're calling the shots on this one," said Audrey.

"Um... ma'am, I don't think so, you... you...um, never mind..." His words drifted.

"What were you about to say?"

"What I was about to say, you might take the wrong way, so I stopped before I started."

"Well, now you have to tell me."

"Why is that?"

"It's the rule," Audrey said.

"The rule?"

"The rule. If you start saying something, then stop mid-sentence, you have to finish it if the other person insists."

"Oh, THAT rule."

"Yeah, what were you going to say?"

"About who got to call the shots with this romance."

"What -- you think I get to?"

151

"I think, Audrey, you've always gotten to. I never went anywhere. I was always here."

"You mean, here, as in, here for me?"

"Yes."

"Why did you think I'd take that statement the wrong way?"

"Because it brings up the past - the break-up. And I didn't want to go there if we didn't have to."

"I don't think there's anything wrong going there if it gives clarity to a situation, especially if life has been hard in any way since then," said Audrey. "Has it been hard? For you, I mean."

"Unfortunately."

"Me too."

Oh? How hard? Audrey thought, *so hard you had to go and marry someone else? When is he going to tell me about her?*

"Really?" he asked.

"Can we not talk about that? I'm more interested in what your life has been like these past ten years."

"Got a year to hear it?"

She smiled. The hostess called them, and soon they were seated in a corner booth, overlooking the water.

"I think after that wine and now this beer, I'm done."

"Me too."

They ordered a couple of cokes and some mild hot wings with celery sticks.

"Um…" he said.

She noticed his brow was furrowed. She felt the change in atmosphere from deliciously playful to now serious.

"We should talk," he said, leaning in closer.

She took a sip of her coke and waited.

"Where to begin?" he asked.

"At the beginning, of course," she said blithely, hoping she might spark a lighter undertone to the conversation.

152

"I wasn't going to talk about the break-up, but like you said, it does clarify some things. Um... I'm not going to lie to you. It was rough. The first six months, it felt like life had beaten me up. It affected everything – work, just day-to-day things."

"I....I'm sorry," she said, actually shocked to hear it.

"You have no idea," he said.

"Again, I'm sorry. I mean it." She bowed her head. "C'mon. It was a long time ago. Maybe we should have stayed in touch. Things might have come around."

He shook his head. "I'm not sure it would have worked as a casual thing. I asked you to marry me. I don't know about you, but Jesus, to me it seemed like we had it all, Aud. I guess I couldn't figure it out. Was it the money you wanted instead?"

"No. That's not how it was."

"Whatever."

"That's not fair," she said.

He shrugged his shoulders and looked away a moment. There was a pause. "Maybe I'm just not remembering it right, then."

We're not fighting, just getting closure.

She cleared her throat. "It wasn't the money. It wasn't. I had to explore the opportunity. You could've come. Don't you remember? I begged you, but it was all or nothing with you. You didn't want to compromise."

He looked across the table into her eyes. They said nothing for several minutes.

Is he angry?

"Family's here," he finally said. "My life. Your family. I hate the city."

"I cared.... I"

He interrupted. "It took me so long to get my life back. I drifted a while."

153

Yep, he's definitely angry. She nodded, wanting the chance to tell her side. *He's so determined to make his speech. Patience. Hear him out first.*

"I'm frustrated. I mean, I'm really glad to see you now. There's what, a decade to catch up on? Where to begin?" he asked again.

"It wasn't always easy for me either, Rog. I've got scars, too.*" So much for patient listening.*

"I'm not sure you've been through what I have recently. I mean... I know losing your dad was pretty bad. I'm not trying to minimize that. In my life, things weren't supposed to end up like this, Aud. It just shouldn't have turned out this way.

"I looked you up on the internet over the years," he said. "...the press releases, the articles and photos of your success. I never let go. And then, one day about two years ago, I met Summer. I thought I could finally forget you."

Summer. She said the name again to herself in her mind. *Summer. Sounds like a stripper. Sounds like some white trash, whore bag who gave him nookie as a one-night stand.* Audrey sucked the coke through the straw with vigor, gulping until the sound of air through the ice made her stop.

"I should tell you about Summer," he said, his voice shaking. He paused.

"Go on. But first, I sure as shit hope you're not blaming me if some chick screwed you over. You know it was different between you and me. You knew my intentions... you knew, Roger. I know you did.

"Nobody set out to intentionally hurt the other person in our case. I'm looking at you. I see how hurt you are. I'm feeling you're directing that pain toward me. Is that what you're doing?"

"Don't misunderstand. No. No. Aud, it's not directed toward you. I dunno, I hate to say it, but after all these years it took this situation with Summer to realize I.. I'm confused about YOU. Still. Maybe you haven't had the same experience I have. Call me fucked up, then, I don't know."

"Pretty passionate there, Rog. Just so you know -- a little FYI..." She moved in closer to him across the table to dramatize her point, "Everybody's fucked up," she whispered.

He gave a little laugh.

She leaned back and put the straw in her cup and stirred up the ice. She let those words linger with him a while.

"OK, so you're telling me about how you found this chick and could finally forget me... which fucks ME up, but who cares about that right now, huh? So, I'm still listening."

"Yeah. Well...when I met Summer..."

Right smack over his head. He jumped right back into his story as if he didn't catch it -- that it's fucking ME up.

"...I had a loft in Tampa for a couple of years. Was doing the bar scene a while, got a bartending job over near the Causeway – worked nights. I was going to real estate school, too."

Audrey nodded. She stirred her ice, hoping for a refill soon.

"I'd go to this small gym that had just opened downtown. It was the kind of a place that all the yuppies went to. A few local celebrities were always there -- some of the staff from the six o'clock news, celeb athletes, socialites -- people like those you probably hang with every day on your job."

She tsked, and he continued. *Ah, let him think it.*

"Well, I'm an ordinary guy, but they didn't know that. They made assumptions I came from money or something, and I sorta ate it up. I ate it up and I kept working out, going to clubs, making friends and thinking I was some sort of a player."

155

She listened and offered a few nods. *Not too unlike me in my work environment – getting caught up in a bit of egocentrism.*

"So anyway, one day I had just finished this workout and shower. I was about to leave the gym, when Sue, this girl from Channel 8, comes in. I'd met Sue before, and she had this blonde girl with her. It was Summer, and she had just moved here from California. She was staying with the Channel 8 chick until she could find an apartment. Sue introduced her to me as her cousin, and we all talked for a few minutes. I had to leave for work, and I asked them to stop at the bar later for a drink, and we could talk some more. Ya know, just being friendly."

He looked up and adjusted his position in the chair. Audrey could tell from his squirming around that this wasn't easy for him. *Me either.*

"Um, Roger," she interrupted. "You don't have to tell me this if it's uncomfortable." *And I'm not so sure I can handle this.*

"I want you to know where I've been and where I'm at today. Unless you don't want to hear the story..."

"No... No, that's not it. I'm more than a little curious -- just nervous to hear the rest. I know where you're going with this, and it ain't fun hearing it. Roger, there's not been anyone like you in my life. I'm not sure how I'm going to react to hearing about someone else in your life. Um... some feelings never change, like me about you."

"So anyway, Summer comes to the bar that night..."

He just blew me off on that confession I just shared with him. Hmmf. Summer obsession?

".... and she's already had too much to drink. She had had an argument with Sue, and Sue leaves without her. So here's this girl I don't even know crying at my bar, and it's closing time. I offer her a ride home, and since she's staying at Sue's and they're in a fight, she can't go there.

156

She's got twenty bucks on her, and knows no one else in town. So I bring her home."

He took a deep breath. Sighed.

"So that's how you met your soon-to-be ex-wife."

He nodded.

"That was two years ago?"

"Yeah."

"How long did you know her before you got married?"

He put his hand through his hair and sighed again.

"Not long. She never left my apartment. She moved in with me and we were… um… intimate pretty quick…"

Oh God.

The food arrived, and they were interrupted. Audrey wasn't hungry. The wine was wearing off. Reality was setting in.

"Excuse me," he said to Audrey after the waitress came and left. "Um, I really just want to cut to the chase on this story, but could I just take two?"

"Sure."

"I'd like another coke if the waitress comes again. Be back in a few."

She felt her face turning red, as it got hotter. *Could this get any more painful?* Given a few minutes alone at the table, she imagined Roger and Summer in their most intimate moments.

Pumping, grinding, doing it. Summer, some sexy thing – she's a woman much younger and skinnier than me. He's lying in bed on his back. She's on top of him, straddling his hips. Summer's breasts are so large that they reach his face and mouth as she leans over him. His sweaty body is in motion with hers. He grabs her ass, bringing her closer to him so he's completely inside her. He gropes her entire body. She's physically fit. She's on top of him, moving fast, the way he likes it. She likes it, too. Summer's moaning. He's moaning. She's exciting him until he cannot stand it any longer. Then they lay together afterwards, smiling and catching their breath. Soon, they'll go back at each other again, like animals. Damn it. Damn.

She shook her head, disgusted at the vividness of her own imagination, and her jealousy of someone she'd never seen.

Why do I do this to myself? She recognized the typical Audrey habit of snowballing stories and turning situations inappropriately towards herself – inflicting pain, even in a story having nothing to do with her, specifically. Recognizing the negative behavior in and of itself, was never incentive enough for her to stop doing it. Her mind raced to more images of Summer.

Is she beautiful? Prettier than me? Bleach blonde, tan, skinny, slutty? Did they do wild things together? Make love outdoors? Suck face everywhere they went? Did he hold her face and adore her in the ways he did me? Her heart hurt. So did her head.

She took a celery stick, dipped it into the blue cheese dressing, and put it in her mouth. She chewed it slowly and deliberately, not enjoying it, but not sure what else to do with herself. She searched her bag for a mirror, and reapplied lipstick and fixed her hair. *As if this is going to make me look or feel any better.* She suddenly felt ugly, fat and old, unable to compete with her image of slutty Summer. *Fucking Malibu Barbie. I hate her.*

Roger returned to the table. He wasn't smiling.

"The wings smell good," Audrey said, trying to sound casual and smooth. *Geez, if he only knew what I was thinking.*

He grabbed a few chicken pieces and put them on his plate and started eating. There was silence between them for several minutes.

Whether he was as fucked up as he had said or not, in Audrey's eyes, Roger gave her the appearance of being a strong man who had his shit together. She watched him

158

eat. She observed the sharp lines of his facial bone structure, his prominent jaw, his chin, and his adorable dimples. There were small lines around his eyes. He showed his age, and she found herself deep in attraction to him, physically. He wasn't just her old college flame sitting before her. He was a full-grown, mature older man with features that distinguished him from underdeveloped young studs, like those guys she had dated in Manhattan (most of whom were five or more years younger than her). Here was a whole new category of man – bigger, hairier, older-looking, and definitely more desirable than anyone else she'd ever had.

They ate and didn't talk. Audrey's mind continued to wander to a somewhat unfamiliar, perverted place. She wanted to seduce Roger, do things to him -- turn a few tricks of her own -- that would make him forget that California bitch. She recognized how psychological this want was, how textbook typical, how very, very high school. *Do we ever REALLY grow up?*

The Stone's *Beast of Burden*, played in the background and she was drawn in by both the beat and the lyrics. It was a song that always made her feel sexy – lyrics telling of a man's passion for a woman to make love to him. *Hot. Quite hot.* She reclined slightly with a gentle-but-determined arch in her back, proudly exposing the largeness of her breasts. Then she leaned forward a bit and swallowed a smile when she saw how Roger's eyes flicked to her breasts – and then stayed with them, as she leaned yet more. The fabric of her bra yielded against her erect nipples. *You like that, Roger? Want to see more? My little asshole and my pussy? I want you to notice, Roger, I want you to wonder....*

Their eyes stayed locked and they remained silent briefly. And in those moments, any thought of summer was gone. It was just she and he in the world, with *Beast of Burden* sparking the fire between them.

"I love this song," he said.

"Mmmmm." She closed her eyes and swayed to the music.

She suddenly felt better – better about him and his interest in her, better about herself and how she was able to arouse him, and glad to hear that the Summer thing was a split.

"Rog. You were telling me about Summer?"

"Ah, I forgot my troubles there for a minute, my Audrey. Shall we forget where we left off and get back to just us? You seem a bit flirtatious, and I'm finding myself liking it."

"Maybe I like flirting – a little, but... no way, sir. I need to know the rest of your story. It's okay. I'm a big girl. I can handle this." *Yeah, that's right. Sounds good. I'll just fake it. Cool Audrey. Open minded. Yeah. Right.*

"A big girl you are," he said, his eyes looking right smack at her chest.

She smiled.

He paused.

"Ah, shit," he said.

"What?"

"Well, it's just not a nice story to finish telling."

"Tell me."

"OK. After Summer moves in, we lived together for about four months. By this time, it's not going so good. She can't find a job, plays the victim a lot, crying... telling me how bad her life was in California and she came here to get straightened out. And I'm sympathetic. Ya know? I'm sympathetic to her."

How quickly his emotions transformed. There was anger in his voice -- deeper, a little louder than a few minutes ago.

"I cut her a lot of slack. I worked extra hours at the bar, took care of her, paid all the bills. Not just the household bills -- her bills -- her credit cards, everything.

160

"And then a few months into it, we started arguing a lot -- mostly about her drinking all the time and going to the beach everyday. Guys were calling her at the apartment, and she always had some story about it being innocent. I was jealous. But I let her stay."

He worked on eating another wing, and the waitress brought them drink refills, finally. Audrey forwent the straw entirely, and instead slugged a mouthful, crunching the ice, nervously.

When Roger finally swallowed his bite, he continued, "I felt sorry for her. She was, well... really like a kid. When it was good, it was good. She thought I was smart. I feel like such an ass now."

Audrey reached her hand out. "It's okay. I understand. I know you. You have a big heart. I understand."

"Wait... there's more. So we're a few months into it, and she tells me she's pregnant. I'm going to do the right thing. I'll get my real estate license and sign up for more classes to get my broker's license.

"I had this trust fund my parents kept for me that I had invested in mutual funds. I could get a house, start the business I always wanted.... So I cash the funds in and that's what I did."

Audrey was chewing the celery sticks faster now, and sucking down more coke. *What more?* But as repelled as she was by the conversation, she was equally captivated.

He paused. He looked into her eyes. He smiled. "Shit. You should see your face right now."

"I'm okay."

"No. You're not."

"Well Mother of God, Roger, this is quite a bit you're spilling out here." She put her hand over her mouth to hide her dropped jaw.

Another pause.

"Get this. She takes off to California for a couple of months. Says she's not sure if she wants the baby, or me."

"Oh Roger."

"I'm okay. Believe me, I've really gotten over it all. But, those months were hell. So anyway... she comes back later and we one day go to the courthouse and get married. No ceremony, nothing. She's miserable. She's scared. She's not sure she wants this baby. I tell her I'll give her a nanny, whatever the hell she wants to be happy. That it will all work out. I really tried. Another stupid mistake."

"Roger, that's really noble. But did you love her?"

He didn't say anything.

"Roger?"

"I've asked myself that, and I can't say that I did after the crap she pulled."

"So then what? I mean I'm freaking out here. Tell me."

"One day I'm at the new building setting up my brokerage, unloading boxes. I was feeling pretty happy, starting my own business and thinking it's all finally coming together. Then out of the blue, get this, Sue walks in -- Sue, you know, Summer's cousin who works at the TV station. I have no clue how the hell she knew where I was. She and Summer hadn't spoken, or so I thought."

"So what happened then?"

"She tells me that Summer's baby isn't mine. I freak out and call her a liar. I figure that because they were pretty much enemies by this point, that Sue is making up this shit about Summer. I tell her off and tell her, 'Leave.' So she leaves.

"I'm sitting at my desk in my new office building, newly married, new house and I'm just shaking my head. It's supposed to be the happiest time of my life, and everything's wrong."

Audrey reached across the table and took his hand. She lifted his hand up and kissed it.

162

Roger continued. "I confronted Summer when I got home. She starts crying. She says that she's sure it's mine. She slept with someone else, she says, one time in California, but the dates for the pregnancy didn't match up with the affair dates and she felt positive of that. So I tell her to get a test. I take her to the doctor myself, and make her get a blood test. Damn results took so long I thought I was gonna die. Then we get a call on a Friday morning. I remember that day like no other…"

"Don't tell me. The baby isn't yours."

He nodded. He was choked up. He was holding back tears. Audrey took her hand back from his and sat silently.

"It…wasn't…mine."

What a relief. "So what did you do then?"

"Whaddya think I did?"

"Kicked her out?"

He nodded. He grabbed another piece of chicken and ate it. They said nothing. Audrey ate a wing.

"I haven't seen her in seven months. I heard she had the baby and is on welfare in California. I got an attorney and she, at last, agreed to sign the papers. It's supposed to all be over by the end of the year."

"Well that's good. Do you still have feelings for her?"

"She's a piece of shit and I wish I never met her."

Audrey nodded.

The waitress returned. "Anything else? A box to take the rest home?"

"No, that's okay," Audrey said, her voice a bit shaky.

"Just the bill," said Roger.

The waitress left the bill, Roger paid, and they got up to leave. They walked hand-in-hand through the restaurant and the parking lot, saying nothing. The wind had picked up more and it was very cold. When they got in the car and Roger started it up, Audrey didn't know where they would be going. *Back to daddy's house?* Her question was

163

answered soon enough as he headed in the direction towards George's house.

Roger popped a CD in the car sound system. It was the latest music of Sting. *Good stuff.* It didn't change the mood though. They were both quiet. She took in the lights of the city as they drove, realizing this was her last night in Florida, and what an emotional ride the whole trip had been.

Her thoughts drifted to her and Roger's earlier conversation that he wouldn't have sex with her because he was still married. *Was that what he said? He didn't love Summer or have any loyalties to her. Why was he using that as an excuse to avoid being intimate with me? That pisses me off.* The more she thought about it, the more she realized that her sympathy to Roger was a mixed emotion, and she was annoyed that he was pining away about some scumbag chick who ripped his heart out. *Why'd he let her whip his ass? Why was he so weak? Maybe he's not the Roger I used to know.*

They pulled up in the driveway. Audrey didn't motion to get out of the car. She looked at Roger, but he didn't say anything.

"Um.. You're going to think I'm a real wimp, but I'm afraid to go in there alone, just, it being daddy's house and all, and it's night. I think I'll just get in Ava's car and drive it back to her house."

He leaned over to kiss her, saying nothing. She let him, but kept closed lips. She was confused. She didn't want to be sucked in, or be on his rebound.

"Tomorrow's Thanksgiving," he said.

"So it is."

"So? What are you doing?"

"Taking a plane back home," she said, waiting to hear his plea for her to stay.

"Will I ever see you again?"

"Will I ever see YOU again?" she responded.

"I'd like that."

"Me too."

"Did I ruin tonight?" he asked.

"Absolutely not."

"This is weird for me, Audrey."

"Me too."

"We're sitting in my car. I'm wondering if I'm supposed to go in the house with you. Maybe I should invite you to stay the night at my house?"

She shrugged. "Um.."

"What?" he asked.

"Can I ask you a dumb question?"

"Please do."

"Why? Why didn't you want to make love with me today?" she asked.

He reached over and took her hand. "Jesus, you always just speak your mind, don't you?"

"I need clarification."

"You need clarification." He was silent for a minute.

"What is it?"

"Um. I thought about it. I coulda. I almost went for it. I had to stop. I can't lose you again. I only want you if -- or when -- I can have all of you. I can't go through it again and be left behind again. The excuse about being married – shit, that was just that.

"Truth is, and I keep telling you this -- I'm confused, Aud. I didn't get over you. You can get on that plane tomorrow and stay away another ten years if you want to. I'll probably still be confused, but I'm not making love and then letting you go. Too complicated. But hey, you wanna go in there and screw like bunnies, let's do. You just better know, I'm not into that love 'em and leave 'em thing. Let's go... Want to?"

"Wow. I'm without words."

"Never knew you to be without words."

"Just – I'm sorry for whatever this is that you're going through. You certainly are more to me than just a good time. Um... hell if I know what the future holds."

He leaned over to kiss her again. Again, she reciprocated, but this time, an open kiss – passionate, long, intense. She stopped and looked him in the eyes.

"I'm confused and fucked up, myself," she admitted.

"Me too. I.. I couldn't stop thinking about you after I saw you at 7-11."

"Me too."

"I saw the obituary. I was there, Audrey. At the cemetery."

"I know."

"You know?"

"When we were leaving in the car -- I saw you."

"I didn't know what to say, I stood back."

"It's okay. I appreciate that you came."

"I loved him, you know."

Audrey noticed his eyes were watery.

"I know. He loved you too."

He put his hand on her shoulder and nudged her closer to him.

"Mmmm, not too comfy with the gears between us," she said.

"Can I come inside? Just a few minutes? It's so fricken cold."

"Okay."

They went inside. *Now what?* She put the TV on very low volume, and they both sat on the couch. He put his arm around her and she got comfortable and closed her eyes. *Sweet, comfortable Roger.* She found herself in limbo between awake/aroused by him, and comfortably numb and sleepy.

"Aud...Aud," he whispered some time later, tapping her arm lightly.

"Hmmm?" she asked, sleepily.

"It's late. Should I stay or should I go?"

She sat up and rubbed her eyes.

"Mmm. Whaddyathink? Can I stay?"

She didn't answer. Instead she got up, turned off the TV, grabbed his hand and led him to her old bed. They stripped to their underclothes and got in between the sheets. He spooned his body behind hers. *Roger in his Calvin Klein boxers, and I in my faded cotton, inappropriate panties.*

They lay in each other's arms all night. His muscular body she'd always taken for granted, now had hidden secrets. She, too, had been no perfect angel, having had her own past. And although his flesh pressed against hers was still sensual, it didn't feel like it belonged to her. Not the way it used to, not the way it could or should, if she had it her way right now. Until the memory of Roger's lovemaking was replaced by a real experience, they were like innocent children taking a sweet nap. Her body tightened and throbbed in frustration. His erection next to her thigh was torture, and she hated him over and over for not making love to her.

"I hate you Roger Hollingsworth," she whispered to him, but he was asleep. *Who's he dreaming about with that big woody?* Even though Summer was gone forever, she hated her. *I absolutely and completely hate her.* She gritted her teeth. Sleep, though restless, finally came.

*****

The phone rang. *It's ungodly early. Shit. Where's my purse? Where's my phone?* Audrey rolled off the bed and her bare feet were instantly frozen when they touched the floor. She grabbed last night's shirt off the nightstand, and negotiated her head through the neck hole as she ran to the living room. The ringing sound led her to the couch where her purse lay on its side -- the bag's contents, including her phone, were spilled out. She snatched the phone up.

"Hello?" she said, as she put one arm through a sleeve and cradled the tiny phone between her ear and shoulder.

"Uh, didja forgot to call your most gracious hostess last night to inform her that there would be no need to leave the light on?" It was Ava.

"Shit. Sorry. Is this your punishment? Calling me this early? What the hell time is it?" Other arm in other sleeve.

"Well, I was worried about getting you on your plane home. It's a little after seven now. When's your flight?"

"The info's on the fridge. My note."

"I didn't see it."

"Um... right next to the turkey drawings the kids made. On the right side by the stove."

"Oh, here. It's a pretty small note, no wonder I missed it."

"So what time does it say? I've forgotten."

"Four ten. You'll want to get there early, you know how airport security is these days."

"Can you take me?"

"That's why I was calling. We were going to go to Jeff's parents for turkey tonight, I wasn't sure if Jeff & I needed to take two cars, or if Roger would be bringing you to the airport."

"Oh yeah, Happy Thanksgiving. You guys decided to celebrate?"

"Happy Fucking Thanksgiving. Jeff's mom insisted. All I have to do is pick up a Publix pie, transfer it to a glass plate, and pretend I made it myself."

"I want you to bring me."

"Really?"

"If you don't mind."

"Not at all, but, I thought..."

168

Audrey interrupted, "Um… no. Just.. I dunno. I prefer having you."

"Everything OK, Sister?"

"Oh, oh, yeah, no prob here."

"Are you at daddy's?"

"Yeah."

"He stayed?"

"Mmmm hmm."

There was a pause. "I see."

"Am I detecting a tone?"

"No. Are you going to give me the 411?"

"Well, let me get up and get myself fixed here. I'll come to the house in an hour or so, kay? I'll catch you up on everything. I've got stories."

"Sounds good."

"See ya."

"Bye."

Audrey put the phone and all the purse contents back in the bag and headed to the bathroom with it, careful to not wake up Roger until she could get herself presentable. *Is there a damn toothbrush in this place?* She sifted through the bathroom drawers and found a few grooming items that she'd make do with.

She washed and put on some eye make-up and brushed her hair.

She couldn't quite sort through a myriad of feelings for Roger. She ruminated the conversation of the prior evening. *Nothing sits well. Maybe Ava will have an opinion.*

Lost in her analysis of the events, she didn't notice Roger right away. As he came up closer, she felt his body heat behind her and saw him behind her as she looked up and into the mirror. He was half-smiling. His hair was mussed. He had a five o'clock shadow. No shirt on -- a tanned muscular chest with more chest hair than she

169

remembered. Her knees felt weak. *Damn him, even at his worst, he looks so good.*

"Morning," she said.

"Hi!" he said, smiling.

"Why are you so cheery?"

"Cuz I'm here with you," he said. He came up behind her and kissed the back of her neck and brought his hands up under her shirt to her braless breasts. As he cupped and lifted both breasts, she arched her back and put her head back on his shoulder so he could kiss the nape of her neck, the ultimate spot for a kiss. It drove her crazy. *Oh God.* She hated him, but at the same time, loved his touch and how he aroused all her senses.

His eyes were closed as he kissed her and caressed her. Hers were open -- she watched their movements in the mirror and how perfectly suited their bodies were for each other. She observed the immense difference between his hard, muscular body against her petite frame in comparison. *Erotic. Beautiful.* He put one of his hands between her legs, and she wanted to fall to the bathroom floor with him on top of her.

I refuse to beg. I'm not ready to make a permanent commitment, either. Yet her body was responding to his and he could take her easily, physically. She was starved for physical attention. *Sooooo long since I....* It was all so confusing. She closed her eyes for a minute.

Mmmm. He smells good. Remnants of cologne from last night, and the scent of a man - indescribable, but distinctly, distantly familiar.

She turned around so that she was facing him, and she reached her arms around his neck. He held her. He pulled her in closer. They were perfectly aligned, the only things between them were the thin silk boxers he wore. *Oh, and the unfortunate faded, cotton panties that won't stop haunting me.*

Audrey and Roger didn't speak. They stood there, half naked in the bathroom, in a stronghold embrace. She wanted to cry. She hated him. She loved him. She couldn't decide.

Mind over matter. She broke away. "I'll see if there's any coffee."

"Hey," he called after her as she walked out of the bathroom.

"What?"

"Whaddyathink?

"About what?"

"About anything?"

"I dunno."

"Me neither."

Just like we used to do when the relationship was new and the conversation was uncomfortable. She smiled as she walked to the kitchen.

"I think I hate you, Roger," she yelled back to the bathroom.

"I think you're full of shit."

"What am I going to do with you?"

"Better figure it out, cause I haven't a clue what to do with you. You're the smarter one."

He came out of the bathroom a few minutes later, shaved, combed and clean. He sat with her at the dining table and they had coffee.

"This is it, Roger. I'm leaving shortly. I mean really shortly – as in, the next half an hour."

He looked into his cup.

"Something in there?" she teased.

He looked up. There were tears in his eyes.

"Oh Roger."

She was choked up, too.

Chapter 11

3:10 PM – TGIF Restaurant, Tampa International Airport – Tampa, FL.

"Another round of Bloody Mary's?" asked the bartender, a stout, chubby young man no more than 21 years old.

Audrey smiled and held up her index and pointer finger to indicate two.

She turned to Ava. "I've never had so much alcohol my whole life as I have on this trip, Sister. Do you always drink this much? I'm getting worried."

"It's temporary. We're in mourning. I don't know about you, but when I have a drink lately, it keeps me mellow, instead of getting pissed off at God."

"I know what you mean. Um, anyway, back to me.. So as I was saying, he tells me that he can't have sex with me because he's not a love 'em and leave 'em guy, and it hurt too bad in the past. I mean, he came right out and said that I had hurt him bad. Then of course, there was his ex-wife's shit she pulled."

"So you mean, even knowing you're still in love with him, you didn't just pursue it? Just let it happen and see where it takes you later?"

"Hell no. I didn't say I'm in love with him, anyway. I can't make a life decision overnight. Plus, I don't think he was asking me to. I think he's confused, and so am I. I need to get home and get into my normal routine.

"I feel like crap. I need to go to the gym, get my hair done, get a manicure. There's so much work to catch up on. I look forward to getting back. I need space and time to deal with dad's death."

"What are you going to do about Roger?"

"We exchanged numbers and email addresses. I don't know. I really don't know. Hey, what time is it?"

The drinks were brought to them.

"We've got time to finish these drinks," Ava said. "I can't believe you're going back – I was getting used to having you here and was really enjoying our time together. We were sisters, again."

"We're always sisters."

"Not really, you get wrapped up in work and forget about me."

"Well, I'll try not to. You can always look at the painting I gave you, and just know how I love your place and being with you guys."

"Shit. Just move here."

"I've thought of it. I got a big ass job, sis. I mean, I can't make that kind of money in Florida. Besides, they're supposed to make me a partner soon. You want me to give that up?"

"I only want one thing for you."

"What's that?"

"For you to be happy – whatever that is for you."

"Don't get corny on me."

"That's all I'm sayin'. I'm not talking no more."

There was a pause and then they chatted for a few minutes more, sucked down the rest of their cocktails, and decided it was time for Audrey to go through the security gate to Airside B, where the plane would be boarding. Audrey grabbed her rolling suitcase and gave Ava a big hug. They both held back tears.

"I'll call ya."

"Bitch – you better," Ava said.

They waved as Audrey got on the tram and the doors slid closed between she and her sister.

The plane ride was uneventful, and Audrey slept through it. When she stepped out of the airport to the taxicab pick-up curb, she found that New York City had turned a bitter cold in the time she was gone. The coat she was wearing wasn't the right one.

"Midtown, East 42nd Street, please. God, I'd give my right arm for a hat and gloves right now."

"Where ya coming from?" the cabbie asked as he made a left turn.

"Just got in from Florida. I was there a couple weeks."

"Yeah, the weather sure changed in the last five or six days here. They say snow this weekend, can you believe it? Kinda early for the year."

"It smells like snow. I love New York." She buttoned the top button of her coat and put on her seatbelt. "Yep, I love the big apple."

Almost home and back to some sort of normalcy. There were ordinary things that needed tending to -- bills, the job, -- all routine. She dug in her bag to find a pen and her date book, and she made a list of things to do:

     1.   Call Randi for scoop
     2.   Fri. - hair, nails, gym, office
     3.   Apt. lease renewal
     4.   Funeral Thank You Notes
     5.   Gift - Bella

6. Bills
7. Groceries

That's enough for now. She lit a cigarette, read over the to-dos, then put the date book away. Her mind wandered. *I haven't thought about Roger for over four hours. Daddy either. It's cold as shit. I hope my electric bill is paid up. I'm starving.*

As the taxi turned the corner of her street, she diverted her worries and looked ahead in the distance. She flicked the cigarette butt out of the window. She smiled. The lights over the door of her apartment building shined brighter than any other on the street. *Welcome home!*

Audrey practically ran up the stairs – the suitcase and bags in tow, bumping and banging her legs along the way. The excitement lasted all of ninety seconds. Whatever happiness she had about being home quickly waned as she walked through the door. The apartment was dark inside.

Of course it's dark inside. What did I expect? She hit the light switch, and realized that it wasn't so much the lack of light that was the problem. *Maybe I should get a cat to greet me?*

Newspapers plus mail stacked as tall as a sequoia tree overfilled a basket in the dining room. A big bowl of fresh fruit – apples, pears and bananas - was on the dining room table with a pink envelope leaning against the bowl. *Bella!* Audrey opened the card. A picture of two stuffed teddy bears was on the front. "Sometimes we just need to know that someone cares…" Inside, "This is one of those times, and I'm that kind of someone. Love & In Sympathy, Bella & Family" Bella's kind gesture wasn't expected. It left Audrey with a lump in her throat, an emotional response to discovering what a true friend her neighbor was, and how lucky she was to have her in her life.

She wasn't quite ready to settle into a quiet evening alone with her list. Now she was feeling chatty and wanting to see her friend. She searched for her cell phone and made a call to Bella. It rang three times. *Shit, the message machine.*

"Hey Bella, it's me. I just got in. Call me when you can. Thanks for the fruit. Happy Thanksgiving. Let's catch up."

Guess it's a quiet evening alone. Audrey made the best of it -- a long hot shower, comfy clothes, laundry sorted into whites, brights, and darks, and a load started. *Need food. Food? What food? Do I have anything?*

When the door of the refrigerator was opened, something seriously dead-smelling reeked out. "Whoa." She put a new bag in the trashcan, and emptied the contents of the refrigerator into the bag. Much of the contents were unrecognizable due to age, and any food appearing to be cemented to Tupperware Audrey threw out along with its container. *I'd rather lose a $3.49 Tupperware bowl than spend fifteen minutes soaking and washing it. Hey, when you have more money than free time, you do these kinds of things.*

Done and clean. So very clear to see the limited options - — some sad looking pickles, a full jar of maraschino cherries, ketchup and other assorted condiments, and some cheese. Gross. She settled on a can of Chicken and Stars soup from the cupboard and a glass of water. *No time like now to start a diet. Not very satisfying, but does the job for getting fed.*

After eating and leaving the dishes in the sink for tomorrow, she plopped on the couch and rang Randi's home number.

"Hello?"

"Randi?"

"Yes."

"Hey, it's me, Audrey. Sorry to bother you at home. Happy Thanksgiving."

"Happy Thanksgiving to you. No problem. Actually, I'm glad you called. So sorry about your dad."

"Thanks. I just got in from my travels. Um... I was wondering if you were on vacation this week, or planning on being in the office tomorrow or this weekend? Anyway, the reason I'm asking is, I wanted to get caught up. I... I really appreciated your email updates, and as you might imagine, I have several concerns about what's happening at the office."

"I have a ton to tell you. Bill went ahead and called tomorrow a holiday as a surprise to everybody, so the office isn't open. I wasn't planning on working this weekend, but we should probably meet before Monday, for sure. Want to meet for a drink tomorrow night at Clancy's?"

"Oh, Randi, you're a peach. I would love to meet you. You're great. How about seven?"

"Works for me. Listen, I'd give you some of the scoop right now, but I'm on my way out...."

"Oh, don't let me keep you, I've already waited this long, I'm sure I can wait another day."

"Just... brace yourself."

"Don't say things like that! It will drive me crazy."

Randi laughed. "I can't wait to see you. Hey, again, my sympathies on your dad. I'm so sorry. We'll have a lot to catch up on."

"You have a good evening, Randi."

"See you tomorrow. Bye."

Audrey put the phone on the coffee table and then looked across the room. The pile of mail summoned. *Please. Do I hafta?* She dragged herself over to the basket and used her foot to slide the basket across the wood floor to the couch.

Ridiculous. 137,000 fashion catalogs. She usually welcomed shopping reading material. Now, with so much of it, getting started was daunting. She considered spending all night flipping the pages of the sales, and ordering new outfits online. She grabbed the Fall & Winter Sale edition of *Casual Connection*, which featured an easy style sweater and matching tan corduroys with western boots on its cover. *Ava's carefree style is like that, and might be nice for me.* She thumbed through the first ten pages of the catalog. *Damn sure, none of these outfits will qualify as office wear. Oh, what's the use?* She tossed the catalogs on the side of the couch without further consideration. *Throw away pile. All the newspapers -- throw away pile.*

Ninety-nine percent of the envelopes went to the throw away pile. The rest of the mail she considered important, and was stacked neatly on the coffee table for later. *Online bill paying. Later. Much.*

But going online for other reasons, definitely a possibility. Curiosity hung over her. *What's on email?* She hadn't received any telephone calls from Roger. Would there be an email from him?

She set up the computer and waited through the computer start-up process until her email account popped open.

Yay. There it was.

```
From:    R Hollingsworth
Subject:  Hey
Message: Hope you made it home safe.
RH
P.S.   I have a violin.
```

She smiled big. *The P.S.* She remembered. It was a sexual play on words that they used to make back at college. In like-mindedness, she quickly hit reply,

```
Subject:   RE: Hey
Message: Home safe.
AB
     P.S.   I have a velvet-lined violin
case.
```

She resisted the urge to write anything more, even though she greatly wanted to. The message was filled with enough innuendo. *Who knows where this will really go, anyway?*

She dropped an email note to Ava to check in, and asked for a list of names and addresses of the funeral guests to begin sending thank you notes. Then, she went to Smith-Anderson's Website. There were a dozen or more emails, meeting updates, new staff introductions from the Human Resources Department, Policy update, Cleaning out the fridge notes, and more. *Nothing too exciting. Nothing revealing about the Essential Earth account. Bummer.*

She flipped back to Roger's email again and reread it. She closed her eyes and remembered his face, his smell. She flipped the screen shot to her email reply. Then back to his again, smiling. Loving it.

Audrey's eyes were now slits and her head hurt. *Long day.*

At 10:30, sleep seemed like a reasonable next action. She slipped into bed, which was unmade to begin with. *Typical. But it's all mine.* She reveled in that it's-so-good-to-be-in-your-own-bed-with-your-own-pillow feeling. But the moment she rested her head down, she realized that the laundry in the washer was done and sitting there, having never made it to the dryer. *Fuck.*

When the alarm beeped at 5:30 A.M., Friday, the day after Thanksgiving, her mind race began, excitedly and frenetically. *A day of my own to seize!*

First stop - the gym. Audrey arrived as soon as the place opened in order to snag them treadmills before the other bitches got there. She ran for 30 minutes. Hard. She worked on the upper body weight machines to tone her arms, her bust, her back and shoulders. Hard. The more she focused on her anger about losing dad, the state of her affairs at work, and not knowing the deal with Roger, the better her workout was.

Finally, she relaxed in the hot tub. Two other women soaking there were planning their Christmas shopping and talking about putting up their trees and lights. Audrey rolled her eyes. *Bah Humbug. I can't take the incessant babbling any longer.*

She dried off and headed for a twenty minute snooze in the tanning bed, where she fantasized about Roger and the morning bathroom scene at George's house. She pictured herself there in much better shape than she had been, with a deep native tan. In her fantasy, Roger didn't resist the tentativeness between them. He pursued her fully, and she was confident and beautiful, and... and.... Click -- The auto-timer of the tanning bed shut off (maximum time allowed and not nearly long enough for bronzing, a nap, or a good daydream.) She showered, got dressed in some weekend duds, threw her long hair into a flip, and headed to the office.

Yes, the office. No one will be there and I can see what's what. All part of the plan to save my own ass.

It was a long walk from the health club to the office building, but it was a time alone to smoke, feel the cold air, have a hot Starbucks coffee, and think.

The security guard greeted her out front -- Mr. Mooney, who had to be 120 years old and shrinking shorter in height every year. Audrey greeted him politely, then used her security card to get all the way through the door to the office suite. Her office door, which was usually closed and locked, was left open, and the light had been left on.

She was sure she was the only one there, and it annoyed her how careless her staff must have been to leave the door wide open and the lights on.

When Audrey turned the corner to enter her office, she noticed the profile of a platinum blonde, fuzzy headed woman who was wearing Audrey's office cardigan (used for chilly days and kept conveniently at the office), who was pouring over some papers on her desk. *That big head. Who else could it be? It was the one and only, Elizabeth.*

Chapter 12

"Kicking me out and taking over so soon?" Audrey teased Liz from the doorway. *Truth in humor?*

"Wha? Jesus, you scared the crap outta me! Audrey? How are you? Oh my Gawd."

Elizabeth stood up, walked around the desk and gave Audrey a sideways hug. Audrey's shoulder bag was hanging between them, and the other hand was conveniently holding the Starbucks cup. She didn't return the hug.

Elizabeth was wearing hippy, low-rider washed out bell-bottom jeans, high-heeled mules and a tight, white sweater that was short and showed off her belly.

Is that a...? It is! She's wearing a belly ring -- with a dangling silver ball. You can tell she just got it done, her piercing looks new, slightly infected and swollen. What the hell is she doing wearing that HERE?

"Nice piercing," Audrey said deadpan, pointing at it.

"Yeah, well..."

Audrey interrupted, "I know it's not a regular workday, but just make sure you cover that thing up if anyone comes in, kay? Nothing personal. No offense."

"None taken. I just got it done and wore this to keep the wound open -- let it heal. I have a long jacket if anyone, well, shows up today. I didn't know you were back yet."

"Yep. Got in yesterday." She looked into Liz's eyes and gave her a half smile.

"How was it? The trip and all?"

"Emotional," Audrey sighed.

"Sorry. Condolences. I'm sure it was hard for you."

"Yeah."

"Um... you're probably wondering why I was sitting at your desk." Liz nonchalantly slipped out of Audrey's sweater and draped it over the desk chair behind her.

She thinks she's inconspicuous. Hah.

"Not at all," Audrey lied. "I'm sure it gives you a bit more room to spread your papers out. The cubicles are pretty tight." There was a pause. "So, whatcha got going on there?" Audrey asked, walking closer to the desk and eyeballing the papers. She took a sip of her coffee. Waited. Tried to read the upside down paper.

"Oh, this? This, here? Nothing. Nothing really," Liz said, as she quickly scooped up the papers and straightened the pile. She drew the pile in close to her chest.

"No, really," Audrey pressed.

"Um.. Just some drafts and ideas."

Audrey nodded, her glare at Liz unyielding.

"It's not something I'm keeping from you, please don't think that."

Liz's body language tells me otherwise: arms are crossed as she hugs the papers to her chest. Her voice sounds a bit shaky.

"I wasn't thinking that," Audrey said. *Lie.* And that was the end of that, as well as any speck of trust she ever had for her right arm assistant.

"I'll need to get in here, though, so I hope you don't mind."

"Don't mind at all. Let me grab the rest of this and make some room here."

"That'll be just great," said Audrey. She took off her coat and hung it on the coat rack in the corner. Elizabeth picked up a pad of paper and some post-it notes and a pen she left on Audrey's desk.

"Um... I'm not sure what you're working on, but I have a lot to catch up on with the Essential Earth account. If you've got a few minutes while you're here, maybe you could update me?"

"Yeah. Sure. I'll need to get my files and, well, I guess I'll meet you back here in a few minutes."

"Great."

Audrey settled in her seat. Her desk faced the outside of the office and she could see Elizabeth walking down the hallway. Instead of turning into her cubicle, Elizabeth turned left, entering the workroom. The familiar sound of the shredder machine echoed to reach Audrey's office. *What papers are being destroyed? Something's definitely up.*

Audrey rolled her chair a little to the left so she could see better. A man walked out of the workroom. *Who's that? Bill? Blurry. Damn, I need to go to the eye doctor! It's him, but he's got a goatee and isn't wearing glasses.* Audrey squinted, she saw he was wearing a green sweatshirt, jeans and running shoes, not in his usual conservative suit.

Audrey stretched her neck to see through the doorway. She tried to think of an excuse to walk down the hall. Just then, Elizabeth came out of the workroom to the hallway and walked up close to Bill. Audrey could see from afar that Liz whispered into his ear. They embraced. They kissed. It was brief. *He put his hand on her ass! What the...?* Then he quickly walked out of sight, probably out of the office building. Elizabeth crossed the hall to her cube, casually, as if it were nothing.

Office affairs are disgusting. But, I'm sorry – that vision was more than slightly amusing. She turned her attention back to her desk.

Hard to concentrate. Not sure where to even start. The in-box was filled with files, and she began reading through things. *Correspondence-nothing interesting here. Invoices, seminar announcements, more typical stuff. Nothing good. Nothing about Essential Earth.*

Liz returned, carrying a briefcase and several large foam boards with paste-ups of the Essential Earth marketing campaign. She placed the boards against the wall so the fronts were hidden, and placed the briefcase on the desk across from Audrey.

"Are you ready?" Liz asked.

"Present me the campaign," Audrey said, folding her hands and placing them on the desk.

"Well... I took the research you did on all the products manufactured by Essential Earth, and reviewed the product life cycles and introduction of their new line of soaps and shampoos." Liz took a copy of Audrey's report out of her briefcase and set it out. "Because the new product line -- the all natural soaps plus the skin care products -- offer the highest projected ROI through point of sales, we will focus on a campaign that launches the new products. A secondary campaign of the hair care line will follow in the second quarter after a successful launch of the first line."

"Well done. Textbook perfect. You've learned well," said Audrey. "I'm listening..."

"Actually, credit is due you. It's your research. But anyway, when you left for Florida, you had approved a creative program that focused on a "Back to Basics" theme, a concept that would show the product line used at every demographic level, from infancy through teens to adulthood, with a focus on the purity of the ingredients of the products. If I'm not mistaken, the slogan we had for that was something about "In touch with nature..."

"You're correct. But when I received your email when I was in Florida, you said that you were taking the campaign in a new direction - something edgier. You said you and Bill were meeting with Nancy and Doug at Essential Earth. I haven't heard the follow-up to that meeting or when the presentation is going to be."

"Oh. I really should have been a better communicator. Geez, that seems like ages ago and so much has happened since. Um... the meeting with Doug and Nancy went just great. They were sorry they couldn't meet with you."

Audrey interrupted. "Yeah, Nancy and I go way back."

"So anyway, at first they were resistant to our new suggestion of narrowing the target to 18-34 year olds, but you know yourself, Audrey, that this group is highly coveted for selling personal products." She looked up to see Audrey's reaction.

"Mmmmm... I might disagree somewhat with narrowing the target based on contrary research I'm aware of, but I still think you could have a strong enough campaign based on that premise. I'm being open-minded." *Did I just say that? I'm such a professional bullshitter. Let's see if she pulled this thing off.* "I can't wait to see the campaign. Can I see it now?"

"Well, I just wanted to prepare you first. It's a little less conventional than what you're used to seeing or what you, yourself, ever created. It's really groundbreaking for Smith-Anderson. At least, that's what Bill says. He says it might put us on the map for even larger accounts. Well, I should preface that in saying, he said it MIGHT put us on the map IF we're able to pull it off."

Audrey nodded. "When do we present it to the client?"

"Oh. Audrey. Um… we already did that. I thought you figured that out."

Audrey's eyes opened wider. "Liz! I thought you guys were going to just meet. I mean in two weeks you formulated plus presented an entirely new campaign? Why in the hell didn't you consult with me, or, at the very least, let me know what you were doing? I had no idea you went all the way with it."

"I…I..I was just keeping to the project timeline you outlined. I thought you'd be happy that I was using that project software you started making us use. It was a critical date in the project. It was your schedule."

"You're not getting it," Audrey said. "Keeping to timelines is just great. Just great. It's commendable that you did that. But Liz, I secured this account based on a lot of selling and after six months of negotiations. It could have been perceived as less than professional to them to have anyone other than the account principal - uh, that would be me - go in there. I'm not criticizing you, Liz, I'm sure the presentation went well and that you're fully capable of leading it. It's just that I could've given some guidance so it wouldn't look like I sent in a junior associate on such a big job. A simple call or email from you, I would have been only too happy to give some tips."

"I don't mean any disrespect to you, Audrey, but Bill is the president, so he handled the politics and negotiations and paved the way for me to make the presentation. He introduced me as your counterpart, on equal grounds as you, and as a seasoned professional. I'm just telling you this so you understand that it was a tremendously professional show. Bill really pumped me up to them."

"Oh, really? In that case, I take back my criticisms. Um.. Is there something I don't know about your position and authority around here?"

"No, no, no. You're making it sound like something slimey happened. I was stepping up my role a notch as your right hand. Bill was just being really supportive and sweet. I thought you'd be pleased..."

Am I hearing this right? Right hand? Feels more like a backhand or upper hand. Bill is sweet? Sweet? Maybe I'm showing insecurity here, but look at her - so intimidated. So inexperienced. Nope, this couldn't have gone down good. Be nice, Audrey. Hold back.

"OK. OK. Calm down, Liz. I just take the account very seriously, and I want every step to be strategic. So, ok, you said you went in for the presentation. Could you do that for me now, just as you did for them?"

"Do you mean, just give you the highlights?" Her voice was pitchy and shaky. "Or do you want me to do the presentation exactly as I did it for them?"

"I would like to get the whole picture of how it was done. Tell me what you said, what you showed, and what they said and how it ended. You don't have to do the entire presentation word-for-word."

Audrey noticed a tear in the corner of Liz's eye. She pushed a box of tissues on her desk closer. For a brief moment, Audrey felt sorry for her. There Liz was -- biting her bottom lip, and her eyes were wider than normal, making her look like a scared puppy about to get her first shot at the vet's. Audrey quickly recognized what her employee was feeling, because she, herself, had been made to feel that way by Bill at least a hundred times before in similar work confrontations. *An epiphany?* That thought sickened her. *No. No. Not me like HIM. Am I giving Liz enough benefit of the doubt? Or is she a snake? Am I wicked? Or am I insecure?*

"Wait, Liz, let's start over here. I feel like I'm making you nervous and I don't mean to. That's not my style. I'm intense about this project. That's all. I don't mean to sound as if I'm scrutinizing every step you took. Let's do this, I'm going to step out of here and go get a can of soda. May I buy you one?"

"Yeah, that would be great."

"When I get back, we'll sip our drinks and go over the account. And I'll lighten up a bit."

Audrey bent down to get her wallet out of her bag and found money for the coke machine. While she walked the hall, she shook her head. *Confused. Fearful of a fucked up account. Not sure I trust Liz to do a good job. Yet scared she did a great job. Why can't I just do my job and not give a damn? Why do I even care?*

She returned to the office with the sodas and sat back down. *Liz seems to have her shit together now.*

"OK, Audrey. Here's the thing. I went in there and did a PowerPoint presentation about our company, followed by graphic charts showing your breakdown of the demographics. Bill added a couple of slides with more research he found, and we did a market share report that basically guaranteed the client an increase of market share by 12% after the launch of the campaign."

Audrey cleared her throat. "You did what? Tell me that again about the guarantee."

Liz adjusted her position and folded her arms, as if to protect her body from flying debris, or Audrey's words and tone. "Um... Bill directed me to say that."

"The numbers don't support that kind of a gain, Liz. Where did he pull that number from? His ass?"

"I really don't know. He's, he's the boss. I trusted him."

"Here's the thing. A company president always has the authority to make a final decision on the direction of something, but the boss isn't helping himself if all he does is hire a yesman or a yeswoman. Hell, cheerleaders are a dime a dozen, Liz. Don't be one. You're being looked at for bigger jobs here. You won't last if all you do is kiss ass. I know you know better. That number is ridiculous and unreachable.

"The way I see it, I was hired to fill a hole in a large corporation. If Bill knew everything there was to know about marketing, why would he hire an executive for a rather hefty sum, just to have that person execute everything he says? Anybody can do that. Anybody. The manager who arrives on the scene who challenges the mind of the leaders, who brings new data that they never knew existed, who makes recommendations never thought about before... that is the marketing professional that brings value to her job. That is the person who enhances a company in its industry. That is who I am, that is what you absolutely need to become. Sure, you can get a job just doing as you're told and it's sweet and all, but I'll bet you my year's salary, you'll never last any place, or if you do, you'll be stuck in that spot and never get promoted.

"Did you think the numbers support that kind of market share increase in such a short time, Liz? Knowing... knowing what you know from your college courses in marketing? Knowing what you read in my research report? Knowing the competitive environment?"

"Absolutely not. I know it's an irresponsible projection."

"Did you tell Bill that?"

"Oh, God, no."

"Did you tell anyone that?"

"No. No, I didn't."

"Why not?"

"Audrey, I just wanted to get the account firmed up."

"THAT was irresponsible. Now what? Who's the fall guy when their market share doesn't increase 12%? There's long term consequences here."

"Bill thinks the campaign is so good that it will."

"I haven't seen the campaign yet, but he's dreaming. And you say that the campaign was changed overnight from the creative I spearheaded eight or ten weeks ago?"

"That's right."

"Let me ask you this, Liz. Does anything good come from a campaign thrown together overnight?"

"Some good ideas."

"Usually raw, good ideas," Audrey said. "We worked our asses off on the first campaign. Why the sudden change in direction?"

"Um."

"I'm waiting." Audrey took a sip of her Coke.

"Bill said he wanted something hotter."

"Hotter? Hotter, he said? He knows what hot is?"

"He thinks I've got something unique - that I could take some of your good ideas and sex them up a bit."

"Sex them up? Is that what he said?"

"Maybe I shouldn't be telling you this... Um, it wasn't even something we discussed right here at work, so maybe I shouldn't say what we personally talked about."

"Personally? I didn't know you knew Bill so well..."

"Oh, well. It's nothing, really. We just... well, had some late nights at work, and grabbed a bite out while you were gone."

"Mmmmm. Hmmm," Audrey was getting the picture. "I guess, Liz, some things are better left unsaid. Let's leave it at that. Just show me the boards, and then you can go back to whatever it is you came in here to do. Which, by the way, what is it that you were here working on?"

"I'm working on a new account. International. Bill wanted me to get started before you arrived. I have to go to London on Tuesday. I was going to tell you on Monday."

"I see. I think I need to call a meeting with Bill since he is making all these decisions and not informing me. No problem, Liz, this isn't about you - I really need to talk with Bill. I'll get it squared away on Monday. Whatever you have for me, feel free to send emails over the weekend or call my cell phone. OK?"

"Mmmm. hmmm."

"I'll look over the boards later."

Liz nodded.

As soon as Liz took her briefcase and walked out, Audrey shut her door and turned the marketing boards facing her.

Holy shit.

The first board showed a nude woman sitting on top of a grassy hill. Her arms strategically cover her breasts, and her legs were crossed. A stream of water was below the hill. The woman's head was poised as in a slightly erotic, backward incline, and her long, blonde hair was blowing in a breeze. The photo had an artistic layer to give it a foggy, steamy feel. The logo for Essential Earth was in the right lower corner of the ad. The slogan at the top said, *Nothing Artificial. Essentially down to earth.*

The second board featured the same female model, nude, but this time, a muscleman was behind her holding a bar of soap, his other hand around her waist, as they stood under a waterfall in a Hawaiian-looking paradise scene, showering together. The slogan said, *Essentially in touch.... With Nature.*

There were several more boards, each one as seductive as the one before it. *Not at all BAD, per se.* Audrey admitted to herself that the photography was quite well done. It was sexy, perhaps enough to cause intrigue in the market that they would buy. *Yeah, yeah, yeah, sex sells. But... something isn't right.* She couldn't figure it out and thought it would be best to ponder the situation over the weekend to determine what was troubling about the campaign. Or, if the trouble was with herself and ego for the campaign not being led by her.

After several hours of office work, mostly routine stuff, she decided to leave and passed by Liz's cubicle to say goodbye. But Liz was already gone.

Audrey's tanning session had kicked in over the past several hours and the warmth of the tan was felt on her back and buttocks, despite the ice cold wind ripping right through her outside the office building. She decided to walk the city a while before going home and ended up at a new hair salon that was having a grand opening. The sign on the door said, "walk-ins welcome" and Audrey went for it.

"Welcome to Maison Salon, I am Julian," said the obviously gay, but handsome Latino. "What can we do for you today?"

"Can you make me beautiful?" Audrey asked.

"Why, yes. What is it that you'd like?"

"I don't care. I have had this style for the past five years. Transform me. I really don't care."

"Come."

Two hours and two fifty dollar bills later, Audrey left the salon about ten pounds lighter in the head area with much less hair and a new flippy bob, and a set of pink and white acrylic nails. *And damn if I don't look great.*

By the time she got home, she only had an hour before she had to meet Randi at Clancy's. She looked in her closet for something cool to wear, but everything staring back at her screamed, Corporate Nerd Girl. *Where is my red sweater? Laundry? Shit.* She remembered she never took the wash out of the washing machine to the dryer the night before. She started the load again and made a mental note to put the clothes in the dryer in forty-five minutes, before she left for Clancy's.

On her way back to her bedroom, she put on the Bose loud to get her in that going-out mood. She looked again in the closet -- this time, trying to have new eyes in her search. *Think positive. What will match my new hair?*

193

Audrey settled on a low cut, basic black criss-cross top from The Loft, which was a classic look that always did well on her. She put on tight, black jeans and her Payless boots. *Something about the new sassy hairdo calls for a little more drama, though.* She put on a black beaded choker and matching earrings. *Suddenly a star!* She even went for red lipstick. *Bold.*

She felt like a star when she entered Clancy's. Heads turned and they were the heads of attractive men. She was alone and had no ring. She might get picked up. *Imagine!* The thought of it both frightened her and excited her. It had been so long since something like THAT happened.

Randi was sitting in the back of the bar at a booth with several men. She saw Audrey's entrance and waved to her almost immediately. Audrey walked over.

"Oh my gosh, Aud, you look fabulous! You guys... you guys, shhhh. Listen up." Audrey could tell Randi was drunk already. She was slurring. "Thiths is my wonderful bothss, Audrey. She is the coolest, swankiest, smartest lady you'll ever meet. She's too cool for you, so don't try anything!"

Rich, George, Sam and Will shook her hand. *Not that I can remember any one of their names. They are all beautiful men. Ah, boys, really. But nice to look at. I feel young, right now.*

Audrey ordered a light beer. She wasn't interested in getting sloshed on this night. A little buzz would do fine and she could manage light beer pretty easily. It was her first time at Clancy's -- a nice place decked out in green décor and Irish Pub signs hung on the walls. She liked it.

The four guys lingered around the booth, drooling over Randi, and it seemed to Audrey that she and Randi wouldn't be getting any real conversation in about the job. A band started playing and the music was so loud that nobody could hear anyone speak unless they screamed in the person's ear.

Audrey smiled a lot. *This fucking sucks. Just keep smiling.*

"Woo hoo," Randi wailed to the music, throwing her arm in the air with her hand in a fist. "Yeah, man."

Oh, Jesus. Not that I recognize this song at all. What a waste of make-up. I hate going out. Why don't I see what they see in all this? I'd rather be home folding laundry. Fuck this. I AM going home to fold laundry.

"I can't stay, Randi," Audrey said.

"What?"

"I said, I GOTTA GO."

"What?"

"BYE!" She waved in Randi's face so she'd catch the clue.

She turned to leave. Randi caught up to her at the door and they stood in the entranceway briefly, between the exterior door and the glass door to the restaurant. It wasn't so noisy in this area.

"Why so soon, Aud? I thought we were going to catch up on Smith and Anderson?"

"Randi, please call my cell phone this weekend when we can talk long. It's noisy. I gotta go. OK? I gotta go."

"Is everything okay?"

"Yeah. Oh, yeah. Your friends are great. I just can't make it a long night tonight, ya know? I got a lot to do just back from Florida. You know how it is."

"OK," Randi said. "I'll call you this weekend."

During the cab ride home, Audrey's cell phone beeped, telling her she had missed calls. She played back her voice mail and it was the sound of Bella's excited voice asking to get together. She'd call her in the morning. There was also a message from Roger.

"Audrey. I'm just sitting here thinking of you. Are you out? Are you home? Call me. I miss you. I would love to talk with you tonight. Call me any time. No time is too late."

She wanted the conversation to be good. She waited until she got home, got showered and into her pajamas and between the sheets before she dialed the number. The lights were out. She cuddled up with the phone.

"Hello?"

"Hey, it's me," she purred.

"Heyyyyy. Great to hear your voice. I'm so glad you called."

"Is it too late?"

"I'm not asleep yet, but I just got into bed."

"Me too. I'm in bed, too."

"Mmmmmm. That sounds great."

"Yeah."

"What are you wearing?" he asked.

"Nothing."

"Aren't you cold?"

"I went to the tanning bed, so I'm hot right now."

"Mmmmmmm. I wish I were there."

"I do, too."

"Um... So how was your trip back and your day today?"

"Fine. I went into the office today. Well, let's just say I have my battles there."

"I suppose if I hadn't been running my mouth so much when we were at Hooters, I coulda gotten the scoop on your life these days."

"You'd be bored."

"I would not!"

"Why don't you come visit me? I'll let you see my life firsthand."

"Really? Stay at your place?"

"If you like."

"Tempting...."

"You should think about it."

"I will."

They talked for about a half hour longer, much of which was an exchange of flirtations. When Audrey hung up, she rolled over and tried to get some sleep. *The damn laundry again! Shit.* She failed to put the wash in the dryer, AGAIN! *I'll do it again in the morning.*

She closed her eyes and reviewed the day's events. There was something gnawing about the ad campaign. There was something about that first slogan that was disturbing. It was familiar. Had she heard it someplace else before? *Where? What was the slogan again?* She searched her mind to remember. *Damn.* She couldn't remember, but it bothered her enough to know that something just wasn't right. Something was very, very wrong.

Chapter 13

It finally clicked. Some sort of revelation. The minute Audrey woke up Saturday, her eyes were fixed with a new determination. Her ninety words per minute typing skills went into full force, and her mouse danced around the mouse pad as she conducted a little at-home, online investigation. It was a diligent effort to confirm her suspicions about the Essential Earth account that came to her serendipitously during the night.

Aha! She hit the print button, after finding the right piece of research. *Aha, again.* More pages printed. An hour later, and she had all the information she needed.

Wanting to share the exciting findings with someone -- anyone, she called Bella. She could always count on Bella to take interest in scandals, or, actually, anything Audrey dramatized to be scandalous. Bella came over with the baby, and the two friends had coffee while the baby played with stacking cups on the kitchen floor. Coffee, that is, minus any milk or cream on account of no groceries. *It'll have to do. Friends let friends be half-assed about these kinds of things.*

"It's funny, and I don't mean ha-ha funny," Audrey said as she swallowed some of her black, too strong coffee. "When I was sitting in my office yesterday reading over the campaign slogans, I recognized the slogans, but I couldn't figure out from where. I jumped on the Internet today to search phrases. And it was hard to find, but there they were, plain as that mole on your cheek.

"Nothing artificial... Essentially down to earth. It's on a billboard for a Canadian firm that launched a personal products line a few years ago. Someone from my company probably thought that they could get away with copying it because the use of the slogans crosses nations. It's likely someone presumed that the U.S. Trademark and Copyright laws don't apply. But here's why that's wrong...

"According to a press release online, the Canadian firm, called Green, Inc., applied for North American copyrights last September, and they have expansion plans in the northeastern states of the USA."

"How did you make the connection to start with?" Bella asked.

"Something was bugging me since yesterday. I finally realized I had seen the words before. You see I always study advertising wherever I am, in whatever I'm reading. It was quite some time ago, but the Green ad made an impression on me. I remembered the billboard from when I stayed at the Blue Victorian Inn in Canada on business."

"That's right. I remember that trip."

"Um... I haven't confirmed it for sure, but I suspect it was Elizabeth who copied the slogans. She's smart enough to get around the internet to have found Green's information, but not smart enough to dig deep into all the legalities."

Bella nodded and added more sugar to her coffee.

"Sorry 'bout the coffee."

"It's fine."

"So anyway, here's the dilemma... Essential Earth signed an agreement with us for millions. I have yet to see it, but I know that's protocol when an account is secured. We assume ownership of the creative and the legal ramifications. It's in the contract."

"Hmmm, this is a little hard to follow, Aud. So now what?"

"Let's just say that this campaign absolutely cannot be launched with this threat of exposure. Liz already presented the campaign to Essential Earth, and they accepted it. We need to do the right thing and pull it. If not, we're unethical, and it could cost the company its reputation, and possibly its very existence."

"C'mon. Really? That big a deal?"

"Hell yeah, that big of a deal."

"You'll be the hero. You'll get partner when you reveal this to the boss and offer solutions."

"I already thought of that."

"You do think they'll do the right thing, don't you?"

"Of course, they'll do the right thing. I may get pissed at my job stress frequently, but after ten years of working there, I think I can trust them."

"When can we celebrate?"

"I dunno, but soon, I'm pretty sure. I can't wait until Monday to have a showdown. And don't worry, I'll be professional, not a bulldog."

Bella nodded and looked under the table at Shandra.

Bella doesn't seem as excited as me. Damn. Bored?

"Finish telling me about Roger, after you left Hooters," Bella said.

"Later."

"Why later?"

"I guess it's secondary right now to where this Smith-Anderson thing is going. I can hardly stand waiting until

Monday. I want to put a full report together with a strategy that will resolve this and leave us clean."

"Oh, Geeze, here we go."

"Here we go, what?"

"You're going to be obsessing all weekend, with your face glued to the computer screen."

"You remind me of my sister and all her judgments about my time spent working. What's so wrong with doing a little work?"

Bella shrugged and then sipped her coffee. "You're not going to be up for anything else. I know you. I was going to ask you over for supper tonight. We could get a couple of the neighbors and play poker. Maybe have some chili or tacos like we did the last time. It was so much fun."

"I'm so busy. I gotta get groceries. Shit! The laundry! I keep forgetting to move the load to the dryer."

"I do that sometimes. You know, you're really a wreck. You need to relax a little. So, will ya come over tonight? Even for a little while?"

"Can't."

"Mmmm hmmm."

She looks ticked off. I swear, I'll make it up to her.

"Bella, I want to, I just can't. But I swear, soon."

"Well, thanks for the coffee, Aud, and the chat. It's always good to catch up. I know you've got a lot to do. Why don't you call me later if you feel like it."

"Mad at me?"

Bella made a pouty face. She shrugged.

"Oh, don't be mad. I'm sorry. You know I'm a freak."

"A freak you are. I miss Fun Audrey. Where did she go?"

Bella put the coffee mug in the sink and scooped up the baby. "It's going to snow today. If you're going to get groceries, you should do it soon."

"You're right. Do you need anything while I'm out?"

"No, I'm overstocked right now."

"Maybe I'll call you later."

Audrey walked her friend to the door. She took Bella's advice and ran out for food before the snow began.

And boy, did it snow. When Audrey returned from the grocery store, the sidewalks and stoops had a blanket of white on them. Being inside, warm now and sipping hot tea, having muffins, and a mission for her report, Audrey was able to concentrate and work for several hours straight. She stopped only to go to the bathroom, light a cigarette, or refill her teacup.

Saturday was a blurr. The trashcan near Audrey's desk overflowed with crumpled first and second drafts. Her report was finally completed before dark, and ready for presentation on Monday. *Ah, this is good. Perhaps what's best of all is the confirmation that Liz took the credit for writing the slogans. That little tidbit, compliments of Randi.*

Audrey recounted her brief phone conversation with Randi from earlier in the day, and ruminated over the finer points of it. *Let's see, Liz is cozy with Bill now. There's an intern working there whom everyone hates. There's a mystery account in London that Liz is heading up, and she's going there on Tuesday for a week. That's all? Old news after yesterday's visit to the office and subsequent research.*

The rest of the weekend was as productive as the first part. After the fourth rewashing of the laundry load, Audrey remembered to put it in the dryer. All the loads finally got washed, dried, folded or hung up, and even some ironing of the important work outfits was done. She chose to stay in all day on Sunday. She cleaned the apartment until it smelled like the pine solution she used everywhere. She put things in their proper places. *Clearing the clutter also clears my head.*

The hours of work had paid off. By evening, Audrey was able to collapse on the couch and enjoy an escape -- watching the old romantic flick on cable, *The Goodbye Girl*. During the final moments of the movie when the theme song played, and Paula is professing her love to Elliot from an apartment building window, she felt it come on -- tears. *God, I miss Roger. That's it. I'm calling him.*

"Hi, it's Audrey. Did I call too late?"

"It's never too late for you to call. I love it."

"I was just watching an old movie and feeling sad. Missing you, I guess. Feeling the Sunday night blues. Back to work tomorrow."

"I'm glad you called."

"So, whaddya think?" she asked.

"I think I have a rocket ship."

"Oh really? Well, I have a launching pad."

He laughed.

"Seriously," she continued, "I wanted to talk to you. I'm in a pickle."

"I've got a pickle for you."

"Don't tease. Really. I have this scandal going on at work, and I uncovered some secrets."

"Sweet. Tell me."

She told him the Smith-Anderson account saga, just as she had told Bella. *Why is it I don't tire of repeating this story?* She loved the spotlight shining on her for the moment, being the heroine in her own life's story. But that fantasy was quickly quashed.

"You might be overconfident," was all he could say after she spilled her passionate feelings about the Essential Earth account.

His comment shocked her. "Why do you say that?"

"You might be giving the company more credit than they deserve. I'm not so sure they'll take the high road."

"Oh, Roger, you think? I hadn't considered that."

"Well, I just think you should develop a Plan B. What if they decide to go with the campaign after all? You have to think if that affects your reputation with your clients. I mean, you're pretty well known in your field, right? I think you've got to consider where the line is that you don't want to cross."

He's right. He's so right. She felt her face get hot and adrenaline pump through her. She didn't say anything.

"Aud?"

"Um. Yeah. I'm hearing you. You just kind of took me off guard."

"I'm just looking out for my girl."

"Oh, you make me feel good when you call me that."

"You gonna be okay?"

"Not sure."

"Of course you will. There's an old saying that goes like this, 'Tough times never last… tough people do.'"

"I like that. You're good for me."

"I know. I'm very good. In more ways than you might remember."

"Are you flirting with me, again?"

"I can't help it. I have this image of you in my mind. My favorite vision of you on your trip here was when you were sitting across from me at Hooters and that song, <u>Beast of Burden</u> came on. Aside from you looking absolutely delicious, it was then I realized something else."

"What's that?"

"That despite my mistakes and failures, you still want me."

She remained silent, pondering that thought.

"Do you still want me?" he asked.

It was a fair question. There was a pause.

"Oh, Roger, I do. But I don't know how to integrate our different lives and how it would work. This long distance stuff isn't going to work, you know that."

"We're going to have to give it some time."

"Did you think about coming to visit me?"

"I wasn't sure if the invitation was serious."

"It was. Come."

"OK. When?"

"Now."

"OK."

"Let's coordinate later this week. But for now, I should get some sleep, Rog. Big day tomorrow."

"Let me know what happens. I'll check the airlines and see about a short visit. You sure you don't mind me staying with you?"

"I want you to."

"Should I bring you a hammer? You know, for the toolbox?"

It took a couple of seconds, then she laughed. "Sure Roger, bring the biggest hammer you've got. I've got a toolbox that's been empty a very long time. Oh, one thing, though. There's a lock on the toolbox. You might need to try a key."

"Hey Audrey?"

"Yes?"

"I'm falling for you."

"I'm glad."

"Good luck tomorrow."

"Kisses."

*****

Flowing white pants with no-waist styling and a crisp, black jacket with notched lapels, goldtone buttons and fobchain detail – the power outfit for Monday back to work. *Don't forget the shoes – classic black pumps.* It was the kind of ensemble that Audrey relied on to give her that boost of authority she needed for a power meeting, interview, or whatever. Although confident (and clothing always made for confidence -- or not), she temporarily lapsed into a fit of what ifs...

What if they don't pull the campaign? What if they think I'm trying to save what's left of this pathetic close-to-middle-aged woman's career that might be given to a woman a generation younger? What if they think I'm on a wicked-ass witch hunt? Oh, hell, what if they just think I'm my usual pain-in-the-ass self? The latter might be the best I could hope for, and that sucks, too.

There was one important incentive for going through with the uncomfortable confrontation with Bill. *What if I save the account, become the heroine, and be made partner with a huge salary?* She'd do it for that. *Oh, and I suppose because it's also moral and good. Even that, I wonder.... When there is material gain in the equation, it's hard to know if the motivation is based on righteousness or selfishness.*

Even Audrey didn't know for sure. She made a quick silent appeal to God for blessings and guidance right before she entered the office suite.

She knew immediately that Bill was in his office. His door was ajar, and the light was on. She saw his back through the crack. Quickly, she hustled to her office where she dumped off her coat and bag on her chair. *Best to get this over with before the troops arrive.* She took out the folder from her briefcase and went directly to Bill's office.

She peeked in. "Bill?"

"Yes, come in."

She walked in and sat down. Bill sat at his desk.

It was hard to get past her memory of him in the office on Friday – the guy who grabbed Liz's ass in the hallway. *Oh Bay-bee... Sexed up Bill*, she thought, along with a few other crude and funny things. Actually, she wanted to burst out laughing. Bill was sporting his new goatee, had a new shaved haircut around the ears with remaining hair on top long and highlighted in blonde streaks. His eyes were now a shade of aquamarine, quite sparkling and dramatic from his previous gray-blue shade. *Color contact lenses – as if anyone would think the eye color was real. He looks like something out of a transvestite review show. He probably thinks he's hot. So hard not to laugh. God, don't let me be like that as I age.*

"Audrey, I'm so glad you're back and I'm sorry about the loss of your father. Did you receive the bouquet of flowers at the funeral?"

"Yes, thank you," she lied, and had no idea of who sent what.

"It's good to be back," she said. "Bill, I'll get right to it. I was here on Friday and acquainted myself with the status of projects in my department. I wanted to have an immediate meeting with you about our progress at Essential Earth and some important concerns I have."

Bill scoffed by moving his hand in the air as if to whisk away a bug flying around him. "No time. I'm leaving for the airport in ten minutes. I just stopped in here for some papers."

"Oh. I didn't realize. I heard that Liz was flying into London tomorrow. Is that where you're going, too?"

"Yes. I'll have to give you an update on our newest account either in an email or when I get back."

"I'm sure the trip is important to you and the company, Bill, but I have to talk to you about Essential Earth. Pardon the pun, sir, but it is essential I speak with you."

"Audrey, don't fret. Liz is handling that one. Be a good role model to her and let her take it to launch. This is no time for micromanaging."

Why did I think this would be even remotely easy?

"Bill, I need to insist I have some of your time. Maybe I could come along on your drive to the airport. Maybe we could chat on the phone on your commute. It is very, very important to this company that we talk about this."

His forehead was furrowed.

"Yes, sir. I'm serious."

"You can come in the car. Meet me in front of the building in five minutes. You'll have to arrange your own ride from the airport back to here, though."

"Thank you."

She flew through the office to collect her bag and coat and embraced the five minutes to smoke a cigarette in the freezing cold out front of the building. *My nerves are already shot.*

Five minutes became ten and Audrey went back in to defrost a moment, before Bill appeared out of the elevator.

"Stay here and I'll pull my car around."

"Sure. Thanks."

The Mercedes pulled up and Audrey got in.

"Okay, Lady. You've got my undivided attention for the next twenty minutes, so let's hear it. What's up?"

"Let's start with the change in the campaign creatives. We had built a campaign that took the department almost eight weeks. It changed overnight."

"That was my direction."

"That's fine."

"Did you participate in the development of the slogans?"

"Audrey, we have a talented team. Liz led the effort and presented the slogans before we hired models and scheduled the photo shoot. I approved it. What of it? You don't like it? Is that what this is about?"

"Did you know that the slogans are the property of another personal products firm?"

"What? Where did you get that?"

Audrey pulled the report out of her briefcase.

"I've worked all weekend on putting the information together in a report for you. I'd like to leave it with you and hope maybe you'd read it on your plane ride."

"I think I'll do that. I find it hard to believe that Liz would take someone else's work. There's such a thing as coincidence, you know."

Audrey looked out the window. Paused. "Can I smoke?"

"No."

"Would you think it a coincidence if all the slogans were linked to one company?"

"What company?"

"Green, Inc."

"I never heard of them. What are they, some podunk company in Alabama?"

"No sir, they're a large firm in Canada that's expanding to the northeastern U.S. They purchased an office in Boston and will launch their products here early next year."

He didn't say anything.

"Here's the thing, Bill. We've got big problems. We sold a bill of goods to Earth Essentials. They signed a contract as well as signed off on the campaign, from what Liz tells me."

"Wait. Just stop. What does Liz say about all this?"

"I haven't spoken with her about the slogans. It was this weekend I pulled the sources off the internet. I recognized one of the phrases from a billboard I saw in Canada the last time I was there."

"Well, I'll read your report and I'll see Liz when she arrives in London, probably Wednesday. We'll see what we need to do."

"Meanwhile, I'd like your direction to take the original plans for a campaign and get it produced."

"That's too expensive. Not an option."

"Not an option? What would you consider to be a better option?"

"Let's use the current photos and change a word in each slogan to throw off any backlash."

"That concerns me greatly."

"Tough."

There was another pause.

"Audrey, I'm not sinking any more money into this. You guys fix this by changing a word here or there, and be done with it. The client doesn't need to know a thing about this, and I would appreciate your limiting communications with Doug or Nancy. Is that clear?"

"But, I'm not sure I can support that."

"You will support that. Hell, you know where the numbers are at as of last quarter. This account puts us financially right where we need to be. I'm not fucking it up."

"Bill, there was another concern I had."

"Jesus."

"Liz told me that you directed her to guarantee a 12% increase in market share as a result of our campaign."

"So?"

"That's ridiculous."

He smiled, crookedly. "OK Audrey, tell me why that's the case."

"The market share they have right now is only 10%. They've steadily increased over the past decade, but you're suggesting now a jump to 22% in a short time."

"So, they know that other factors are at play – the economy, the war, things that we certainly couldn't control."

"So why did we use that number as leverage? Is it founded on research?"

"They're just words, Audrey. We needed to get the account official."

"I worked my ass off to negotiate getting it. We were there."

"Not when it came down to the signing of the agreement. We needed something to seal the deal. That was what we said. I think you're overreacting."

"It's my job to protect this company in all deals."

"I want you to go back to the office once I find a damn parking spot here, and go out and solicit another large account. I've assigned Liz to lead this one, as well as the London account, if we get it. Your schedule is clear. I need you to work on other priorities."

He parked the car.

"Is that your final answer?"

"Yes, ma'am. I will, however, read your report on the plane."

"Will you at least call me or drop me an email after doing so? This is very important to me."

"I'll contact you if there's any other direction. You have your instructions."

He got out of the car and opened the truck to get his suitcase. She got out of the car.

"Do you have cab fare?"

"I do. Do you have time for a coffee? Maybe we could talk some more?"

"Actually I'm running late and I do have some international calls to make." He pointed to the left side of the parking lot. "If you just walk down that ramp, ground transportation is right around the corner and you should easily find a cab. I'm headed the other direction."

"OK." It was all she could say.

He walked away and got on the elevator.

Audrey stood and watched him leave. As she turned to walk the other way, she took a glance into the Mercedes. Her report was on the seat. He didn't even take it with him.

Chapter 14

The impenetrable Audrey Beane held her head up high as if nothing was wrong, and she walked briskly down the parking lot ramp to the sidewalk. A lineup of cabs approached after the traffic light turned green. She made a slight wave of her right arm to signal her need, and the first car pulled over to let her in. The meter was running, and she had twenty-two minutes (based on her own calculations) estimated time of arrival to the office. It was all the time she had to plan her next step and any communications with her staff.

She gave the driver the address, then lit a cigarette and asked herself a really hard question. *Why am I numb? Why, at this very moment, don't I give a shit? I feel nothing -- nothing at all. Not anger. Not defeat. Nothing. What the fuck is this?* She hadn't felt the deadness to this extreme before now – not ever. *Have I been through so much emotional strife in recent months that there's nothing left? No tears? What's wrong with me?*

Audrey closed her eyes. She was worried that she wasn't worried. It scared her that she wasn't scared. She suddenly cared that she didn't care. And she thought that this might be the end. *So this is what it feels like when you finally lose your marbles. Empty. Vacant. A shell.*

Seventeen minutes left E.T.A. and she hadn't even started developing a new strategy. *I guess it really doesn't matter. I have no influence. I'm a pawn in someone else's chess game. It's all so stupid.* She remembered the entire weekend spent in vain, researching and writing a report that probably nobody would read. *My own fault. So typical of me. What an ass.*

Audrey worked closely with so many clients over the years that she learned about all kinds of corporate dirt. It wasn't as if she was completely ignorant that many companies -- even the major players -- practice unethically or sell out. *But not MY company. Or, have I been blind all this time?*

The cab stopped short when someone tried to cut into the taxi's lane, and Audrey's purse flew off her lap. It jolted her, and she snapped out of deep thought to realize that she was getting close to the office now, still having no inkling of what she was going to do.

I should fire Liz. That would be grand. She imagined Bill at London's airport waiting for Liz to walk off the flight to greet him. There he'd be, watching the passengers deplane, waiting until the last one exited, and not find her there. *The look on his face would be priceless.* She had half a mind to just do it. Firing Liz was certainly an option. *Even if Bill terminated me for it, isn't it over anyway for me? Wouldn't that be a great way to go out? I could still be the hero in the story of my life, doing what's good, keeping some dignity.*

She lit another cigarette right after the first, aware that she was overindulging lately in the smoking-way-too-many-cigarettes department. *Last one.*

"I'll turn here, Miss. I can let you off at the corner, or we can try to pull up close after the light," the cabbie said.

"It's fine. The corner's fine."

He let her off, she paid, and the freezing wind battered her face as she walked to the building. But that was nothing compared to the smack in the face of reality she got from Bill not but a half hour ago. She threw the half-smoked cigarette butt in the street and watched it burn out immediately against the muddy snow along another of New York City's infamously filthy dirty and littered curb.

When Audrey walked through the doors of the office suite, she was surprised to receive such a warm welcome from the employees – even those who weren't in her department. Raymond at the front desk got up and hugged her with a tear in his eye, saying how sorry he was to hear of her father's passing. "We've missed you so much," he said. Darla from HR extended her hand as she walked past the reception area. Hugs, hellos and waves followed from several others.

"There are Krispie Kreme donuts in the break room," someone called from the accounting area. "There's still a box left, but they're going fast."

"I'll get one for you, if you want, Audrey," said Randi. "Go put your stuff down."

"Oh, that would be great, thank you."

Audrey walked into her office and got settled in. Randi was close behind with a paper plate that had a glazed donut on it. She also brought Audrey a cup of coffee, prepared as Audrey liked it, with cream and sugar.

"Thanks, that's awfully sweet of you."

"Well... Bill's secretary said you went for a ride with Bill to the airport to catch up on things. I'm sure with the drive and the weather and all, you're probably in need of a nice cup about now."

Audrey smiled. "You have no idea."

214

Randi looked adorable. *She really is a pleasant girl. She has a bright aura about her that exudes innocence and sweetness. The leather pants and high-heeled booties she's wearing are more appropriate for a night out than a work day, but what the hell? Randi carries a classy air about her. She looks professional with those pants paired with the work-appropriate blouse. What am I – fashion police? I'm too tired to care.*

"Hey, Ya got a minute? Shut the door and sit with me a sec," Audrey said.

"Kay." Randi shut the door and bounced back to the chair at Audrey's desk.

"Whassup, Boss Lady?" said Randi. "Everything all right?"

"I'm going to confide in you, Randi."

"Sure. You can always count on me to keep a confidence." Randi's face adjusted to Audrey's tone of seriousness.

"Oh, I know that. Um... Things aren't good at this moment. There's a problem with the Earth Essentials account and we have to redo all the boards."

Randi smacked her palm against her forehead. "What did we do?"

"You didn't do anything. The layout on the ads is great. You did a fine job."

"You're forgetting," Randi interrupted. "I didn't even touch those boards. It was Liz's cousin, the new intern, remember?"

"Oh, yeah. You'll have to bring her in and introduce me."

"Liz told me this morning that she's gone now. She was temp, just for the Earth account."

"Well, we're not done yet on the account. Either the temp comes back, or maybe, it looks like you're going to get on this job now to fix it."

215

"Oh, really? That's fine. I was so bummed that I didn't get to be a part of the biggest job we've had since I started here. What do we have to do, exactly?"

"All the slogans have to be redone. I'd really like to get Jack on the rewrites. He's so good at wordsmithing, but..." Audrey put her head down and paused.

"But? But what?"

"Can't get ahead of myself." She shook her head, still looking down. "Bill insists that Liz -- and only Liz -- be the project manager on this account. I guess my directing you on the new layout is overstepping. You should double check with Liz on who should do what."

"Oh, come on. You're my boss, for chrissakes, not her. What the heck is going on around here? Liz starts sleeping with the boss, and she gets to be in charge? Are you going to let that happen?"

Audrey shrugged. "I honestly don't know what to do any more."

"How come the slogans have to change?"

Audrey looked up. "This is the part I'm asking you to keep to yourself." Audrey put her finger over her pursed lips. "I found out Liz plagiarized the slogans."

"Shut up!"

Audrey nodded.

"Does she know you know?"

"No. But you know what? Do me a favor."

"Anything."

"Just keep me posted on the case, tell me what Liz tells you, and how she corrects the campaign. I'll be talking with her today about the slogans so she can begin fixing things."

"What do you mean? Aren't you going to take back the reins?"

"This is Liz's little game. Bill put her in charge to see it all the way through. He's fully aware of the situation. He told me this morning that she's to handle it." Audrey took

216

a bite of the donut and remained perfectly unemotional. "I'm out of it," she said casually, talking with her mouth full.

Randi looked at Audrey intently, a questioning look on her face.

"Look Randi, I'm just handing her the rope."

"Rope?"

"Yeah."

"I don't understand."

"The rope is for her to hang herself. Haven't you heard that expression before?"

"Oh."

"I just mean… I'm not doing a damn thing further to make it right. I tried to intervene, but it wasn't accepted. I'm done. This is how Bill wants it. Fine."

"It should be interesting."

"Well then, you can go back to your desk now. Drop me an email of your current task list, if you don't mind. I'll see if we need to reprioritize anything you're working on. I'm going to be in the field much of the week at appointments, and I want to make sure I've got you kept busy."

Randi got up to leave.

"Oh, just one more thing… Could you please send in Liz if you see her?"

"Sure. Good to have you back, Boss. And don't worry. I won't breathe a word of what I know."

"Thanks."

While waiting for Liz to stop by, Audrey checked emails, including her personal email account. There was a message from Ava that included the list of people to send thank you notes to for the funeral flowers. *Yeah, yeah, yeah, I'll get right on that.* A joke from Bella was in her inbox, and finally, an email from Roger.

```
From:  R. Hollingsworth
Subject: Intoxicating You
Message: The Honor of your Company
```
is requested by Mr. Roger Hollingsworth,
for a Romantic Dinner the second
Friday of December at 6:30 PM at New
York's, Upstairs at 21 Restaurant.
Please dress formal. Following
dinner, please join Mr. Hollingsworth
for a weekend of planned events and
surprises, which includes three
romantic and fun-filled nights.
Regrets Only.

She read the email several times over, pausing long over the subject header. Just two little words -- two tiny words he chose out of all the words in his vocabulary – were written to describe her – Intoxicating You. It had great impact. She felt a drop in the pit of her stomach, a familiar-yet-distant rush -- a feeling she compared to riding a Ferris wheel -- that brief ecstasy of fear and fun mixed together.

She'd never been to Upstairs at 21, but she knew celebrities went there, and that it was an award-winning and very high-end place. *Yay! How exciting.* Roger's whole plan for romance, the fact he was arranging his own transportation from the airport and not even troubling her with the flight details, impressed her. *A man who leads and takes control, plus, who concerns himself with what a woman would like -- Imagine that!* Most guys she dated didn't have what it took. Roger was different. He was no pushover, and he knew how to take control as well as please her.

Roger was, perhaps, the only man who was man enough to keep her down. He could arouse her senses to make her feel like a lady – a genuine, regal and feminine girl without that chip on her shoulder – a chip, real or not, that others perceived.   Yet he wasn't overbearing or condescending - ever. Because of Roger's inner strength combined with his outer mild-mannerisms, she listened to him and trusted him. Roger was the only man with whom she ever shed defenses to be soft – with whom she could simply die in his arms. Until now, she had forgotten THAT power he had over her.

That's it! She smiled. She had figured it out. It was that "it" factor – that hard to identify quality about him, that certain masculine strength he so effectively showed, -- that was "it". It was magical and perfect. Just reading his note sparked fond certain memories that characterized the "it" factor.

In the early nineties, Audrey was an intense college student who insisted on being the best of everything. When she struggled to get through a Statistics course with high marks, she broke down into tears on many nights before tests and papers due. She'd often end up in a full-blown panic attack. More times than not, Roger would be with her, witnessing her freak-out sessions.

God, how I remember that fear of failure. The migraines, the sleepless nights, the over-inflation of the importance of each and every test. She shuddered with embarrassment thinking back to how Roger had to see her falling apart so often. *But boy, he fixed everything.* Roger would refuse to go down a path of negativity with Audrey. She recalled that once, he even grabbed her by the shoulders and shook her, literally shook her, to put some sense back into her that nothing was THAT big of a deal. "You're smart. You're worthy. You're good." These were the things he'd tell her over and over and over again, until she'd finally believe as much as a tenth of what he'd praise. Nobody had told her those things for a long, long time.

Audrey remembered the sights and sounds of back then in 1993. Sheryl Crow's, <u>Strong Enough to Be My Man</u>, was one of year's biggest song hits. She tried to remember the tune. *The lyrics? Something about throwing punches in the air and being broken down and unable to stand.... then... Would you be man enough to be my man?* That song reminded her of young Roger's enormous inner strength. He had ability at such a young age to put up with an emotional, bigger-than-life character who didn't yet know how to channel her energy. *I'm still that girl. But I'm better than I used to be.* Audrey made a mental note to conduct herself with Roger as that better person. *It's comforting that even if I fall back – he understands me to my core.*

She closed her eyes and thought about Roger's face. His kisses. She wasn't sure if she was falling in love with him all over again, or, if she was in love with her memory of being in love with him. *How to reply to his email?* She was lost in a daydream, again.

Liz appeared at the office door.

"Hi Audrey."

"Oh. Hey Liz, come on in."

"Good weekend?"

"Yes. You?"

"Fine, had to get sorted for the big trip to London."

"Yeah, I heard."

"Um… Randi said you wanted to see me. Is it about the Earth account?"

"As a matter of fact, yes it is." *I'm working without net under me. I'm just going forward, no plan, let's see where this goes.* "Uh, the slogans. I wanted to ask you about the slogans."

"What about them?" Liz seemed to lose her footing, standing there.

Check her out! I wish I had a camera.

Liz took her pointer finger and started twirling strands of hair around her cheek. She took a seat in front of Audrey's desk, twirling away.

"Oh, I just wondered if you thought far enough in advance of using Green, Inc.'s slogans, or how you would battle their attorneys on a copyright lawsuit?"

Liz didn't say anything.

"You know, Liz? I mean, I was wondering if I should put a few hundred thousand dollars into next year's budget for fees for that? Or, were you planning on doing next year's budget, too?"

"Audrey, I... I.. I don't know exactly where you're coming from on all this. Am I fired?"

"Fired? Why would you think that? No, you're not fired. You're going to London tomorrow to meet up with Bill on a key account."

"I'm really not prepared to answer your questions about the Earth Essentials account, Audrey. It sounds like you're accusing me of something that I'm not so sure was intended to be a threat to our company."

"Exactly what were you thinking, Liz, when you obtained another company's creatives, and used them for our account here?"

"I didn't think I was doing anything that would get us into trouble."

"I see. Um.. Do you remember that conversation we had on Friday about bringing value to a company?"

"Yes."

"Did you think you were hired to surf the net to find other slogans that you could pass off as your own creative work? Did you think that was bringing value?"

"I don't like whatever game it is that you're playing," Liz said. Her eyes were welling up. The tissues were at the end of the desk within reach, right where Liz had them the last time the two of them met in Audrey's office. Liz finally took a tissue and let out some of her held-back tears.

"Game? You think I'm playing a game?" Audrey asked.

"I'm just saying…. whatever it is I'm in trouble for, just say it and let me fix it."

"Oh, okay," Audrey said sarcastically. She sat there saying nothing long enough to let Liz squirm a bit.

"I talked to Bill this morning before his flight."

"WHAT?"

"Mmmm. Hmmm. He told me that you are to take this account to the finish line, Elizabeth. Whatever that means to you, that's what you need to do to fix it. Just keep in mind, Bill has indicated that the budget will not allow a total re-do of the campaign materials. You've already sold something to the client that they love. You'll need to make changes to bring the campaign to compliance without incurring costs. Meanwhile, you need to appease the client on those changes. All in a day's work, my friend. You're a professional, right? Here's your chance to get back on board and impress. Let's see you tackle it and do well."

Liz shook her head and looked down in embarrassment. "Oh, Audrey," she said. "I never, ever meant for THIS. I wanted to get your approval on a job well done and advance my position here. That's all I've ever wanted."

"I'm afraid, Liz, you've taken this account down a shortcut path I, myself, am not empowered to fix. This is something you will have to do yourself. Maybe Bill will provide you some direction – that, I don't know. But I, myself, have some new assignments now, and I am going in another direction."

"But I have this new London account to focus on," she said, sounding pathetically childlike.

"Oh, poor Liz. What are you going to do? Welcome to the world of multi-tasking. Our accounts don't always permit breathers between them."

"Can you just give me some advice? I admit it, I made some mistakes. I need some help."

Audrey shook her head. "I feel for you, but I know that Bill believes in you. This is your chance."

"It doesn't feel like a chance."

"Who said project management would ever be easy?"

"Aud, I look to you as a mentor."

"Mmmm. Hmm." Audrey half smiled. "Tell me this then, why didn't you bring me in on the campaign? A simple email or phone call when I was in Florida would have sufficed. You told me not to worry, that you had this whole new direction that was edgier, or whatever word you used to describe something that apparently my earlier ideas just didn't have."

"I wasn't trying to compete with you."

"Well, whatever it was you doing –- perhaps trying to make a name for yourself -- you've got to take it to the finish line. Even a mentor would have you complete a job or solve your own problem. I'm not stepping in. Bill doesn't want me to step in, either."

"Is he upset with me?"

"That I don't know. You'll see him in London, I guess. I'm sure you guys will work it out."

Liz nodded as if to agree. "Um…. does anyone else here know about the slogans?"

"Just Bill. I guess you can tell the team whatever you want if you need them to work on the campaign. I won't utter a word."

"I would appreciate that."

"Hey, it's your first project to manage. You know all the senior managers are watching you – no pressure, of course, but ya gotta know we're all watching. I guess you've got a second chance on this account, Liz, that's all I needed to tell ya. Good luck and have a safe flight to London, okay? I'll be working on drumming up some new business for us here while you're gone."

223

Liz nodded. She got up and walked out without saying anything further.

Now, what about a new dress for the Upstairs at 21 affair? A little cyber shopping was definitely in order. *My work is done here, at least for a while.* So Audrey spent the next couple of hours adding items to online shopping carts and charging her credit account for anything and everything.

It's just another day at Smith-Anderson and Associates.

Chapter Fifteen

By Tuesday of the following week, the packages started to arrive. The UPS guy came to the door about the same time every evening, and he and Audrey were on a first name basis by Thursday. By Friday of the next week, the final box arrived -- drawing to a close Audrey's Internet shopping spree from nearly two weeks before. *Drawing to a reckless crash, is more like it. Every fucking thing is going back except one item. Net loss - $57.95 in shipping charges, plus whatever the hell this shit is going to cost me in postage to return, whenever I feel like actually going and standing in a post office line with some of New York's finest.*

Return reasons? Respectively: cheap material, too tight in the boobs, too long, too big, too tight in the boobs, and again, too tight in the boobs. When are they going to make real clothes for real women over the age of nineteen? The one thing worth keeping after much contemplation was a red slinky dress for the formal dinner with Roger. It was either that, or the back up plan: a classic black dress in the back of her closet, an old stand-by for a formal event.

I dunno, it's iffy if I can pull this off. She stood looking at herself in the red dress in the bathroom mirror. *They weren't kidding in the description of this neckline as plunging.* She turned for a sideways view. *No bra required is nice, though. Support in all the right places. A slit up to my thigh? I'm not sure about this.* She did the sit-down test, putting the toilet seat down and parking her rear on it, looking at her side view reflection as the silky material draped over her long, tanned legs. One wrong move (or would it be a right move in the case of Roger?) and there would be no secrets between her and the world. She tested her movements, crossing and uncrossing her legs so there would be no accidents, only controlled motions to hide or reveal her flesh. She had the maneuvers figured out after only a few minutes.

One final test if the dress would be a keeper. She got up and went to the closet. Among her thirty-seven (maybe more) pairs of shoes, she found some to match the dress. *I have to keep the dress now. That just proves it's meant to be mine.*

Everything was ready for Roger's arrival...Freshly laundered Egyptian Sateen sheets on the bed, a strategically placed nightie over the bed post (for a hint of sensuality rather than to actually wear), a candle next to Audrey's favorite book, Robert Frost's Collected Poems, on the nightstand. *Could I be cornier? So what. He'll love it.*

She phoned Ava to catch up.

"Hey."

"Hey."

"What are you doing?"

"I just got the boys down. I was about to read Cosmo in bed. What are you doing?"

"Just getting ready for Roger's visit."

"What did you decide on for the dinner?"

"Slutty red dress."

"Cool. Did you decide to renew your apartment lease?"

"I still have two weeks to decide."

"Are you waiting to see what happens with Roger?"

"Oh, Geez. I can't think about that. We're early in the relationship."

"So what happened with the job?"

"Nothing. It's actually been nice without Bill and Liz around. They were supposed to be back last weekend. Bill's secretary confided to me that they took a side trip to Pair-ee. Voulez-vous coucher avec moi? Ooh la la! I still haven't heard what the London account is about."

"Dogs! They didn't call or email you?"

"Nope. I just can't see those two together. Makes me want to hurl."

"What have you been doing in the office?"

"Oh, taking full advantage. I took Randi with me to a long lunch today, then, we went to the gym. Everyday, I've been on at appointments in the city, then cutting out early for home. I think I got a new account, not that Smith Anderson deserves it."

"Sounds like you're still pissed."

"Not pissed. I think I'm over it. I don't give a shit about the company at this moment."

"That's good. You can be like most people in the world. Go to work, have lunch, come home, get paid for it."

"That's not my style."

"You know that's what your problem is. You always think everything you do must have some long-reaching meaning in life."

"Um… yeah. Wouldn't it be a better place if we all tried to do that?"

"You're living in the wrong century, era, place... something. I feel sorry for you. You make your own pain. Why can't you just loosen up?"

"Can we change the subject? You're depressing me."

"I'm just wondering, if you can't get that lovin' feeling back at work, then what?"

"Don't know."

"You know what I think, don't you?"

"Yeah. Yeah. Yeah. You're going to tell me to quit, pack up and go stay at Daddy's."

"So you know, I put a Fed X in the mail to you today."

"What is it?"

"It's papers from Daddy's attorney's office. You have to sign where they highlighted and return the pages, and then we get to cash in the accounts."

"Ugh. It makes me sick to receive Daddy's money. He wanted to take us to Ireland next year with some of it."

"I know. I know."

"He could have enjoyed his last years a helluva lot more if had spent a little more on himself instead of saving everything. I'd rather have HIM here than have the bucks."

"I know. Me, too. But it's a nice sum for both of us. You could live ten years without working if you did it right. I'd show you how to clip coupons and stuff, and you could even work part-time to get whatever that need-to-be-in-business-shit is out of your system. You'd have time for your painting and gardening. Just an idea."

"Ya know, here's what's wrong with that. It just seems like a cop-out. It seems like a compromise. Just give up New York and the life I made here? How convenient for Roger. I don't want to do that. It just feels wrong. I really don't want to set myself up, and set him up that way. It seems too easy."

"What the hell is wrong with easy? You think there's something noble about the proverbial road less traveled bullshit? Here we go."

"Are we going to end up in an argument, again?"

"It's just, Sister, you make everything some sort of moral theme. Some sort of... I don't know... big dilemma. It's not. I mean, it's just another part of the country. Your roots are here. You love it here. I don't think you're thinking of those things. You think you'd be running away from something – bad job, whatever, and that you have to stick it out and overcome. Nobody cares or is watching you. You're sucked in and filled with ego. And you know what else?"

"Oh, I'm sure you're gonna tell me..."

"You've always yearned to come home. Now, because you're having work issues, you think you're running away. You just need to get your head right."

"Whatever."

"Yeah, whatever."

"Anything else new?"

"No."

"Want me to call you again this weekend?"

"Yeah, let me know how it goes with Roger."

"I'm nervous and excited."

"Think about what I said about everything."

"Mmm hmm. See ya."

"Bye."

Before turning into bed, Audrey fired up the computer to see if there were any messages from Roger. There was one.

```
From:    R. Hollingsworth
Subject: Breathless
The  thought  of  seeing  you  at
Upstairs  at  21  tomorrow  leaves  me
panting.  I can only imagine the vision
of you before me.
   Don't worry about a thing. I'll find
my way there. Please be there at 6:30
```

```
sharp.   I don't want a minute lost of
the precious time we have together this
weekend.
     Yours,
     Roger
```

Oh God. She felt like a virgin again, preparing for the first time. A shiver for the unknown ran through her body. On seeing Roger's name, the excitement and impatience rose in her, and she trembled as she typed her response,

```
     From:    A. Beane
     Subject:  It's getting warm in here
     Look  for  the  lady  in  red  tomorrow
night.
     With Intimate Thoughts of You,
     Audrey
```

After sending her note, she turned out the light and slid into bed and closed her eyes. The quiet darkness inspired sleep.

*****

Once upon a time a beautiful princess stepped out of a horse-drawn carriage, to be escorted by a handsome and chivalrous doorman to a beautiful castle where her prince awaited her. *Or something like that*, she thought, as she stepped out of the cab with her umbrella extended, hoping the up-do she had spent half an hour pinning up wouldn't fall into a stringy mess. *Typical. Typical. Typical.*

A doorman did greet her, surprisingly. But he wasn't handsome, and he didn't smile. But he did hold the door open, which was nice. Audrey folded her umbrella quickly, and removed her damp coat. She checked the items with the coat checker, and then turned to see if Roger was there.

He wasn't in the lobby. She turned and saw the Bar Room on the first floor and realized it wasn't a cocktail lounge, rather, another restaurant. A hostess directed her up the stairs to Upstairs at 21. *Duh, hence the name of the restaurant, upstairs. God, help me. I'm nervous.*

On her way up the stairs, she saw him at the top looking back at her. He had on a black suit and a red tie. He was holding a dozen long stemmed red roses, tied with a beautiful red bow. Whether there were a hundred people in the room or just the two of them, their intensely held gaze connected them as one. Roger broke their stare first by glancing at Audrey from top to bottom, then bottom to top, then smiling, as if he approved of the pretty woman standing before him as his date.

She walked up to where he was standing. "Oh, Roger! For me? They're beautiful."

Roger put the roses in her arms and kissed her on the lips, then whispered, "You look ravishing." He extended his arm to show her to their table. She placed the roses on the extra chair. He held her chair out for her. As she sat down, the slit on her dress opened. Her left leg all the way up to her hip was exposed when she did so. When he gently pushed her in, the tablecloth covered her skin. But he caught a good view. *I know he did.* She smiled a little that she had bettered Ava's suggestion to wear thong panties, and she wriggled in her new and slightly uncomfortable crotch-less lacy number.

A bottle of fine red arrived, and the server gave Audrey a glass to sample. She gently took a taste and nodded approvingly, after which, the waiter poured two full glasses. Audrey turned to Roger. "It seems you have a good memory for things I like."

"I think I remember quite a few things you like."

She wondered if his mind went where hers did when he said that. She gave him a slow, seductive wink.

The ambiance of the restaurant was dazzling and inspiring. Audrey looked around at the gold wallpaper, the murals of New York City, the sprays of silk flowers, the mirrors and chandeliers with their romantic low glowing lights. *Intimate and classy.*

"Roger, how was the flight?"

"Long. I couldn't wait to get here to see you." He smiled.

"Me too."

They avoided chatter about ordinary things, like work. It seemed like there was little to say, not that it mattered. It was as if he could read her mind anyway. He'd look at her, knowingly. She'd feel embarrassed and exposed for what she was thinking. Words weren't satisfying enough, and she felt dizzy with desire to be in his arms all night and loving every inch of his body. It wasn't that she wanted this glorious dinner to end, either, but not having had sex for such a long time, she wanted to do everything two people could do all in one night, for as long as he could go to keep up with her.

Is it safe to believe we will make love tonight? Not knowing was part of the mystery and fun.

By the time they finished the bottle of wine and their main courses (which were sizable), the thought of dessert was no longer appealing.

"Did you want to unwind at my place? You're probably tired."

He smiled. He shook his head no.

"Oh. Okay, then. What did you have in mind? Coffee shop?"

He shook his head again, keeping his smile.

"What's that look for?"

"You'll see. C'mon."

He picked up the roses, then reached to take her hand to usher her away from the table and down the stairs.

"Where are we going?"

"Can't a guy have a surprise? Shhh. Don't ask."

They picked up their coats and umbrellas.

"Roger, if we're going someplace, maybe you should tell me because we'll need to direct the cab driver, and I know what to tell him."

"There's no cab driver."

"Oh, if we're walking, we should…"

"No. Aw, Jesus, Audrey, c'mon before you ruin the surprise."

They put their coats on. He opened the door to the cold outside. The rain had stopped, but it was chilly. There was a stretch limousine in front of the restaurant, and a chauffer standing beside the parked car.

"What is THIS?"

"Madame…" Roger bowed.

She put her hands over her mouth in surprise, and a tear formed in the corner of an eye. The chauffer let her in the back, and Roger followed.

An opened bottle of icy champagne was in the console, along with two flutes. Roger poured them both a glass and toasted, "To us." She raised her glass and shook her head in disbelief.

"Where are we going?"

"I've never seen the lights of New York City, Audrey. Let's go for a drive, and I wondered if you'd mind if we looked at the tree and the skaters at Rockefeller Center. Um… it's Christmastime. Or, have you forgotten?"

She put her head down and for a moment, wanting to cry. "I was avoiding the holidays all around this year. Ya know, being in mourning."

He put his arm around her and drew her in close. "Shhh. It's okay. I know. I know. Do you think Big George would mind if I took his little girl to see some pretty lights and maybe some kids ice-skating?"

She looked up at him with her big, sad blue eyes. "It will be wonderful. He'd be so happy for that. Thank you. Maybe I do need a little of the Christmas spirit."

They kissed. Open and long. They paused only to set their glasses in the cup holders so they could better embrace. Audrey's coat was off by now, and her dress hung on her with gaping openings at the bust-line and at the legs – and she liked being alone with him like this and watching him respond with the eyes of a hungry wolf each time he looked at her.

Roger closed the sliding partition to privatize the backseat from the driver's view. He mentioned that it was soundproof in the back. A CD was playing Joni Mitchell's, Both Sides Now from a movie soundtrack. It was the kind of a slice-of-life event that a girl remembers her whole life – looking her best, next to a guy she was hot for, hearing music that set the mood, smelling a mix of roses and men's cologne and her own fragrance, and the cold, winter air surrounding the passionate heat stirred by two old lovers just reunited. They continued to kiss until their bodies slid horizontally to take up the entire back seat. He lay on top of her, kissing her mouth, her neck, her exposed and slightly sunburned and sensitive nipple.

She directed his hand under the slit of her dress to between her legs. He caressed her and quickly discovered the crotch-less panties; and when he did that, he let out a slight groan, and inserted his fingers deep inside of her until she, too, groaned.

"Oh, Roger... We need to stop or go all the way, I can't take this much longer."

"Shhhhh." His hands under him were quick to unbelt his pants, open the zipper and allow his throbbing hard-on to escape the confines of clothing. Audrey brought her hips up higher on the seat to better align her body with Roger's. Although he was large, he slid into her easily. He thrust hard and fast, the way she liked it. She intensified the thrusting by wrapping her legs around his hips and gyrating in harmony and against his movements.

If only this could last all night.

He let out another moan and lifted his head up. She looked up at his face and watched his eyes shut and his head shudder slightly as he climaxed inside of her. No fear of pregnancy for being on the pill, she was completely at ease. And seeing him in ecstasy made her, too, reach her high point, yet needing desperately still a few more thrusts. Realizing it was unlikely that Roger could continue, she reached her hand down between them, and touched herself to the motions that matched Roger, giving him a break, yet yielding her to the climax she was so desperately seeking. And it came, and it lasted and it was strong, and it made her shake and sigh aloud. He watched her as she touched herself, and him watching her made her feel sexy and alive and satisfied.

The song was over, just as their lovemaking ended. She lay under him, unable to believe what just occurred. *Magical.*

"Audrey," he whispered.

"Mmmm?"

"Audrey?"

"Yes, Roger."

"My God, Audrey. That was incredible."

"Mmmmm."

"I think I'm in love."

"Me, too."

"Is that okay with you?"

"Mmmm hmmm." She sat up. All the pins in her hair were out and her blonde locks draped around her face and shoulders.

"You are a beautiful woman. Not like the girl I once had. You're a real woman."

"Oh, Roger!" She kissed him on the cheek. "Look out the window, check out the Big Apple."

He zipped up his pants and took his champagne glass and watched out the window. She cuddled under his arm and pointed out some of the sights as they neared Rockefeller Center.

"There's Radio City Music Hall. I saw Tina Turner there last year."

"Cool."

Soon the car pulled up to let them off at Rockefeller Center. The driver opened the door and they grabbed their coats. Roger told the chauffer that they'd be back in a half an hour.

The tree was spectacular. There was a group of violinists playing carols and they strolled up and down, enjoying the music and holding hands.

"Audrey. Audrey. Audrey."

"Yes, Roger?"

He stopped and faced her. He drew her in close to him and he kissed her again. "It's official."

"What's official?"

"I'm in love with you."

"You're killing me. Really? I mean really? Really?"

"Yes. Does that do anything for you?"

"I've... I've just been afraid to admit my feelings about you to myself. I didn't want to get hurt. I live here and you in Florida. I.."

"Do you love me, damn it?

She looked up in his beautiful eyes.

"Do YOU love ME?"

"Yes, damn it. I do love you."

He kissed her. "I never stopped loving you."

"Me, neither."

They grabbed a cup of coffee along the walk and walked hand in hand, without speaking. The wind seemed to pick up and it was freezing out."

"I think it might snow again," said Audrey.

"Let's go home and get warm."

"Okay."

They returned to the limo, which took them back to Audrey's apartment. All the ride home, Audrey wondered how they would make this long-distance affair work. All she knew was, she loved him and she wanted him. And she hoped he had it in him for some more of what happened in the limo as soon as she got him inside the building.

Chapter 16

"Whaddya think?" he whispered to her, as he reached over to the nightstand to turn the clock towards him. The clock flashed 2:37 A.M. He blew out the candle, which had filled the room with an earthy fragrance of lavender and sage.

Audrey rolled away from him and put the covers over her head. She didn't answer immediately. Her body shook from the last several hours of lovemaking, and it felt like she'd had more exercise than a full day at the gym. Her head felt drunk from all the bedroom talk, sweet compliments and I love yous that Roger so openly gave. It wasn't even the effect of all the wine -- that had worn off long ago. Her jaw hurt, and she had forgotten how strenuous oral sex could be – if done good and given with extra love. But despite all that, she was finally, completely and perfectly sexually satisfied.

"Ya hear me? Whaddya think?"

"About what?" she whispered, sleepily.

"You know. Me. Whaddya think now? Of me?" He put his hand on her shoulder and rolled her toward him. The moonlight from the window lit their faces.

"I love you?" She said with a question, knowing --just knowing -- that it wouldn't be enough for him.

"C'mon Audrey. What else? There's got to be a new answer to that silly question. Whaddya really think now?"

"That you're the king of lovemaking?"

"I wasn't exactly looking for you to stroke my ego. I'm pretty confident in that department."

"Sweet, sweet Roger." She put her hand on her forehead, sighed and closed her eyes. "Please. I don't know."

"What's wrong?"

"Nothin'. Don't misunderstand. I love you. Scared – just scared, plain and simple. You have managed to totally take my world and stir it up, and make me feel things I've never felt. So. That's what I think."

"Scared, why?" He rolled from his back to his side, closer to her, interested and concerned.

She paused to think. "I don't know the words. I suppose I'm afraid of love."

"It's precious. These are some strong feelings. You have to knock down a lot of walls to find them. We've both had a lot of walls put around us. I can understand what you're saying."

"Mmm. Hmm." She was holding back a tear, trying not to reveal it - an intense emotion she didn't understand. "Life's been hard and unfair, if ya ask me." Audrey wiped her eyes, and then closed them. She noticed she was all tensed up – her jaw was clenched, her legs – stiff. She inhaled deeply, and made a conscious effort to loosen her body.

There was a silence between them. She turned to kiss him. He was again on his back with his eyes closed, and his slow breathing told her he was already asleep. That quick. She watched him in his stillness for a while, not touching, looking at him. *A beautiful body. A beautiful mind. A beautiful man.* The rhythmic sounds of his breathing brought her own breath and heart beat in unison with his, and she cuddled up close, and the two became one as they slept.

*****

Roger was an oblivious rock, but the usual sounds awoke her several hours later – the dog barking next door and the sound of Mrs. McCuddy's door shutting, just like every morning at dawn when Mrs. McCuddy took Snickers for a walk. *Damn shaky, nervous, barking Chihuahua with bulging eyes. Love dogs. Not snippy Snickers, though. Little fucker bit my thumb when I tried to pet him in the hallway.*

The brightness of the dawn poured through the window -- Audrey had forgotten to close the drapes in all the rushing around and passion of the night. She looked out the window and saw that most of the snow had been washed away by the rain. She gasped at how irresponsible she was not to tend to the outside balcony. Five or six potted plants were spilled over the fire escape. Where once were green healthy herbs were now brown sticks as remnants. *Another season, another dead backyard.* Staring at the pile of dirt, she thought for the millionth time what it would be like to have a real backyard where she could establish not only an herb garden, but vegetables and flowers, too. *I love sweating in the sun, putting my hands in the earth, and....*

She remembered what Ava told her last night about her being from another era or time and place. *Maybe I would be a better fit for a simpler life. Could it work?* She looked at Roger and imagined being with him – living with him, and not being a career woman. *Well, not a Manhattan one.* The thought both excited and scared her.

She didn't want him to wake up and see her. *He called me beautiful last night. What a wreck I must be now. There may be nothing more indecent than a woman who's had too much to drink the night before, who turns into a lascivious lush, then crashes without washing off all that make-up.* She bolted to the bathroom to smear baby oil all over her face to ease washing mascara off. She jumped into the shower.

When she returned to the bedroom all fresh and clean, she had on no make-up. Her hair was twisted in a towel, and one was wrapped around her torso.

He was sitting up in bed, watching her. Smiling.

"Don't be smiling at me. I'm not remotely attractive yet."

"Yes, you are."

She opened up her dresser drawer to find a long-sleeved shirt and some underwear.

"Don't."

"Don't what?"

"Don't get dressed."

"Why not? Don't you want coffee?"

"Um… okay, make coffee. I want a shower, too. Can we meet back in bed – naked with coffee?"

"That would be dangerous."

"I'll behave."

"Promise?"

"I promise. Are we allowed to have a cigarette and the paper in bed?

"I'll make an exception for you."

So they met back in bed and had coffee and cigarettes, and shared sections of the paper, fighting over the entertainment section. They talked. They napped. Again, they talked, and talked about everything. And every third or fourth topic they fully exhausted in conversation, they made love again. The clock said 3:57 PM, and they hadn't eaten all day.

"I don't want to get up, but my stomach is growling," Roger said.

"We need to get our lazy asses out of bed, for God's sake. I mean, we're reverting. This reminds me of Saturdays in the summertime with you, back in college."

"Do you remember the afternoon when we got whistles from the gumball machine at the grocery store?"

She laughed. "I wish we had some now." She recalled how they made love with the whistles in their mouths, and every time they started breathing hard, they would trigger whistle sounds.

"How come when you're young, you do stupid shit like that, and then one day you don't do fun things any more?" Roger asked.

"I guess you lose your sense of humor when you get older. You're not tarnished by life's abuses until you live through some shit. Funny changes when you age."

"Yeah, I guess," he said.

"I remember my dad used to ask me the same kind of question. He'd ask, 'How come one day you want to ride the horse – you know, the kind you put a quarter in at a strip mall – the horse ride that rocks for a few minutes? You beg for it when you're a kid. Then one day, you walk by the horse -- no interest whatsoever. Why?' Roger, when is that defining moment we go from being a fun-loving kid to it being over? Why does it happen just like that?" She snapped her fingers when she said the word, *that*.

"I think this conversation is going someplace that I want it to."

"What do you mean?" She flipped a towel at him. "You better not be making something sexual out of this."

"No, I'm not. It's just interesting to me that you would bring this up right now in the context of our lives right now."

"What are you getting at?"

"It's just, before you know it, you're old. You've got to swim in the sea of fun while you can. Just do it."

"Swim in the sea of fun? You're a cornball. And your point is?"

"The point is, consider doing something in life that you might want to do, but are afraid might be too free-spirited. Just do it."

"Like what?"

He answered softly, jokingly and very quickly, without hesitation. "Like move to Florida and live with me, and let's get married." He put a pillow over his head after he said it, as if to protect himself.

Audrey did hit him with her pillow. "Um.. What was that? If that was a proposal, it was a pretty pathetic one."

"Um... no, that wasn't a proper proposal. It was a feel-you-out-question-before-I-go-and-blow-three-month's-commission-on-a-ring proposal."

She laughed.

"Audrey, I'm starving, I want to go to the kitchen and see what you keep in there. So, I want you to quickly tell me if the improper proposal I just made could get an answer."

She looked at him guardedly. "Rog, are you being serious?"

He put his hand on her face. There was a tear in his eye. "I've never been more serious in my life."

She paused and swallowed hard. "I.. I.. I don't think I could say no to you. But my God, isn't this a little fast?"

"Fast? Are you kidding? I've waited ten years."

They embraced. Their bodies were spent and satiated, so all the energy they had went into simply holding each other and sobbing softly.

They were interrupted when Audrey's phone rang. It was Bella, and she and Mike wanted to meet Roger.

"I just wondered if you'd like to walk up the block to the new pizza place with us."

Audrey covered the phone receiver and whispered the question to Roger. He shook his head, yes, happily. "I want to try authentic New York pizza. Hell, yeah."

"It's nice out today for a walk, not too cold. Sure, we'd love to!"

"Great. Call me when you're ready and we'll meet downstairs."

"OK, bye."

"Perfect timing," Roger said.

"Sure is. Let's get dressed."

The five of them clicked immediately, and Roger was quite taken by little Shandra. He asked if he could carry her, and he placed her up on his shoulders for the duration of the walk. Shandra found herself a great friend in Roger. At dinner, Roger had a way with her that kept her smiling and happy throughout the meal.

"Will you come to the ladies room with me?" Bella asked Audrey.

"Of course."

When they entered the ladies room, Bella immediately burst out, "I love him for you. He's your soul mate. I see it. Oh my Gawd, he will be a wonderful father. I approve. I approve."

"Really? Do you think he's cute?"

"Only absolutely adorable and a perfect match for you. You'll have great looking kids."

"Bella, really? You like him?"

"He's funny. A great sense of humor. You'll need that in a marriage."

Audrey's face beamed. "Well, we haven't made any official plans."

"I'm sure you will. You should see yourself glowing right now."

"Well, we've been a little busy reuniting." She blushed. "Oh, Bella, it's been incredible."

"Audrey. Audrey. You been gettin' crazy, girl?"

"We'll have to get together to talk -- just you and me. Hey, I thought you had to go to the bathroom."

"Fooled ya."

They returned to the table and the check was paid. Shandra was looking a little tired. Bella put her in the stroller and they ambled homeward.

A street vendor was selling very small, live Christmas trees for $20. The adults laughed as they walked by, reminiscing about the old Charlie Brown cartoon and the poor boy's sad, bald Christmas tree.

"Aud, let's get one for your apartment. Kind of as a joke. Let me buy you one."

"Oh, Rog, I don't know. We really don't need one."

"Come on."

"Oh, if you want. But I'm not sure it's so funny to have a Charlie Brown tree."

"It's funny. I want one. Ya got decorations at home?"

"I do."

Roger paid the man and carried the tree all the way back. They separated from Bella's family and went up to decorate the new tree.

Roger helped her unravel the lights out of the storage box.

"I was going to skip the whole tree this year," she said.

"Ya gotta have a Christmas tree."

He started at the top of the tree and draped the little white lights vertically, going down and then back up again.

"Uh... no, that's just wrong."

"Nah Uh."

"Roger, please. Let me do it. That's not the right way."

"I think I know how to hang up Christmas lights."

"You start at the top and circle around. It won't look right going up and down."

"This will work."

"It's ridiculous. Take them down, please. I'll show you."

"It's fine, Audrey. Damn."

"I insist." She walked over to the tree and took the string from his hands. He gave her a puzzled look.

"Here's how you do it." She started at the top and began wrapping the tree.

Roger stood back and watched, tapping his foot, nervously. "It's the same thing, basically. Same results."

"No, you're wrong."

He walked over to her and touched her hand. "Let me try it, then. If it looks bad, we can take them down."

"What's your problem? Believe me, I know what I'm talking about."

"I disagree."

She dropped her hand from his touch.

"You disagree?"

"Yeah, watch how it's done."

"Um, it's a waste of time. You'll see."

"Fuck it, then. Here ya go." He threw the lights at her, hitting the pointed plug part against her leg.

"Ow."

"Oh, come on."

"No, ow. You threw that at me."

"I didn't throw it."

"I didn't want the tree, anyway. It's not Christmas without daddy." She ran to the bedroom and slammed the door. She fell down on the bed and hugged a pillow. *I just need some time here alone. I hate Christmas.* She sobbed as she thought about the holidays -- about being an orphan.

As she lay there, she looked out the back of the fire escape to the alleyway that broke the property lines to the neighboring brownstone. Just daydreaming, getting her head right, and letting the tears dry up.

What the? She got up and ran over to the window and squinted to see the garbage cans below. There was Roger, stuffing the Christmas tree and the lights into a garbage can. He was in a fury, using all his might to shove the tree in the can. It overflowed the top of the can, and he couldn't get the lid back on, so he threw it down - hard.

He looked up to the window and she hid so he wouldn't see her. She started laughing at the ridiculousness of it all.

Seconds later, he was back in the apartment.

"You can come out now. The tree and lights are gone."

She opened the door. "What the hell?"

"I'm not gonna break up with the woman I love because we can't agree how to hang lights. You don't want a tree? It's gone."

"But you spent $20 bucks on that tree."

"Fuck the money. I should have been more sensitive that this is a hard holiday for you."

She didn't know whether to laugh or cry. She just stood there.

"Can we be done now?" he asked.

"Yeah."

"Our first fight?"

"Yeah."

"Think we can survive more of them?"

"Yeah." She sniffed.

"OK, then. Come here."

They hugged. She smiled.

"I love you," she said.

"I love you more."

"Did you see anything good in the Entertainment Section this morning? You want to go into the city tonight? Party?" she asked.

"Not at all."

"Not back to bed?"

He smiled. So they spent the rest of Saturday night in bed.

Chapter 17

"It's all fun and games until somebody loses an eye." That was the saying on the tee shirt Roger was wearing.

"I want that shirt," Audrey told him, checking it out from across the kitchen table.

He looked down at his chest to see which shirt he was wearing. "Ooooh, noooo. They don't make 'em like THIS any more."

"I'll trade ya something for it."

"Maybe. I'll think about it."

They were sitting at the kitchen table eating a big Sunday brunch that Audrey had prepared – fluffy egg casserole topped with bacon, homemade banana muffins with real bananas, sliced cantaloupe and Hazelnut Coffee ground fresh from the fancy coffee shop.

"Are you going to cook like this for me every day when we're married?"

She felt a rush of adrenaline. *Fear of domestic responsibilities and marital expectations.*

She sipped her coffee. Cleared her throat. "Um… about that…"

"Oh, Audrey, I'm only teasing. I don't eat breakfast. You don't have to cook dinner either, I'm damn good at grilling these days, and vegetables from a can are fine."

"I didn't say I wouldn't. Besides, I think I'm a good cook and I'm excited about showing off some of my culinary skills. I was just thinking that, well, we've been so wrapped up in romance this weekend, we haven't really talked about some pretty important stuff. Moving to Florida, this partnership – aren't real to me quite yet."

He got up and poured himself more coffee and filled up her cup, too. "Alright. What do we need to talk about?"

"Several things. You should probably know that I have sucky housekeeping habits. I keep my front rooms clean in case someone pops over, but I never make the bed. The bathroom counter looks like a clown factory with all my potions and lotions, and I often have a pile of dishes in the sink. I do laundry infrequently, and I hate ironing. I tend to skip dinner altogether, and I drink a glass of wine every night, usually. And, sometimes I'm on the computer all night, and I like to go to bed when I feel like it, not because of what a clock says."

"I have no problem with any of that."

"I'm just being honest."

"Audrey, Jesus Christ. I'm not buying a car and comparing features. I love you, and I take all of you, good or bad. You know I'm not a fanatic about any of that stuff. I just want you to be happy, and I think I can give you some things that will make you happy. I also know for a fact that you will make me happy."

"Two-part question, then. What about me makes you happy? What is it that you think will make me happy, because I sure as hell haven't been able to figure it for the past 34 years."

"35 years."

"Not for another week. I'm still 34."

"You make me feel alive, and I haven't been happy without you all these years. I can give you stability and life choices. Heck, I don't care if you want a career if that makes you happy. I do care if you want a career that takes you away from me for long periods, but it's fine if you want to work. I would love it if you chose to do nothing and stay at home. Of course, if you did that, you really should do the dishes." He smiled. "If you're worried about finances...."

"Well, not really. I know I'm getting some inheritance, and you do seem to have a successful brokerage company."

"We can talk about money, specifically, if you want."

"I'm not about the money. The times I cared about money, I hated myself. I could live in a trailer -- a cardboard box, if I had to."

"I noticed you really have become down to earth. That was an interesting revelation to me. I thought you came to Manhattan for this high-powered job because of the money. I learned a lot yesterday when you told me where your heart really is – what you've been through. The things that make you happy are simple things, at least I think I'm right about that. Heck, you're looking at Mr. Simple."

"I'm scared."

"OK, why?" He pulled the chair out and moved it closer to her.

"Well, I'm just so busy all the time. Chaotic busy. What if I get into this new lifestyle and I don't have all the mental stimulation. Will I die?"

He laughed. "You will find trouble no matter what, or make it yourself wherever you go. You'll never be bored. It's not in you."

"I've never functioned in a non-dysfunctional lifestyle. Abnormal, crazy busy is normal to me."

"You might be surprised. Look, Aud. I can't make decisions for you, but the way I see it, your reason for not making any changes is that you're afraid of the unknown. Understood. That's normal.

"Only you can make the hard choice about what's right for you. I have a proposal out there to you. I hope you take it. I'm not going to beg. Tomorrow I go back to Tampa. You can never see me again. Or, you'll spend some time here and think for yourself what you want the rest of your life to be like."

He's fair. He's good. He's right. I do need to spend some time alone and sort through these feelings.

"What do we do after tomorrow, when you go home?"

"I go home, and I pray that you'll come home to me."

"Live with you?"

"We could talk about getting our own place, if you wanted. Frankly, I have some bad memories in my bungalow. I could sell it easily. It's circa 1910, and I restored much of it. You could sell your dad's place. We could get something together on the river. You should see my boat. It would be a happy, sweet life. Just you and me. A couple of kids, if that would make us complete."

She nodded. She felt a rush of fear and excitement.

"Hey," his fingers intertwined with hers. "Whatever you want, Babe. I'm just throwing out ideas that might appeal to you. I've got the city covered with real estate possibilities. That's all I'm saying."

They continued their conversation as they cleared the table. He washed, she dried and put the dishes away.

"I'm not going to pressure you. I want this to be your decision because it's what YOU want. Don't make this something because your lease is up, or because you want to run away from that asshole you work for. Give it time. I've waited ten years for you to come home. I'll wait some more."

She nodded again. She didn't know what else to say.

The dishes were done. The apartment was closing in on them. Even the bed was becoming unappealing after so many hours spent there. Outside, the weather looked sunny and crisp. The exhilarating desire to walk the streets of New York allured them both. *Destination unknown. An adventure wherever it takes us.*

They walked hand in hand through the streets, indulging in cigarettes. Audrey wore Roger's tee shirt in a fair trade that she would spend the rest of the week giving full consideration to his proposal. The shirt was hidden under her coat, but the cotton against her skin gave her a reminder of Roger's embrace, and who knew? Maybe she would get to show it off if they stopped someplace maybe to eat, and she could take off her coat.

They walked together quietly, and Audrey's mind drifted to the possibly of choosing her current existence, as opposed to living in Florida as Mrs. Audrey Hollingsworth. *The hard question was, Can I live with that?* She looked at his profile as he walked next to her and she realized to the depth of her soul that she would not be able to live without him. *But wait. How will I feel when I see everyone at the office? That would be yet to be determined.*

They took a turn down a street Audrey was unfamiliar with. There was a Cuban restaurant and just a few doors down, a painted sign that read, "Psychic Readings."

"Oooh. Let's get a reading, Roger. Maybe I'll get some clarification."

"Absolutely not."

"C'mon, I figured you'd be up for an adventure."

"Need I remind you Audrey Mary, that you are a Catholic and this, my love, would be a sin of the venial kind? Or have you completely lost your mind? It's witchcraft."

"It is not. Most Catholics I know are intrigued by such things. It's just for fun. Please? Let's see the crystal ball lady."

"I refuse."

"Refuse? Roger, I'm shocked."

She stopped dead in the street. "What about swimming in the sea of fun? You said it yourself."

He pulled her past the building and kept on walking.

"You're not the boss of me," she said.

"Oh, please, don't use this against me, or think that this is a thing to come. I'm not being a jerk, I'm protective of you, Aud. I don't want anyone messing with your head. Just forget about it. Geez. Sometimes you really.."

"Oh, fine then."

"See what I mean? Like I said, you'll always find your own trouble. God, you worry me."

"I'm telling you, I'm not an easy person to love. I'll admit it."

He stopped and pulled her closer to him. He kissed her. "You are so easy to love. As much as you are a woman, you equal that in your childlike pursuit of new ideas. I love that about you. But you do need someone strong to look over you. I can be that."

"You do a mean sales pitch."

"I don't mean to."

They walked some more and ended up renting a ride on a horse and buggy through the park. Neither had done so previously in their lives. The air was filled with uncomplicated, child-like energy. Audrey realized that even at her age and perceived level of sophistication about the world, there was yet to be many more firsts in her life. She tried to describe her feelings to Roger.

"I'm dizzy. I'm swept away. I feel new. I know it sounds like a sappy romance novel, but I can't breathe or think, or get myself together. I feel butterflies inside when I'm with you, and I seem to not care where I am, or who's around. I could take you down right now, and strip you naked, and attack you right here on this stinky buggy ride."

He grabbed her hand and put it on his crotch, and smiled.

"I love you. I love you. I love you. I want to go home right now and just be with you. We only have hours remaining," she said.

They held hands on the walk back to the apartment, and stopped to eat hotdogs with sauerkraut and mustard, bought from the street vendor. *Another perfect day.*

*****

The alarm buzzed at 7:00, jolting her. A rush of adrenaline and heart flutters. *These are no ordinary Monday morning work jitters.* Roger was asleep on his back and she rolled completely on top of him in a panic and said, "Wake up, I only have about an hour before I leave for work, and I want every second I have left with you." She kissed his lips. He opened his eyes and rubbed them.

"Geez. Okay, woman."

"Help me get ready for work. Let's take a shower and get you packed up, too. Chop. Chop."

He closed his eyes again, ignoring her.

"Roger!" She whipped the covers completely off the bed, leaving him there nude.

"Rude ass. It's cold."

"Hurry up. We don't have time for fartin' around."

She pulled him off the bed and into the bathroom. She turned on the showerhead to get the water hot. While the water ran, they brushed their teeth. Audrey hid none of her tears. Roger had an extreme calm about him.

"I just don't find teeth brushing that emotional, Audrey."

"Quit it. You know this isn't easy for me."

She pulled him into the shower and pushed him against the tiled wall and kissed him. She took the bar of soap and lathered up her hands and rubbed all over his body. He didn't reciprocate - he simply leaned back and let her wash him. She washed his hair and caressed every inch of him. Crying. Crying. Crying. "Oh, Roger. Oh, Roger."

He stood under the showerhead to wash off the soap while she washed herself. She stretched out her arms to brace herself against the shower wall, and then stabilized both feet on the floor with her rear towards Roger. He responded to her invitation immediately, and penetrated her from behind, caressing both her breasts at the same time. The steam and the rush of the hot water on the back of her head combined with the sensation of Roger's propelling and driving force into her, made her short-winded. The encounter was quicker than she wanted, but hard and powerful and vigorous -- just what she needed. She turned to face him and give him a dozen quick kisses of gratitude. "You're awesome."

They got dressed, and Audrey made sure she wore something to make her feel confident. *It might be a rough day.* Roger put on jeans and a casual shirt. He put all his things into his suitcase, folded up the fun and games tee shirt and placed it on Audrey's desk for her. They had enough time for a quick cup of coffee and a few good-byes.

"You can just lock the door behind you. Oh, and make sure you leave enough time for traffic to get to your flight on time."

"Don't worry so much."

"I just... I just can't believe we've reached good-bye. I can't bear it. This was the greatest weekend of my life."

"Mine, too."

"I love you, Roger."

"Me, too. You better go downstairs. The cab is probably already waiting."

"Do you want to come downstairs for one last goodbye?"

"No, I might be crying and it wouldn't be good for my manly image."

256

She looked at him with her sad eyes. But, she didn't cry. For him – she didn't cry. They kissed at the door, and Audrey pulled it behind her. She didn't look back.

The cab was already waiting for her. The driver was one of the regulars. "Smith and Associates, ma'am?"

"Yes, please."

Chapter 18

Bill's door was closed. His secretary, Margaret, said he wouldn't be in until tomorrow. She said this morning she'd synchronized her computer calendar with Bill's Palm Pilot updates, and there was a notation that said, "Dinner with Audrey and Goldstein, 7 PM" for Tuesday.

"Maybe you ought to check and see if he sent you an email about it. I haven't the foggiest what it's about," Margaret said.

"Thanks. Just let me know if you hear anything more," Audrey said as she walked by.

"Sure thing."

Audrey started up her computer as soon as she walked into her office. While waiting for the server to connect, she sauntered to the break room for coffee, all the while pondering over the strange conversation with Bill's secretary. *What's up now?* Goldstein works as Smith-Anderson's corporate legal counsel -- a little man with gray on black hair and a long beard. On the rare times Audrey saw him, she always imagined him wearing a Yamukah when he wasn't doing business. *How dreadfully clichéd of me.*

She passed Liz's cubicle on the way back. Liz was there, spreading cream cheese on a bagel.

"Good morning. How was London?"

"Morning. Um. Good, I guess. I'm a little tired, still. We didn't get the account yet. Still negotiating."

"No one's told me what the account is. So, ya wanna get me up to speed?"

Liz stood up and did a prairie dog. She peeped her head over the top of the cube to see if her coworkers were around, as if she didn't want them to hear her.

"Can we talk in your office?"

"Absolutely. Grab your breakfast and come over."

"Let me get coffee, too, and I'll be right there."

Audrey used the brief moment alone to check her email, and there was a note from Bill.

> Subject: Tuesday Dinner Meeting
> Message: Please plan on staying late on Tuesday night. Mr. Goldstein will be in the office and I have asked him to dinner to discuss a new direction. It's important you're a part of this. I will be in the office Tuesday morning and will provide information then. I'll expect you to attend.
> Thanks. B.

Fuckin' A! Why the mystery? What new direction? Audrey felt her mood more than a bit feisty today. She was ready for anything, including a fight, if one came her way.

Liz came in and shut the door. She put her coffee cup and bagel on a napkin on the desk in front of her.

"So?" Audrey asked.

"Well, first off, I wanted to talk to you about the Earth account. I think you know it really bothered me how we left off, and I know you were making this an integrity thing. It's not that way at all. I talked to Bill at great length about it. I explained to him that... no offense... but I thought you were overreacting to something creative folks do all the time. Ya know, even the best companies use competitor information to spin ideas around to a different product. From what I know about slogans and copyrights, I think that the Green Company in Canada would really have to fight hard and spend a lot of money to go toe to toe with us in a legal dispute."

"Oh, really?" Audrey tightened her leg muscles, bracing herself from wanting to leap across the desk and grab Liz's head of snarls.

"Yeah. Bill agreed, too. What I'm saying is, we're going to use the current campaign, and everyone should feel good about it. I thought you should know."

"Well, thank you, Liz." *Was my sarcasm detectable when I said that?* "Look, I put my professional opinion out there. I think I told you this before. I don't own this company – all I can do is offer up the recommendation. If that's Bill's decision, then so be it. I think you're both making a mistake, and I'm disappointed. The issue is dead, as far as I'm concerned. It's your baby. Hopefully it'll work out to your benefit, and it's a successful campaign."

"Oh, but Aud, just so you know... your concerns were definitely taken into consideration, so you shouldn't feel bad about speaking out about what you believe in. I've always admired that about you, that you speak from your heart."

Oh, thank you so fucking much for the vote of confidence and cheerleading routine. Remind me how I feel about you when it's time to put in for bonuses and raises.

Liz continued. "...It's just, well, as Bill says, time is money, and business is business. We need to move on."

"I see." Audrey felt the hairs on her arms stand up and a twinge in the back of her neck. She imagined herself looking like a cartoon character with steam blasting full force out of her ears.

"Well then, I guess that's that. Fine then." Audrey paused, and Liz stared at her with a questioning look. "Really. Fine," Audrey said.

"Oh, good. I was hoping you'd be cool about this. Whew! I'm glad I got that off my chest."

And sure as shit, that's not the only slimy thing that's been on your chest, I'll bet. Audrey imagined Bill's hard dick sliding between Liz's tightly-pressed-together-in-her-hands fake boobs on a squeaky bed in a dirty, tiny London hotel room.

Liz continued. "So, onto the London story. This opportunity is huge. Bill has known Guy Dupont from his journalism days in the U.K. Guy's a real sharp businessman. He's a major investor in a specialized computer firm that manufactures computers that are virtually unbreakable. They're little clamshell-looking things with the power of a full Pentium that can go underwater, or be dropped from a mountain-top, or anything like that."

"I don't get it. Why would anyone need that?"

"Well, these computers took off in Europe. For one, they use them in the panda cars."

"Panda cars?"

"Oh, sorry, that's English for cop cars."

Jesus Christ, excuse me while I throw up. We've got ourselves a regular Bridget Jones talker now.

"Mmm. Hmm."

"You can use them in the field – great for mountain climbers, archeologists, UPS drivers, whatever. So anyway, there are plans for international expansion for the

261

company. They want a major ad campaign and a launch of their new SF-2 model. I've got one of the units at my desk. Want me to go get it?"

"Yes, please."

Liz ran out of the office and returned quickly, closing the door behind her.

"This product is top secret, Audrey. If this got into the wrong hands, it could be total devastation to Paws Computers. That's the company name."

Audrey grabbed the computer, which looked liked a CD player. It was heavy and made of aluminum or metal. It had a paw print logo on it and the letters, SF-2 in red.

"How does it work?"

"The switch is on the bottom. Here." Liz grabbed the unit and turned it on, and returned it to Audrey. "This one isn't programmed with anything but Windows, but you can see how fast it is and how clear the readout is. It's a touch screen. It can communicate vocally with other units. It manages signatures and fingerprints. It's incredible. We went on a field trip with the police, and saw these units in use. Totally fascinating."

"This is pretty cool. So tell me. Where does Smith-Anderson fit in?"

"I know that we were close in negotiations to be the ad agency of record, but negotiations took a really bad turn. The last night we were in London, Bill went out with Guy alone, and he was not at all happy when he returned to the hotel. I never saw him so bad off. He said he still had a lot of number crunching to do, and he was going to talk to you about some math formulas when he got back to New York. He said you're the best we've got, and if anyone could make it come together, you'd be the one."

Audrey gave a questioning look. "I wonder what he means by that."

"He thinks you're brilliant. He told me so himself. He told me he's a bit worried about you. You've been distant ever since you went to Florida, and he needs your full commitment now more than ever – the way you used to be. I told him you've been through a lot, and he should ease up on you a bit."

Oh Geez, thanks a heap for making me look like a wimpy girl.

"So what went wrong with negotiations?"

"I think the males got their egos twisted up. Bill didn't get into details with me, but he mentioned that he needed a real schmoozer to handle Guy – maybe a woman. Guy is King, but so is Bill. Someone needs to break through."

"Is that why you went along, Liz? You know, to be the woman to break through the battle of two egos?"

"No, not me." Liz blushed and continued, "You and me are friends, right?"

"Um... okay, sure we're friends."

"Can you keep this totally confidential?" Liz asked, checking behind her to make sure the office door was closed.

"Yeah."

"Well, fool I am, I thought Bill wanted me along on the account because he was so impressed with my leadership on the Earth account. I feel like such a jerk now because I know the real truth."

"Real truth? Don't tell me, he's interested in you -- romantically?"

Liz looked up and into Audrey's eyes, innocently.

"That's such a sweet way to put it, Audrey. I thought that was maybe it, too. And I wouldn't have minded that…. Oh, God, I can't believe I'm telling you this."

"It's okay. I've seen a lot in my time. I'm sure you can't shock me."

Liz pushed her bagel aside, as if it made her nauseous. "Either reason would have worked fine for me. I would love to be respected for my work, but I would also love to be loved as a woman by a respectable man, such as Bill."

"Good God, what happened?"

"Let's just say, I let him get the best of me. Oh, don't go feeling sorry for me, I was a great seductress in all this and certainly, I'm half to blame. I'm not sure where my head was. I thought an affair could turn out beneficial all-around. Ya know? Like it would make us even more a team in the business, and a permanent relationship, too."

"So what's the status now? Not good?"

Liz shook her head and looked down. "I'm not going to cry about it. As fast as it all happened, is as quick as it's over. We talked long about it. He was kind, too. Didn't want me to come back to work all wigged out or something." Liz shrugged.

"Wow. Um.. Is he okay now, too?"

"Yeah. We had a few nights here and a few nights in Europe that were spectacular. Drinking, dancing, flirting. It just went too far, and it wasn't meant to be for the long haul, I guess. It was better in my fantasies, anyway... his lovemaking was..."

"I'm stopping you right there, Liz. I want no image of Bill that way, please." *Ew. Ew. Ew. Ew.*

Liz gave a little uncomfortable laugh. "Please don't tell anyone. I would just die."

"Of course I won't."

"So, where's my lecture from you about the sins of promiscuity, all about responsibility and professional decorum?"

"Oh, shit, Liz. I don't have it in me. Would you even listen anyway?"

"Probably not."

"I can see you've been hurt in all this. I'm not going to rub your little Clinique-powdered nose in it."

"Thanks. I use Lancome powder," She smiled. "I'll be fine."

"I know you will. Hey, I appreciate the information about the Paws account."

"Yeah, well, Bill is supposed to get with you right away on it. And to answer your question.... as for needing a pinch hitter in negotiations, it was never going to me, sad as that is to me, but it was always going to be you, Aud. I was invited along for the ride only, and you know what ride I mean."

"Oh, Liz, I'm so sorry."

"Hey, I'm glad we're back like this. You know, I look to you for many things."

It was a nice moment.

Liz left the office, and Audrey felt like a two-faced piece of shit, acting like she was concerned for Liz -- inside pissed as hell at her for her stupidity in business, at the same time feeling sorry for her.

And shame on Bill.

*****

Roger called about 9:30 that night to tell Audrey he had gotten an early Christmas present. The lawyers had called him to tell him the divorce from Summer was finalized.

"Yeah. My cell phone rang just when I landed in Tampa. I'm so happy. I'm all yours now, not just my heart, but I'm free legally, too."

"That's terrific. My heart is dancing."

"I miss you already."

"Me, too."

Audrey told Roger about her day. "At first, I thought the meeting with Bill was going to be about the Earth account – some strategy for revising the account to make it bullet-proof from scandal. But after that conversation with Elizabeth, it's definitely going to be something different. That scares me."

"You think he's going to want to send you to England to win the account?"

"That's exactly what I'm thinking."

"Oh, man, I don't want you overseas. No place is safe these days. Damn terrorists."

"I agree."

"Are you going to go?"

"What should I do?"

"Fortunately, you've got a little time to ponder the different possibilities before you meet with them. What an asshole he must be to work for. He's going to lay it on you Tuesday morning, and then at dinner he's going to corner you with the attorney to give you the skinny on what you need to negotiate. I don't like my girl being a pawn."

"Everyone's a pawn in someone else's game when you work for a corporation."

"Be strong, Audrey. You have good instincts. You don't have to do what you don't want to do. You have choices, Babe. And I'll take care of you if you reach a standoff with them. If it's really uncomfortable, and you don't know what to do, then do what I do..."

"What's that?"

"I call it, the Twilight Break."

"Twilight Break?"

"Everyone needs time away to make a major decision. You need to sleep on things to see how you feel about issues in the morning. You go to bed with the problem on your mind. You'll have your answer, the real answer – in the morning. It will be in your heart. I don't know, maybe that's what they call prayer. I just call it the Twilight Break."

"Do you really do that?"

"Yes."

"That's beautiful."

"Thanks. It works every time."

"How'd you get so smart?"

He laughed.

"Rog... I should go. I need to charge this phone up. I'm probably going to lose this connection."

"Okay. Hey, Audrey?"

"Yeah?"

"I love you."

"I love you, too."

"Could I ask you to please take a Twilight Break about us, and think about my proposal soon? Will ya? Don't let my proposal be contingent on what happens at work. It'd mean so much more to me if you chose me on the merits of our relationship, alone."

"Oh, Roger. Please don't feel like you're second to my career."

"I don't. I'm just saying..."

"I understand exactly how you feel. You don't have to say it. My God, I'm sorry I haven't been more thoughtful ... I.. I..."

"It's okay. It's okay. Get through this work thing first. Be strong. I trust in our love. It's all going to work out the way it's supposed to. I have faith."

"Kisses."

"Take care. Call me after dinner no matter how late."

"OK."

Audrey stepped into her bedroom and plugged in the phone to overnight charge. She looked in her closet to find something that would go nicely from day to night for the big meeting. Nothing struck her as the right outfit that would give her confidence. She honestly didn't want to impress. She was feeling rebellious. She wanted something to wear that said just that.

It'd be so predictable to throw on a conservative job-interview type of suit. Such an outfit would say, "I'm a mini-man. I'm here to impress and be your Yes Girl." Bull fucking shit.

Audrey pulled off the rack a clingy, zebra-print low-cut dress and hung it on the outside of the closet door. She located her highest-heeled pumps. It was an outfit that she felt all-girl in, and all-powerful in her sexuality.

Fuck the world, it's all about me. You go, girl.

It was getting late. Her head hurt. Her kick-ass attitude waned as soon as she slipped into bed and turned out the lights. *Twilight Break? My ass! Why are problems so huge at night?* She was scared. She lay a while, quietly.

My Dear Heavenly Father, I have been so far from prayer lately that I feel unworthy to even come to you now... and then the silent tears started as they often did when Audrey prayed, for the guilt of infrequent communications with God, initiated only whenever there seemed to be trouble. *So few reflections of thanks for Your many gifts to me. I am so sorry, and so weak and unfit.*

When she got choked up like this and couldn't find the words, she'd recite all the prayers she knew, sometimes twice, on occasion – three times. Tonight, it was three times. Finally, she felt okay enough to put her problems out there, offering them up, and asking for help to be guided to do the right thing. Her tears continued until sleep came, but she slept well.

A door slammed, and Snickers was barking down the hall. It awoke Audrey, and she turned to look at the alarm clock, which flashed half past seven. *Damn alarm didn't go off. Saved by that SOB rat dog. Thank God!*

She would've been late, but by having the clothes laid out, it wasn't too hard to catch up on getting ready and getting to work on time.

She walked into the office and heard a loud, "Whoa!" She walked by Raymond and rolled her eyes at his teasing.

"Hot mamma," he said in his charming Jamaican accent.

Why is it, sometimes by being pressed for time, what you do throw together with hair and makeup works out to better than times you spend over-primping?

"Puhleez."

But she loved it. This is just what she needed today to keep her mood light and playful, and not intensive and confrontative.

As soon as she got in, her phone was ringing. She reached across the desk to grab it.

"Good morning, this is Audrey Beane."

"Good morning, Miss Beane. This is Bill. I'd like to see you in my office now."

"Yes, sir."

He hung up. Instead of Audrey getting angry that he didn't politely end the call with a good-bye, she laughed.

She walked into Bill's office and didn't get out of there until lunchtime. They reviewed the entire operations of Paws in England and the expansion plans for a U.S. office. That expansion would not occur for two years – operations were staying right where the company was.

"Guy is looking for a joint venture with Smith-Anderson to open a full service ad agency exclusive to Paws and their subsidiaries in Europe. It has to be run professionally, just like Smith-Anderson's Manhattan office. It will be a two-year stint."

The plan was to send Audrey to London to open the office, hire the talent, build the team, and run the company for two years. Liz would replace her in the New York Operations.

Bill held no information back from Audrey *(refreshingly unfamiliar)* – he showed her the profitability and all the supporting numbers. "It makes great business sense to move forward in the venture.

"So, tonight Audrey, we will be presenting to you an offer and a new compensation plan, along with our vision for your position with us for the rest of your life. I view this as a celebration and reward for your long tenure here. You've waited long, and I'm so happy to finally offer you something that is comparable remuneration for your talents.

"I'm not at liberty to disclose the package to you at this time. Our attorney is integral in the terms and conditions, and I want us to carefully discuss them over dinner. Do you know 21?"

Audrey about fell over.

"Audrey? You okay? You look a little piqued."

"Fine. I'm fine. Uh, yeah, I went there once before. It's very lovely."

"Great. I'll stop by your office around six or so, we can head over and get a start with cocktails before Mr. Goldstein arrives."

"Uh, sure. Sure."

"Here. Please take all these printouts and study them today. I'd love to get your recommendations to tighten it up a bit. We'll need these presented to Mr. DuPont next week. Check if your passport is up to date. OK?" He gave her a big, toothy smile. "Good day, Ms. Beane."

"Thanks." She was almost out the doorway, then turned back to look at him, "Oh, Bill? One last thing."

"Yes?"

"I secured us a fairly large account this week."

"What's that?"

"That new Bookstore and Internet site, Booksters."

"What's it worth?"

"Half a mill."

"Well done. Look, I don't need the details. You might as well hand it off to Elizabeth. She'll be in charge in U.S. from here on out. Thank you, Audrey."

She nodded and left, smiling a big smile. It was the day in her career she had always dreamed of. Everything she had worked for. And today, she received all the validation she ever yearned for. *So overdue. So desperately sought. So wonderfully received.*

*****

270

Maybe it was she hadn't eaten all day. Maybe it was she was still in a state of shock of the last several hours. It was all foggy, and had yet to be worked out about what specifically she was going to say, or how she was going to do it. *How will I endure the reaction of someone who's so optimistic? How will I watch happiness and hope turn to pain and injury about my decision?* Although she was completely and totally sure of what she was going to do now, a break-up of any kind isn't an easy thing to do.

Chapter 19

At 6:00 Audrey applied a fresh face of make-up and swept her hair into a feminine, sophisticated up-do. When she returned from the ladies room, Bill had his coat on, and was standing in front of her office teasingly flashing his watch at her.

"C'mon. C'mon. I got the car's engine running downstairs, and the security guard keeping an eye on it."

"Alright, already. Geez, just let me get my bag."

When they got downstairs, Bill politely held the car door open for her, treating her like a lady.

It was almost dark, and the radio was playing some slow jazz. Bill was chewing gum, looking casual and comfortable as he drove. He smelled like expensive cologne. Audrey looked over at him and felt like she was on a date. *A woman always feels like she's on a date when she's alone with a man in the evening, even when she's not. It's a given.*

Although it was bitter cold and the car hadn't warmed up yet, Audrey's brow had beads of sweat. *Where the hell is my confidence, now that I need it most?*

She thought about how she'd react to the compensation package, realizing it really wasn't so much about HOW MUCH it would amount to in her pocket. It was, rather, WHAT the dollar figure represented -- the company's perceived value of her at a place she'd given her heart to. It was personal.

It was that simple, really.

What if the offer is rudely too low? What if it's shockingly high? Can I keep a poker face? Be professional? Be gracious, but firm? Will I stand by the decision I already made, or will I weaken? And will being in a restaurant where I had my most romantic evening throw me into freakish emotionalism? There's only one solution – wine and more wine. Just drink wine.

"I didn't know you were such a wine connoisseur," Bill joked at the bar after she finished the first glass in minutes.

"I guess I was a little quick. I do like fine wine. It goes down so smoothly."

"How did you know about this vintage? It's not commonly ordered."

"I had it last time I was here with someone who knows wine and knew when the grapes in France were best in season. Mmmm - it was lovely last time. It tastes good now, too." Audrey smiled a little, remembering how good she felt sitting across the table from Roger -- a bit buzzed, looking into his sparkling eyes and feeling in love.

Bill's cell phone rang. He picked it up immediately, and after a few seconds said, "Great, meet us upstairs. We'll get seated."

The waiter brought the bottle of wine up and showed Bill and Audrey to a table in the middle of the room. When

Mr. Goldstein arrived he came over to Audrey and kissed her on the cheek. *He never did that before.*

The waiter knew Mr. Goldstein by name. He brought him a Manhattan on the rocks.

"I highly recommend the Sea Scallop Sashimi with mussel dressing and caviar for the appetizer," Goldstein said. Audrey nodded, and so did Bill. When the waiter left, Mr. Goldstein opened up his leather portfolio and brought out a legal contract in triplicate.

"I guess we'll just get right down to business," he said, handing a copy to each of them.

Audrey looked at the top page. *Bunch of legal-eez gibberish. Would it be rude of me to flip to the pages for the compensation part? Please, damn it -- just tell me the money and what you really think of me.*

Mr. Goldstein repeated the entire story that Bill had already told her about Paws. Whatever he was saying, it sounded like, "blah, blah, blah, Audrey, blah, blah, blah…"

Finally, the good part.

"…and, for remuneration, the company will provide, in part, housing paid at 100% at Earls Court Square, which comprises luxury London accommodations."

He handed Audrey a real estate brochure that had photos of the condo. The kitchen had light wood cabinets, wood floors and modern aluminum appliances. It was fully furnished in a sort of Scandinavian style. *Quite lovely, actually.*

The appetizers arrived, and Mr. Goldstein immediately stopped talking and started eating.

I want to turn ahead pages in this contract and see the salary.

Audrey pretended to be enjoying the food. But she preferred more wine. They had finished the bottle, and nobody asked the waiter for another one. She didn't want to be impolite by being the one to make such a request.

As soon as the appetizers were done and the small plates were removed, the main course arrived. *Please can't we eat AND talk?* But the men were busy feasting.

Do pan-roasted lobster and prawns reheat in a microwave well? I should've ordered the filet. It would make better leftovers.

She picked at her plate, taking small bites, and waiting until Mr. Goldstein put his reading glasses back on and spoke.

"Audrey, if you'll turn to the addendum of the contract on page five, you'll see the compensation package we've outlined.

"Now, although the sum is shown in pounds, it is consistent with U.S. dollars that double your current wages. In addition, if the resulting product sales exceed certain tiers, you will note a bonus compensation program as a percentage of the sales levels."

Audrey nodded. The waiter reached for her wine glass to fill it. *Thank God, Gustavo or whatever the hell your name is.* She took a sip and tried to give a nonchalant but considerate perusal of the document. Inside, her heart was doing a flip over this better-than-expected offer. *The value of the housing, alone, is significant.*

"Now if you'll return to page three of the document, you'll see here after a twenty-four month period, the operations will relocate to Manhattan, and a new contract will be written for the continuation of your role here."

That about wrapped up the deal. Both men looked at Audrey without saying anything. *I guess I'm supposed to say something brilliant now?*

Audrey's pause lingered. She put the papers to her left side, and then lifted her wine glass to her lips. The men gaped at her. She looked up at them, gave a half smile, then returned the goblet to the table. She picked up the pages and continued reading. She cleared her throat to break the silence.

"Gentlemen, I'm overwhelmed. Thank you for this wonderful opportunity and generous compensation offer. This is something I've worked my entire career for, and it means a lot to me to reach this high note."

Mr. Goldstein held out his Manhattan, and Bill clinked it with his wine glass. Audrey held back hers.

"As lovely as your offer is, Mr. Goldstein, Mr. Barnes, I am declining the offer."

There was an awkward pause, and Bill and Goldstein looked at one another.

This is a Kodak moment. But she didn't dwell upon it. This wasn't about revenge or spite. This was about making a life decision that was right. And it felt right. Audrey remained calm, and let the words settle in. She took a sip of her wine.

"Audrey, I don't understand. Is it not enough?" Bill asked.

She shook her head no. "It's excellent."

"Then what is it?"

"It's not the offer, the money or even that the work is in London. It's coincidence that the offer has come at a season in my life when I have decided to pursue other interests. I know that that sounds trite, but it's true. I've given ten years to Smith-Anderson. My God, this has been an unbelievable journey. I've loved it. I've watched this company grow up. I've grown up along with it. But I have other stuff to do now.

"Um... I know you know that I lost my father last month."

"Condolences," said Bill with his eyes wide open, obviously still shocked by her decline of the position.

"It was the most difficult thing imaginable." Talking about it brought the memory back vividly. She was a little dizzy. Her hand quivered as she tried to place her glass back on the table. But she continued talking.

"Being back home – I reconnected with my past – family and friends. I realized there are important things in life that I need to make time for. I'm talking about some of the intangibles – relationships with people and family, nature, being in touch with a softer side of me.

"My trip to Florida stirred me. And, I'll admit I've reunited with someone very special. I want to be with him now. In Florida, that is."

The men looked at each other, as if they didn't understand.

"Permanently – uh, effective January, say, the 15th or around there, if that's an acceptable period for me to wrap up my projects to your satisfaction?"

Audrey's face was beaming and she tried to hide it by looking down. *Why isn't this difficult? Why isn't this painful?* She spoke from the heart, and she knew it. She wasn't out to impress them with some shroud of corporate bullshit lines. There were no hard feelings. *Just me.*

They ended the dinner on good terms, shook hands, and even talked about some type of continued consulting work or contract effort for Audrey to assist in the recruitment of a replacement. Her ego hoped they'd beg her to stay. But that didn't happen. Even in Bill's car when he drove her home, he didn't bring it up.

There's only one thing that matters now – Roger.

She ran up the stairs, anxiously dialing his number on her cell phone along the way.

"Hello, Audrey. I'm literally clutching this phone waiting for your call. How did it go?"

"Hi. I just got back. So here's the deal... What if I told you they offered double my salary and luxury housing completely paid for in London if I open an office and run it for two years?"

He didn't say anything.

"Roger? Did you hear me?"

"Um... I guess that would be a hard thing to turn down, knowing how hard you've worked to get to the top. Is that what they offered?"

"Yes."

"I see. I'm very proud of you. That says a lot about your abilities." He said it straight – no emotion.

"Oh, Roger, don't you get it? Yeah, that was their offer, but I turned it down. I turned the damn thing down. That and everything else, too."

She kicked off her shoes at the doorway of her bedroom and fell back on her bed, looking up at the ceiling, sobbing softly.

There was silence on the other end of the phone line. Or perhaps he was weeping too, the silent, happy kind of tears.

Epilogue

6 Months Later – Early Summer

Along River Road in the town of New Port Richey, there's a mailbox painted like a birdhouse, with the name "Hollingsworth" on it, and it goes with the little gray house with white trim and a red door and red awnings over old-fashioned windows. Lacy curtains crisscross the windows, offering a little privacy from the outside.

There's a birdbath alongside the house, where crepe myrtle trees bloom in shades of pink and lavender. A picket fence lined with rows of three-foot sunflowers separate the property from neighbors, and leads all the way to the back, where land meets water. A river runs perpendicular to the house, and a bow rider boat floats on a dock where a couple of Adirondack chairs are arranged.

Nobody is in the house; they're out back, but music is playing inside and speakers blare classic rock tunes to the backyard.

Audrey, in a big straw hat, is crouched over a raised bed of rich soil, harvesting beans. Her hands are dirty and she is wiping her brow. When her basket is full and there are no more beans, she grabs a hammer and sticks a decorative bronze sign in the ground and pounds it into the earth. The words etched in bronze say, "A season for all things and a time to every purpose under heaven..."

She looks up and sees Roger, her husband, standing at the dock and sipping a beer. He's taking a break from mechanical work he's done to his boat. He looks back over to her and waves and smiles. She blows him a kiss.

279

Author Biography

I'm a Florida Girl, originally from Woodhaven in Queens, New York. I live in New Port Richey with my husband of a million years (well, since high school) and our high school/middle school aged children.

Although I've always considered myself a writer, for many years other priorities took precedence -- raising a family plus working outside the home. Time was always precious being a working girl, going to grad school at night, changing diapers and --- well, the things most families know about all too well.

I guess for the past decade or so, I became so entrenched in survival of the American Dream (the big house and some grownup toys), I was spending an inordinate number of hours each day working at the job. Or talking about it. Or worrying about it. I woke up one day and said, "Ohmahgawd, I'm going to be 40! What am I doing?"

I was impassioned to write HER BACKYARD as a creative outlet for all the pains I've known (that which I know so many other women share) in trying to balance work and family. I certainly had enough material that I could build from. I've lived it.

To me, writing is spiritual and when you build characters that you know intimately, I've found that the characters lead you through the plot you've outlined. There is a feeling of loss when an author finishes a book. I had heard that said before and now I know. When I finished writing the story of Audrey Beane, I had to start a new book immediately. Now that I am HERE - writing - I shall continue to write.

HER BACKYARD is my first published work. Since completing the story, my life took a turn that parallels my character's journey prophetically. I was laid off of work for the first time ever. Facing unemployment and losing my large home has made me reassess my dreams. I am choosing a simpler path, now working from a home office doing real estate and writing. The money isn't what it used to be, but I think given time to the new adjustment, I'm going to be in a happy place where I've always longed to be.

Please visit the Author at her website:

www.doreenlewis.com

Printed in the United States
27370LVS00004B/181-201